"Within this compelling suspense novel are stories of loss and redemption, romance and deception, addiction and recovery, and an underlying message of God's grace. I loved it."

—Edgar Struble,
producer, *God Bless the Broken Road*;
music director, The Academy of Country Music Awards, The Billboard Music Awards

"In *Deadly Commitment*, Kathy Harris creates characters you care about and plops them down into a world of deception and danger. I was so caught up in the story I almost burned dinner."

—Patricia Bradley,
author of the Memphis Cold Case novels

"I was captivated by the author's imagination, the things she loved, and her ability to bring the reader into this well-layered, intriguing story. She had me look at Nashville in a new light. This novel makes for a fun read and one that would work well for your book club meeting."

—Nora St Laurent,
The Book Club Network,
Where Book Fun Begins!

DEADLY
COMMITMENT

The Deadly Secrets Series

Kathy Harris

NEW HOPE®
PUBLISHERS
Imprint of Iron Stream Media
Birmingham, Alabama

New Hope® Publishers
100 Missionary Ridge
Birmingham, AL 35242
NewHopePublishers.com
An imprint of Iron Stream Media
IronStreamMedia.com

This book is a work of fiction. Characters and events in the books are entirely the creation of the author's imagination. Any similarity to real persons, living or dead, is coincidental and not intended by the author.

Iron Stream Media serves its authors as they express their views, which may not express the views of the publisher.

Library of Congress Control Number: 2019946848

ISBN-13: 978-1-56309-304-3

Ebook ISBN: 978-1-56309-311-1

1 2 3 4 5—23 22 21 20 19

In memoriam

Larry Harris
God blessed me with you.

Brandy, Ryan, and Michael
Your stories ended far too soon. This book is for you.

Prologue

race . . . No!"

The words ripped Danni from her sleep. Pulling herself closer to the wall, she listened, trying not to breathe.

"Let me go!" Her mother screamed.

Danni clutched her pillow. *Please, God—*

"Grace . . . the girls . . ."

"Don't touch me!" The repugnance in Grace Kemp's voice burrowed into her six-year-old daughter's heart. *How could a mother turn against her family?* Then Danni remembered. Everything had been okay until Chloe was born.

She turned her head, listening for the slow, methodic breathing of her baby sister, who slept less than ten feet away. Danni prayed the two-year-old wouldn't wake up. If she started crying, it might bring even more trouble their way.

The conversation in the next room spiked once again, inching Danni back toward the wall. *Mom will be fixed soon.* Hadn't Daddy promised? But the arguments had become more frequent. The shouting often kept her awake at night.

"Get your hands off me!" Her mother screamed. "And get out of the way!"

"Grace . . . you can't leave—"

"Just try and stop me!"

The door in the next room slammed, and Danni startled. *Leaving?* Her mother was leaving? Danni had to stop her. She would tell her how much she was needed. And that she would do more. She would take care of Chloe . . . and clean her room. *Please, God. My mama can't leave!*

Throwing back the covers, Danni placed one foot on the floor. Then the other. Moving too quickly might awaken the panic that would bring the darkness, and she didn't have time for that right now. She had to get to her mom.

Danni inhaled the cool air of her bedroom, filled her lungs, and then expelled hot breath through her clenched teeth. Just as the doctor had told her. He'd also told her to think about something good—the zoo, the park, even church when they attended as a family. Just the three of them before Chloe was born. Those things could . . . No, they *would* . . . happen again.

She would tell her mom. She would stop her. She had to get—

Danni's stomach started churning. *No . . . not now.* The room began to spin, and she reached for the edge of her bed. If she could just sit down for another minute. But it was too late. Her legs folded, and as the darkness overtook her, she fell to the floor.

CHAPTER 1

Present Day – March 15

anni Kemp stepped from the marble lobby of her downtown Nashville condo building into the brisk March morning. Sunshine cut through the chill as she walked beyond the shadow of the monolithic concrete high rise she had called home for almost two years.

Looking up, she saw scattered clouds dotting the cerulean sky, and a sense of the coming spring invigorated her. Life could be better, and she was about to make it that way. If she had to, she would walk away.

It didn't take long for winter to mock her resolute idealism. A gust of wind from the west shoved her toward the street ahead. Fighting to regain her balance, she danced awkwardly with her invisible partner, her arms flailing, her feet shuffling, until she was jilted at the edge of the curb.

Waiting for the crosswalk signal to turn, Danni clutched the belt of her navy Burberry raincoat, pulled it tighter to her waist, and scanned the concrete cityscape to see if anyone had been watching. A single figure, ragged and unkempt, stood staring at her from the bus stop on the far side of the street. He wore an ill-fitting gray jacket. His khaki pants looked torn and dirty. His unruly, dark hair defied style. But it was his penetrating stare that chilled her even more than the March wind.

She averted her eyes to a metro bus approaching the intersection, a Music City USA logo in the jewel tone colors of a Trivial Pursuit game emblazoned on its side. Hopefully he would board the coach, and she would never see him again.

Air brakes squealed as the massive vehicle rolled to a stop in front of her, and a toxic fog of diesel fumes wafted in her direction. Danni held her breath, willing the man on the other side to be gone. But when the bus pulled away, he hadn't moved.

Too soon the crosswalk light flashed. She lifted her chin, looked straight ahead, and propelled herself off the sidewalk toward the opposite side of the street. Acknowledging the intruder would admit vulnerability, and Danielle Kemp would no longer give in to fear, a new commitment she had made to herself last night. She held her breath as she approached the disheveled stranger, hoping to avoid the expected and unwelcome stench of body odor. But when she held it too long and was forced to gulp a mouthful of air, only the fresh scent of the cool morning filled her nostrils.

Curiosity won the battle over fear, and Danni turned to look at him. He met her gaze, his jaw set, his intense brown eyes piercing through the composure she had championed only a few minutes before.

She tried to smile—a faint offering she hoped wouldn't give away her discomfort. But a hint of disgust flickered in his eyes, and he looked away.

How dare he! Repulsed by *her?* He didn't even know her.

She tucked her chin and walked past, her high heels clicking on the sidewalk as the cold wind—now her friend—swept her along.

What interest did he have in her? Would he choose to follow?

Danni listened for footsteps behind her, but only the soft rustling of the silk scarf around her neck filled her ears. She quickened her pace, and two blocks ahead she took a right on Second Avenue.

Glancing over her shoulder and seeing no one, her anxiety eased. Until she realized that he might have taken another route. He could be waiting for her at the next cross street. As a precaution, she hurried across Second. At the next street, she scanned to the left with her peripheral vision.

It was him! *Or was it?*

She turned her head and stared. The clothes and hair were similar, but this man carried a guitar.

Danni hurried down the sidewalk, which had transitioned from pavement to brick, making it more difficult to navigate with high heels. She slowed her pace and a few minutes later turned the corner into the alleyway running beside Amoré, the Italian restaurant she managed.

She took a final glance over her shoulder.

No one.

Relieved but still shaken she dashed inside the rear service door and came face to face with Amoré's executive chef, Jaycee Alexander.

"Whoa, Danielle." Jaycee sidestepped to avoid a collision. "Did you see a ghost?"

"Why?" She breathed.

"You're pale as one."

"There was a strange man outside my condo. It felt like he was waiting for me." Danni loosened the belt of her coat. "Silly, huh?"

"No. It's scary." Jaycee scowled.

Danni shrugged. "I'm sure it was just my imagination, but the way he looked at me gave me the creeps."

"I know you enjoy the walk, girlfriend." Jaycee wagged her finger in Danni's face. "But I wish you would drive your car to work."

"Please, no lectures this morning." Danni dismissed her friend with a wave and then swiveled toward the dining room, almost knocking over a pastry chef when she turned.

The young man swayed, trying not to spill the tray of desserts he carried.

"Sorry!" Danni reached to steady him.

"You're fine, Ms. Kemp." He maneuvered past her and hurried away.

"It could have been worse." She tossed the remark to Jaycee as she headed toward her office, just beyond the kitchen.

"Yes, it could have been." Jaycee's words echoed behind her.

When Danni stopped in front of the door marked General Manager to search her handbag for keys, Jaycee stepped beside her.

"Just say an extra prayer for me, Jay. I'll be fine." Danni knew her friend hated it when she mocked her religious zeal.

But the chef returned the joust before turning to walk away. "I pray for you every day. But don't come running to me when your guardian angel resigns."

Danni smiled, snagged her keys, and unlocked the door. She loved working with Jaycee. Not only did she enjoy her company, but together they ran one of the most successful restaurants in Nashville.

Jaycee had endless energy and a reputation as one of the best chefs in the city. But more importantly, she was a good friend. Danni spent more time with her than she did with her boyfriend Rob.

Which reminded her.

She stuck her head out her office door and called after Jaycee. "I have two tickets to the symphony next Thursday. Want to go with me?"

The petite chef with flaming red hair turned and walked backwards toward the kitchen. "Where's your lame excuse for a boyfriend this time?"

"On the road with a new act he manages. James Dillon . . . Jamie Dillon . . . Bob Dylan. I don't know. I can never remember their names. He's always out with a different one."

"I'd love to go to the symphony. But you're a sad case." Jaycee clicked her tongue, twisted around, and hurried away.

"I really am." Danni mumbled as she flipped on the light switch beside the door.

But I'm determined that's going to change.

Danni said goodnight to the remaining staff and walked into the cool night air just before eleven. The outside air reinvigorated her after a long day inside the restaurant. While the spicy-sweet smell of a kitchen had an attraction of its own, garlic and other strong odors clung to clothing, hair, and skin.

But her job provided a good living. And most of her friends, peers in the industry, could relate to the long hours. You either devoted yourself to your work or you were replaced by someone who would. Even then you were vulnerable to the next great idea or innovative menu.

Danni enjoyed the challenge and thrill of competition and filled nearly every waking moment with thoughts about the restaurant. She spent full days and long nights, weekdays and weekends, on her work. When she wasn't officially working, she was networking. As the general manager at Amoré, her responsibilities included attending Chamber of Commerce luncheons, women's organization meetings, community functions, and charity dinners—anything that would keep the restaurant's profile high. Even her attendance at the symphony next week was job-related.

She had dedicated the last three years of her life to promoting Amoré, and her hard work had been paying off. Traffic had increased. And so had the profit margin. The groundwork had been laid for a chain of restaurants she hoped to manage one day. Amoré's owner, a family friend in Iowa, had promised her it would happen if she would continue to build the bottom line.

Danni waited for the traffic to pass before crossing Commerce Street and heading north on Second Avenue. Even at this time of night in the downtown historic district, business was still keen. Tourists, locals—and homeless men and women—flooded the sidewalks, sometimes spilling into the street. Those who remained until 3 a.m., when most of the businesses on Lower Broadway closed, were among the most unsavory.

With that thought came a reminder of the homeless man. Would he still be there when she returned? She tucked her chin, shielding herself from the unforgiving wind, and redirected her thoughts. Shoving her hands into her coat pocket, she chastised herself for leaving her gloves at home that morning.

Life as a whole was fulfilling in Nashville. Her career goals were well on track, even if her romantic life was going nowhere. Robert Evans had swept her off her feet three years ago with his good looks and winsome charm. And at first she had been attracted to his work ethic. But he spent more time out of town than he did at home.

Jaycee said Danni would never be able to tolerate him full time anyway. Not that it mattered, because she had decided to break up with Rob when he returned to Nashville tomorrow afternoon. Perhaps walking away came naturally to her DNA, a thought that disturbed her and had kept her with Rob longer than she should have been.

While Rob's inability to commit was obvious even to Jaycee, the truth was more complicated than her best friend knew. The night when Danni was six years old and her mother walked away had left a lot of doubt that she could ever be loved. And perhaps even the doubt that she would even be able to recognize a healthy relationship if she could find one.

Danni stepped up her pace, searching under each streetlight and checking each doorway along her route. The chances were good she would never see the homeless man again.

Turning left on Church Street, she walked the remaining two blocks in chilly silence, seeing only a young woman with a dog, a scrappy teenager on a scooter, and a middle-aged man in a business suit. There was no sign of the dark-eyed stranger.

Once inside the main lobby of Rutherford Tower, she acknowledged the security guard, one she'd never seen before, and hurried to the bay of four elevators. Taking the first lift to the seventh floor, she unlocked her condo door and walked into the darkness.

"Are you okay?" The uniformed Metro police officer scowled at Caleb Samuels as he lay curled up on the Metro bus bench.

"Yes, sir." Caleb nodded, straightening into a sitting position and clutching his lower back. "Just resting my back, sir."

He had staked out the Rutherford for several weeks, enduring everything from mouthy teenagers to bad weather. He had no real complaint, except for the boredom that sometimes numbed his mind. With too much time to think, his past had a way of slipping up behind him, and it could choke him like the fog that sometimes rolled into downtown Nashville this time of year.

Yet, if it hadn't been for the unfortunate turn of circumstances in his life, he would probably be behind bars instead of working for the Tennessee Bureau of Investigation. God had blessed him with a second chance. He would never forgive himself for the price that had been paid for it. Only the satisfaction of knowing he was helping keep narcotics out of the hands of young people made it possible for him to look himself in the mirror each morning.

Caleb eased off the bench and assessed his surroundings, rife with possibilities. The nighttime revealed ugly truths about the drug scene. He had often watched danger shake its fist at the darkness with the audacity of an undisciplined child.

But while the darkness could mask a multitude of sins—and danger—it also danced in the daytime, wearing its everyday clothes. Some people like Robert Evans opened their door to it, fully recognizing the implications of their guest. Others were caught unaware, or unconcerned, at the unknown threat that lived among them while they politely looked away.

Caleb was grateful he had no family at home to worry about him. No one to answer to. Not even a dog. If he had to work eighteen-hour shifts to break a case, he could. No one would be pacing the floor with concern for his safety.

Although, from the looks of things, they would have had no worries tonight. It had been a slow one so far. Three more hours, and he could go home for much needed rest. For both his body and his mind. So far he had been the only agent his supervisor had been willing to assign to this case, but his gut told him it would pay off.

CHAPTER 2

After midnight – March 16

M ove over, Sophie! You're pushing me off the bed."

The big, black Newfoundland raised her head, stared at Danni, and then stretched her body as far as she could, taking up even more space.

"Thanks for nothing." Danni ruffled the fur on top of the dog's head before grabbing the television remote from the nightstand. Danni flipped through more than a hundred channels before deciding on an old movie. She didn't need another sleepless night thinking about Rob, and a black and white B-flick should make her drowsy.

Danni gave her pillow a solid punch, snuggled into the covers, and stared mindlessly at the television. Within minutes the feature cut to a commercial, and a tall blond built like a mannequin glided across the screen. The actress wore a slinky black dress and dangling pearl earrings. She placed her palm to her bright red lips, flung a kiss toward the camera, and then purred in a husky voice, "Make him commit."

The video dissolved to a still of a shapely perfume bottle with a matching red lip print on the label.

"Perfect. Just what I needed." Danni rolled over.

Apparently Sophie wasn't happy either. The dog pulled herself to a standing position, paced to the foot of the queen-sized bed, and flopped down.

"What's wrong, Soph? Did that remind you of someone?"

The dog sighed as if on cue, and Danni chuckled. There was something to be said for canine intelligence. And devotion.

Rob certainly didn't qualify in the latter category. He might have made the right promises, acknowledging that they were headed toward marriage one day, but he would never discuss specifics. And while he was generous with his money, Danni rarely had his time. Or, for that matter, his full attention. Even when he was with her, he was on the phone or daydreaming about his next big business scheme.

His dedication had paid off for him. His success had allowed him to help her with the down payment for her condo; at the same time he'd purchased the unit next door for himself. Their eventual plan, he had said, would be to marry and connect the two spaces to create a large luxury apartment. The oversize space would make a good starter home when they finally decided to have a family.

But was that what she really wanted? And why was she thinking about this again? Hadn't she made her decision last night? She didn't want to raise children by herself. Not after watching her dad do it. Even if her dad had done a great job, it hadn't been fair to him or to his daughters.

With Rob on the road forty weeks out of the year, if they had kids—and she wanted them—he would miss most of their lives. Her dad had been the foundation of their family. He'd had to be.

Dan Kemp had found time to eat dinner with his daughters every night, even though he sometimes worked two jobs. He had attended most of their softball games and every PTA meeting. He had taken them to church. Despite her mother's absence, she had many fond memories of her childhood. But the pace was slower in her tiny Iowa hometown. And there were no homeless men to scare th—

Thump-thump-thump.

Sophie growled. Danni glanced at the bedside clock. Three a.m. No one with good intentions would be knocking at her door at this hour. The face of the man on the street flashed through her mind. Did he know where she lived?

The thought made her skin crawl.

Danni reached for the remote and switched off the television, and the room went black. Easing across the bed, she slid her hand into Sophie's collar, whispering for the Newfoundland to move closer. With her other hand, she grabbed the leash she kept on the nightstand and snapped it into the brass ring of the collar.

"Come on, girl," she whispered. "Let's check this out."

The dog jumped off the bed and padded silently beside Danni down the hall, through the living room, and into the small foyer. Standing on her tiptoes, Danni peered into the peephole on the front door, giving her a wide-angle view of the outer hallway.

No one.

Panic stilled momentarily.

Sophie scratched at the door jam, sniffing. Someone must have been outside a few minutes ago.

Danni rechecked the viewer. The hall was empty. Then, suddenly, a head came out of nowhere. She screamed, her breath catching in her throat. A second later, she replayed the image in her mind and realized it was Rob standing outside.

But why . . . ?

With shaking hands, she unbolted the door and threw it open. "What are you doing out here at this time of morning?"

"I couldn't find my keys. I thought it might be better if I knocked instead of waking you with a phone call."

Danni steadied herself against the door jam. "I looked in the viewer, and you weren't there at first."

A wry smile crossed Rob's face. "I dropped my phone and bent down to pick it up. I guess you saw me when I straightened up. Sorry."

She encircled his neck with her arms. "I'm so glad it's you!" Then stepping back, she looked into Rob's ice blue eyes. "But I didn't expect you until this afternoon."

"We made unbelievable time coming from Tulsa." He straightened his shirt. "It's good to be home, and you . . ." He grinned again. "You look beautiful."

At that moment she remembered she was wearing her flannel pajamas, the ones with a pepperoni pizza design on a bright blue background. Jaycee had given them to her in jest, telling her she "ate, drank, and *slept* her job."

"Right. I'm sure I look amazing." She ran her fingers through her hair.

Rob leaned forward to kiss her on the forehead, stifling a yawn. "Do you have my spare key, babe?"

"I'll get it for you." She pivoted, but Sophie blocked her path. "Move, girl."

Rob patted his chest for the dog to jump up. "How are you, Sophia?"

The dog huffed and followed Danni into the kitchen. When they returned, Rob was standing in the foyer, scrolling through his phone.

"Can you meet me for lunch today?" Danni asked.

"I'll do my best, babe," he said, not looking up. "I have a lot to do before we leave town tonight."

"Tonight?" Danni slumped. "You're in town for *a day*?"

He tucked the phone into his pocket and pulled her into a hug. "You know my schedule, Danielle. It's always changing. This is a busy time for me."

"You're always busy . . ."

He kissed her on the forehead again. "It will get better. I promise."

I can't wait that long. She pulled away. "I need to get some sleep."

Rob frowned. "I'll see you sometime later this morning." He took the key from her outstretched hand and left.

But it would soon be her who walked away.

At eleven o'clock that morning, Danni saw Rob walk through the front door of Amoré. Even from across the room, his good looks caught her off guard. It was no wonder she had fallen in love. She waved him toward the back of the restaurant dining room.

He sidled toward her, flashing a boyish grin, the dimples in his cheeks deepening. "Hey, babe." He gathered her in his arms, enveloping her in the scent of soap and Paul Sebastian, her favorite combination.

Rob might have the accent of a Mississippi boy, but his blond hair, blue eyes, and muscular build were more reminiscent of a California beach bum. She imagined that lifestyle would suit him.

"You smell great." She settled back into the booth where she'd been working, leaving room for Rob to sit beside her. Instead he chose the seat opposite her.

"You look beautiful, my dear. I don't want to take my eyes off you." He reached across the table to take her hand.

He not only had the physical attributes of a movie star, he had the charm, which he always applied liberally with her. She had no doubt he also used it to full advantage when it came to business. Given enough time, Rob could win over everyone he met.

Well, everyone except Jaycee.

"I'm glad you came by. Have you eaten?"

"I had a late breakfast. But I would love an espresso." He pulled his phone from his pocket and laid it on the table between them. "Make it a double. I need a jolt of caffeine if I'm going to stay awake in my meeting this afternoon." He chuckled. "After all, I did get into town late last night."

"And scared me half to death in the process." She pivoted out of the booth and saw Jaycee heading straight for their table. Rob must have seen her too because he let out a long sigh.

"Hey, Robert. When are you going to slow down and marry this pretty lady?" Jaycee thumped her knuckles twice on the table-top for emphasis.

Danni suppressed a smile.

The corners of Rob's mouth twitched upwards. "The truth is I'm saving myself for you." He winked at Danni.

"Please." Jaycee rolled her eyes and walked away laughing.

A few minutes later, Danni returned with a steaming demi-tasse of espresso and set the cup in front of Rob. She retook the seat across the table. "Who are you going on the road with tonight? I thought you were supposed to be home for a while."

His face lit up. "I just signed a new group. Their show needs a lot of work. They'll be my priority this year."

Danni bit her lip and then mumbled under her breath. "Of course, they will."

"What?"

"Never mind . . ." He had no clue.

He took two gulps of his coffee and glanced around the dining room. "How's it going for you, babe? Is the restaurant doing okay?"

"We're doing great." She crossed her arms and forced a smile. "I keep busy with it. I have plenty of time since my boyfriend is never in town."

Rob downed the rest of his drink, apparently unaffected by her comment. "That's why we were made for each other. We're willing to make sacrifices." He stood to go. "Can you have dinner with me tonight before I leave?"

"Yes. I was hoping we could talk."

"Great!" He planted a kiss on her forehead. "I'll pick you up at your place at seven thirty, sharp."

Some romantic dinner. Danni shifted her attention from Rob to the smoldering embers in the massive stone fireplace only a few feet from their table. He had been on his phone for more than ten minutes this time. Since then, the waiter had cleared their plates, refreshed her drink, and asked about dessert.

She studied the diminishing flame. When Rob had suggested they go to Le Grande Steakhouse for a "romantic dinner," he had been right about one thing, the setting was romantic. But no amount of candlelight, firelight, or even moonlight could chase away the shadow that had fallen over their evening. Her so-called "boyfriend" couldn't stop doing business long enough to enjoy his meal. Or his time with her.

Some nights she would have been happy to retreat to her own mental calculations, planning menus, marketing, or brain storming the next milestone for Amoré. After all, she didn't often have the opportunity to dine leisurely at one of her top competitor's establishments, and a lot could be learned from such observation. But her heart wasn't into reconnaissance tonight. What she wanted was a meaningful conversation with her dinner companion, a discussion about their future. Or the lack thereof.

She studied the dessert menu. Maybe something sweet could salvage the evening. Or at least provide her with the courage to say what she needed to say.

There were several options. In both regards.

Crème Brulee. Not sweet enough. *Apple Pie à la Mode.* Too mundane. The tiramisu might be good. But it couldn't compete with Jaycee's. Perhaps *Death by Chocolate*? No, too rich for a queasy stomach.

Rob lowered his phone to the dark linen tablecloth and offered an apologetic smile. "I'm sorry." He nodded toward the menu in her hands. "Do you want dessert?"

"Bananas Foster." She dropped the carte du jour on the table. "What was so important?"

The corners of Rob's mouth flickered. "Like I said, it's just busy right now, babe." He gestured to the waiter across the room, took a sip from his water glass, and then looked back to her. "Did I tell you I'm leaving for a month this time?"

"Rob! I never see you anymore!"

The couple sitting at the next table stopped talking and glanced their way. Rob gave her a disapproving look.

Danni brushed her hands across her shoulders to rally her courage. "We need to talk . . ."

He reached across the table, closing the distance between them and tried to interrupt.

"No." She exhaled the word more than spoke it. "Hear me out, please."

He nodded and withdrew.

"I can't do this anymore." She fought back tears.

"Hey . . ." He massaged his ring finger. "I know you're stressed with everything you have on your plate right now. We've both got a lot going on. But that's a good thing, right? It's for our future. Together."

Anger rose in her throat, strangling the words she had to say, but she was determined to say them. She glanced toward the waning fire, gathered strength, and turned back to him.

"No!"

He winced, looked around the room, and then tried to stare her down.

"No." She remained resolute. "I can't . . . do this . . ." Danni let the taste of each syllable linger on her tongue. "We're done."

"Babe." Rob's expression softened, and he took her left hand in his, cradling it with his moist palm. "At least give me a chance to talk."

She tried to pull away, but he tightened his grip.

"Listen to me for a minute." He lowered his tone, along with his chin, as though speaking to a child. "You knew when we met that I traveled."

He relinquished her hand, which she quickly retracted into her lap. Tears welled in her eyes.

"The truth is, I would love for us to spend more time together," he continued. "But it's just not possible right now. I have too much invested . . ."

Danni remained quiet during his monologue, but there was nothing he could say that would change her mind. *Nothing.*

After he had finished speaking, he leaned back in his chair and searched her face. Seconds ticked by before he reached into his jacket and pulled out a pale blue box. He set it in the center of the table. Two words, Tiffany & Co., were inscribed in gold on the top.

"Let's make it official." A smile slowly spread across his face. "Let's get engaged."

The lump in Danni's throat plummeted to her stomach. This wasn't an option she'd planned for. When she made no movement to open the box, Rob did.

"This is just a promise gift." His hand shook uncharacteristically as he extracted a necklace from the tiny box and dangled it in front of her.

"I picked it up in Phoenix last week. I went to the store looking for an . . . an engagement . . ." His voice drifted off. "Well, let me just say this. I want the two of us to go together to pick out rings so you'll have exactly what you want."

What did she do now? She'd been so sure they were finished. That she was through with—

"Hey, are you going to leave a guy hanging?" Rob's voice wavered. "Will you marry me or not?"

"I—I don't know what to say." She reached to touch the pendant. The exquisite five-point star was encrusted with diamonds, and every facet shimmered in the candlelight. Even its delicate chain had been accented with stones.

"I hope you like platinum." His confidence returned.

Was she about to give in? Did he really love her?

"Even though I don't say it often enough, you're the star of my life, Danielle." He turned the palm of her hand upward, dropped the necklace into it, and then closed her fingers around it. "I hope this will let you know how much I care about you. I want you to wear it all the time, to remind you of my feelings when I'm not here, *can't* be here, with you."

"Rob . . ." Tears blurred Danni's vision, and she ignored the warning inside her head that screamed *walk away!*

Rob leaned back in his chair. "Well, I guess you have a wedding to plan." He raised an eyebrow in the direction of the approaching waiter. "Just don't make me wear a penguin suit like that."

She laughed and wiped a tear from her eye.

"May I take your dessert order, sir? Madame?"

"I'll have coffee. What would you like, Danielle?"

A half hour later, as the waiter cleared her dessert plate and Rob prepared to pay their tab, ideas for a wedding swirled in Danni's head. Chloe would be so excited. She couldn't wait to call her sister and to pick out a ring and a dress—

"Babe, I need to ask you a favor." Rob broke the spell. "I want to give you some money to take back to your place. I didn't have a chance to go to the bank today, and it's too much for me to keep on the road." He nodded toward the black leather briefcase sitting in the chair between them.

"What is it?"

"It's from Jamie Dillon's merchandise sales. Plus, one promoter paid us in cash."

"I don't understand. Why didn't you give it to your assistant Melissa at the office?"

"Because it's a lot of money."

She had to strain to hear him.

"It's not that I don't trust Melissa. I'd just feel better about you keeping it."

"I don't know, Rob."

"Babe, I wouldn't ask if I wasn't in a bind. I need your help. Just stash it in your closet. I'll deposit it when I return next month."

"What if something happens? Can't you just take it to your place?"

"No." He drew a long breath and released it. "To be honest, I have another satchel of cash there. I would rather spread it around, if you know what I mean. The odds are better, you know, that someone wouldn't break into both of our places."

"Okay. As long as you understand I'm not responsible if something happens."

"Of course not." He stood, walked around the table, and took her arm. "I trust you with my life, baby. You know that."

Caleb Samuels watched from the shadows as the couple left the high-class restaurant. He could only imagine the price of a meal in that place. He was certain he wouldn't be dining there anytime soon. Not on his salary.

The blond man's arm encircled the dark-haired woman's slender waist, and he clutched a leather briefcase in his other hand as they walked to the valet stand, exchanged pleasantries, and then stepped aside to wait for their car. A few minutes later, a white Mercedes sedan arrived. The valet jumped out, ran around the car, and held open the passenger door. After helping seat the woman, the blond man handed her the briefcase.

Was it Caleb's imagination, or did she hesitate before she took it? Something didn't seem right. Or maybe he was just making excuses. The dark-haired woman was starting to get to him. He reminded himself that he had a job to do. But what could she see in Robert Evans?

Oh, yeah, the money. It was always the money.

CHAPTER 3

After midnight – March 17

Robert Evans paced the dimly lit parking lot as he waited for the arrival of his tour bus. He checked his Rolex and grimaced. Almost half past midnight. Hank should have been here by now. Had something gone wrong with the drop off?

Rob mentally recalculated the events of the last twenty-four hours. He had parted ways with his driver Hank, and the bus, in Oklahoma a little more than a day ago and taken a flight into Nashville. After leaving Rob at the Oklahoma City airport, Hank had deadheaded to Atlanta to exchange cargo for payment. Even if he had stopped for a nap, he should have had time to get back into town.

Despite the chill in the air, a bead of sweat formed on Rob's forehead. He brushed it away and continued to pace. After a few more circuits around the lot, he pulled his phone from his overcoat and redialed the driver's number.

Voicemail again.

He pocketed the phone and thought about everything that could have gone wrong, from a breakdown on the road to a breakdown in communication with the connection in Atlanta. Anything else was unthinkable. If Hank didn't show up soon, Rob would be forced to call Ramirez and sound the alert that something had gone wrong. Maybe dead wrong.

It was then he heard a diesel engine in the distance, and in less than a minute the sleek, black Prevost crawled to a stop in front of him. The air brakes released with an earsplitting hiss, and Hank threw open the doors.

The driver jumped out, arms flailing in a defensive mode. "I'm sorry, Mr. Evans."

Rob keyed the electronic release for the trunk of his Mercedes sedan. "What happened?"

The driver snatched two suitcases from the car. "I hit traffic."

"At this time of night?" Rob slung his leather carryon bag over his shoulder and studied the driver's face for any sign of deception. Seeing none, he decided the man was too stupid to make up a believable lie. And smart enough to know better than to try.

"Must have been a concert at the—"

"Never mind." Rob waved him off. "Did everything go okay with the drop off?"

"Yes, sir."

"That's all I need to know." Rob turned his back to the sweaty giant of a man and stepped into the familiar warmth of the bus. "When you've finished loading the rest of the bags, let's get out of here."

"Yes, sir."

Inside the front lounge of the coach, Rob shrugged out of his overcoat, folded it neatly, and laid it across the arm of the cream-colored leather sofa running lengthwise along the wall that led to a small galley kitchen. He opened the electronic sliding door beyond the kitchen and walked past the guest bath, Hank's bunk, a long row of closets, and finally into his master suite at the rear of the bus. Tossing the shoulder bag on his king-sized bed, he settled into a chair and waited for Hank to stow his remaining suitcases and hanging clothes.

A private tour coach had a number of amenities, but the best was just that. *Privacy*. Rob preferred traveling separately from his artists. It made his work more relaxing, yet he could stay on top of his game and in the middle of the action by working away from home.

Actually, this *was* his home. Much more so than his condo.

As soon as Hank pulled out of the parking lot, Rob would go to bed and sleep until they arrived at their destination in the morning. It was a luxury ride, an expensive way to travel. But just like all good things in life, they could be bought if you had enough money. That included women and a lifestyle that brought satisfaction.

The road gave Rob the freedom he craved. No one called the shots for him day by day. Each artist's tour manager took care of the minute details. Hank would often caravan with the other entertainer buses and trucks so Rob could still maintain control without dealing with the petty stuff.

He ran a well-oiled machine. Life on tour was almost perfect. Second only to the eventual possibility of lounging in a deck chair on a yacht in the Caribbean. Or relaxing in the sun on an exotic island. Those were future goals, and he was on track to realize them soon enough. Danielle Kemp had a bright future ahead, if she would only give him time.

Unlike his peers in the entertainment industry, Rob had diversified. His artist management business made him a good living. But he had another, much more lucrative means of securing his financial future.

And it had nothing to do with music.

Insomnia had become a habit. Danni switched on her bedside light, illuminating the corner of the room in a soft white glow. Sophie groaned, jumped off the bed, and padded silently across the thick Kashmir rug and into the adjoining master bath. Seconds later, Danni heard the dog drop with a thud onto the Italian marble tile. She smiled as she pictured the big Newfie stretched out in one of her favorite spots next to the cool porcelain of the Jacuzzi bathtub. At least one of them might get some sleep tonight.

Danni reached across the nightstand for a book. If she couldn't sleep, she might as well work. She had yet to crack open the restaurant management guide she had borrowed from the library last week.

Twenty more minutes passed and, after rereading the first page three times, she laid the book aside. It was impossible to focus on anything but the wedding.

The wedding. A shiver of excitement—or was it a cold chill—scuttled up her spine. This was what she wanted, right?

In less than nine months she would become Mrs. Robert Evans. And to think only five hours ago she had been ready to end the relationship. How did you decide to marry someone the same day you had planned to breakup with him?

Because Rob had expressed his love to her, that's why.

Despite the lack of a ring, he had insisted they set a date, maybe even fly to Las Vegas to elope. But marriage was a lifetime commitment, something you did only once, so you had to do it right. Even if she hadn't attended church in the past few years, she wanted to exchange vows in the traditional way.

Rob had agreed, and together they had settled on the second Saturday of the coming New Year, pending his brother Jack returning from the Middle East so he could serve as best man.

Danni would, of course, also clear the date with her family. But it shouldn't be a problem. Her dad and Chloe would drop everything for her wedding. Their support in her life had always been a given, even if they didn't see each other but once or twice a year now.

She grabbed her phone and began taking notes. She had a dress to buy, a church to reserve, and invitations to send out. The list was overwhelming.

Flowers. Catering. Hotel reservations for out-of-town guests. Rob had left it all to her. And she thought she had been busy before. Planning a wedding would soon become the icing on that proverbial cake—oh, don't forget the cake! Hers would be caramel mocha in seven layers and decorated with a bride and groom on top.

She made a note to call Grandma Kemp for the recipe that had been passed down for generations in their family. She would give it to the bakery that Amoré often used for special occasions, because Jaycee would be too busy catering the wedding to worry about a cake.

Jaycee! What would her friend say when she heard about the wedding?

Danni clutched the pendant Rob had given her a few hours before and imagined her friend's reaction to the news. It wouldn't be good. Not at first. Jaycee would wag a finger in her face and lecture her on Rob's shortcomings. But she would eventually come around.

On the other hand, Danni's sister would be excited to hear about her plans. Even though she was several years younger, Chloe was much further along in life. She'd married her childhood sweetheart right out of high school. Now in her mid-twenties, Chloe and her husband had two children. Brian was not only the youngest mayor to be elected in their small hometown of Fountaine, Iowa, he was the youth minister at their church. And, of course, Chloe was the perfect mother. Somehow she had managed to figure that out despite their lack of a role model.

Chloe and Brian were a hard act to follow. Her younger sister had everything Danni wanted and was afraid she would never have. But this milestone, marrying Rob, who was a real catch in anyone's eyes, would finally be evidence that she could have it all. A career, a husband and, one day, a family.

Rob Evans awoke to the gut-wrenching squeal of brakes and the sensation of being propelled, feet first, toward the front of the bus. Clutching the side of his bed, he spat out a curse word as he braced for the impact that was surely coming.

Instead, the speeding vehicle swerved to the right. Rob snatched at the bed sheets that had only minutes before cradled him in a dreamless repose. He managed to hold on, and within seconds he heard the engine housed beneath his king-sized bedroom suite grinding down. The bus rolled to a halt with a final squeal of the brakes.

Glancing at the clock on his nightstand—3:07 a.m.—he pressed the talk button on the intercom that had been secured to the back wall of the coach.

"Hank, what the—"

"I'm sorry, Mr. Evans." His driver's husky voice boomed back, another disconcerting wakeup call at such an early hour.

Rob winced and sat up. "Do you even know how to drive a bus?"

"I'm really sorry, sir. The lead driver in our convoy sent word of a police roadblock a half mile up the highway." Hank's voice quivered. "I had to take this exit if we were going to avoid it." He mumbled something unintelligible and then added, "I'm sorry. I had to stand on the brakes to get us stopped in time."

Rob scrubbed his fingers down his face. His driver might be an overgrown pigpen of a man, but he understood the business they were in. Maybe he was smarter than he looked.

"Good job."

"Thank you, sir. Thank you. I apologize in advance for the bumpy ride ahead. The side road won't be very smooth, but we'll get back on the interstate in about ten miles. We'll make our appointment without any problem."

"I'll leave that up to you." Rob stood, planting his bare feet firmly into the thick carpeting beside his bed. "Call me if you need me."

He headed toward the bathroom, picking his way carefully now the bus was moving again.

That had been a close one.

In times like this Hank was worth the small fortune he was paid. Not just for the lengthy overdrives required to maintain their schedule but also for keeping his mouth shut and watching out for trouble. They couldn't be too careful. After all, they worked in a dangerous business.

CHAPTER 4

Y ou set a date?" The color drained from Jaycee's face.
"January 24."

"Oh, Danni." Amoré's petite chef braced against the door-
jamb separating Danni's office from the kitchen corridor. "You've
had so many doubts about Rob. Is he really the person you want
to spend the rest of your life with?"

Danni straightened a stack of papers on her desk and avoided
her friend's eyes. "You're the one who's had the doubts. I was
just—" She looked up to see that the color in Jaycee's face had
more than returned. Her cheeks now matched her fiery red hair.

The chef knotted her fists. "That's not true, and you know it."

"Okay." Danni leaned back in her chair, increasing the distance between herself and her concerned friend. "Look . . . I
admit it. I had doubts. But it's different now that I know he
loves me."

Jaycee stared at her.

"It's his lifestyle I don't like, Jay. But that will change with
time."

"And how do you know that?" Jaycee shook her head. "How
often does that happen? I mean, seriously, that's the biggest mistake in the book, thinking you're going to change someone."

"Rob says he cares about me." Danni straightened in her chair.
"Isn't it worth the risk?"

"Risk?" The chef closed the office door and stepped toward the desk. "I guess I'm old-fashioned, but I see marriage as forever. Are you sure you can make that promise to Rob?"

"I think so." Danni shrugged. Her conviction appeared to be waning, but she wouldn't let Jaycee, or her fear, win.

Jaycee dropped into a chair in front of the desk. "You're concerned too, aren't you?"

"Concerned about what?" Danni shot back. "That I can't have a happy marriage because my parents didn't? Or, maybe . . ." she stammered, "that I don't deserve one?"

"Danni . . . please." Jaycee's expression softened. "I know how much you deserve one. And you will be a great wife to . . . someone someday. The truth is that Rob doesn't deserve you."

"It'll be okay, Jay. The two of us have been together for almost three years now. At least there won't be any surprises, right?" Danni forced a smile. "I know he's attached to his job, but as long as he's committed to me for the long haul, I'm okay with that."

"I hope you know what you're getting into. I don't think Rob even understands the concept of commitment." Jaycee let out a long breath. "Is he a believer?"

"He agreed to be married in a church."

Jaycee's eyebrow arched. "So where did he want to get married?"

"Vegas. He said it would be romantic."

Jaycee rolled her eyes. "He's just—"

"Would you stop, please? All you can think about are the negatives. I know I've shared a lot of my frustrations about Rob, but there are good things about our relationship too."

"Name three."

Danni glanced away, and then looked back to her friend. "He always comes home to me. He buys nice things for me. And . . . he trusts me."

"Is that all you've got?" Jaycee fired back. "How about I name three? He's selfish, detached, and probably not a believer."

"You'll never accept Rob. That's not fair."

Jaycee studied her momentarily then shrugged. "Okay, you're right. It's your decision." She leaned forward, reaching for Danni's left hand. "So let me see your ring."

Danni jerked her hand away and pulled the star pendant from beneath her sweater. "I don't have it yet. He gave me this pre-engagement gift. It's a—"

"Oh, my . . ." Jaycee recoiled in mock distress. "That's not exactly your style."

"You're so dramatic." Danni chuckled then glanced at the cluster of diamonds. "It is a bit much, isn't it?"

"Un-huh." The chef nodded, the corners of her mouth turning slightly upwards.

"Well, the good news is that we're going together to pick out rings when he returns to town next month."

"Good idea." Jaycee winked as she stood and turned toward the hall.

"Hey . . . wait."

"Yes?" The chef pivoted.

"Since you're okay with the wedding now." Danni stood and hurried around her desk. "Would you be my maid of honor?"

"Of course, you're my best friend." Jaycee gave Danni a hug and then took a step backwards. "But you don't get off that easy." She wagged her finger. "I'll be hoping you change your mind in the next nine months. In fact," she said as she spun back around. "I'll be praying for it."

Although traffic had been brisk in and out of the Rutherford ear-lier, it had finally begun to dwindle. Caleb checked his watch. The Timex strapped to his wrist with a frayed canvas band kept per-fect time, probably just as good as the Rolex Robert Evans wore. And it came with a lot less guilt. Not that Caleb cared to compare himself to Evans. Nor was he envious. Peace of mind couldn't be bought. Especially with dirty money.

The Timex, and everything he was wearing, had come from the used clothing store on Charlotte Avenue. One perk of an undercover gig, he hadn't spent much on clothing—or razor blades—in the past few weeks since being assigned to stake out the Rutherford. But what he had saved on clothes he had spent on hot water trying to wash away the street grime that clung to both his body and his mind.

He ran his hand through the coarse stubble on his face and counted the number of hours remaining until he could go home and take one of those hot showers. Although the thought invigo-rated him, he still had to worry about staying awake.

This time of the night was always quiet. By two or three in the morning most of the party crowd had gone home. Or crashed wherever they were. Caleb lowered himself onto the nearest Metro transit bench to sit out the rest of the shift, which had been unusually uneventful. Only a few rowdy kids and a couple drunks had roused his suspicion.

Quiet wasn't necessarily a good thing. If something didn't happen soon with this case, his supervisors would shut it down, and that would be a shame. His gut told him he was close to breaking it wide open. That same hunch reminded him that lives were on the line.

What he needed was a significant lead. And a little more time.

He glanced around the Nashville cityscape and whispered a silent prayer. *Lord, please bless the work I'm doing here. You know how important it is and how many lives will be saved.* He paused. *And You know what this means to me.*

When Caleb returned his focus to the Rutherford, a solitary figure loitering in front of the high rise caught his attention. In the few weeks Caleb had surveilled this building, he had become familiar with its residents. There were occasional strangers, of course, but this man, at this hour, didn't fit that profile. The Rutherford had a young, upwardly mobile clientele, and this character looked out of place, leaving cause for reasonable concern.

Caleb watched as the lanky, dark-clothed man lingered near the entrance. He appeared to be studying the keyless entry system, and his hesitation indicated unfamiliarity. Caleb counted ten seconds before the suspect raised his hand to punch in the code. When he did, the main entrance doors opened.

The stranger wasted no time entering the building. He hurried through the lobby, past the empty guard desk, and stopped in front of the bank of elevators visible through the front window.

Caleb crossed the street to improve his sightline. From the shadows he watched the lift doors slide open and the man step inside. Within seconds the floor indicator lights began to illuminate. One by one, the elevator crept upward toward the penthouse, stopping short at the seventh floor. The floor where Robert Evans lived.

Bingo!

Like any good cop, Caleb trusted his hunches. And he didn't believe in coincidences. Both of those tenets had kept him alive for the five years he had worked with the Bureau. With his right hand he pulled his phone from his pocket and dialed for backup. With his left he pounded on the front door of the Rutherford.

A drowsy-looking security guard, evidently just returning from his rounds, ambled in Caleb's direction. Caleb flashed a badge and pointed toward the elevators.

"I'm TBI. I have reason to believe a felony is in progress on the seventh floor."

The guard blinked but didn't move.

"Come on, man. Let me in!"

Caleb pulled his 9mm Glock from the holster secured to his ankle and pounded on the door again.

The guard nodded, released the locking mechanism, and stepped away from the door.

Wasting no time, Caleb pushed through, stopping only to ask directions to the nearest stairwell. If he was going to surprise the suspect, he needed to avoid the elevator.

"Over there—"

The guard moved to follow Caleb, but he waved him off, shouting over his shoulder. "I've called Metro. Stay here and direct them to the seventh floor."

"Yes, sir." It appeared the young rent-a-cop hadn't witnessed this much action in his entire career. Now was his chance to be a hero.

Caleb jogged toward the stairwell—thankful he had only seven flights to ascend and was in good enough shape to accomplish the task quickly. Taking the first flight of stairs two steps at a time, he calmed his mind by anticipating how it would feel to cuff the thug and question him for information that might move this case along.

As soon as he reached the seventh-floor landing, he paused to listen and assess his surroundings. Only silence and the sound of his own heavy breathing filled his ears.

Caleb cracked open the stairwell door, stopping to listen again. This time he heard a faint scraping noise.

Confident the intruder was far enough from the stairwell door, and distracted, Caleb sent up a silent prayer of protection and widened the opening enough to pass his head and shoulders through. About fifty yards to the left, the suspect hovered in front of the entrance to one of the residential units.

If Caleb had been afraid the man would see him, that fear was soon forgotten. Within seconds, the intruder breached the door and stepped inside the premises. Immediately the elevator doors opened, and two uniformed officers rushed into the hallway, guns drawn. Turning first in one direction and then the other, the cops scanned the hallway and then leveled their firearms at Caleb's chest.

He acknowledged them with a flash of his badge, arms raised. "TBI undercover. Your man's down the hall." He pointed toward the open door at the far end of the corridor. "I've got your back."

One of the uniformed men nodded, and the pair sprinted toward the breached apartment while Caleb crossed the hall to watch from behind an upright architectural beam jutting from the wall. If this ended up being a routine break-in, he might not have to break his cover.

He watched as the two officers took positions on either side of the unit door, the taller man on the right, the shorter on the left. After pausing to listen to what was going on inside, the smaller officer stepped into the opening and shouted. "Police. Come out with your hands up." Seconds later, the burglar alarm went off.

Caleb's first impulse was to shield his ears, but there was no time. Someone was opening the door to the apartment next to the compromised unit. An innocent life was about to be put in jeopardy. His mind flashed back to a drug deal gone bad more than a decade ago. That mistake would haunt him for the rest of his life, and he wouldn't make it again.

He would have to act fast if he was going to neutralize this situation.

Danni fumbled with the locks on the front door of her condo. Right now, she would love to get her hands on the person who had set off that obnoxious alarm. And if the voices she had heard were coming from Rob's apartment, as she had suspected when she was first awakened, that person would be Rob.

Why did he keep forgetting to tell her he had changed his schedule and was coming home early? His lack of respect could be frustrating. Nothing seemed to change with him.

She stood on her tiptoes to stare into the peephole, remembering the last time he had hidden beneath it. Sophie pushed against her, almost knocking her off her feet.

"Stay back, girl." Danni forced the dog into a sitting position. "I'll take care of this." She stroked her head. "Then we can get some sleep."

The Newfoundland stared at her with a blank expression that told Danni she wasn't buying any part of her story. If Danni hadn't been so tired, it would have been amusing. Sophie could always manage to provide levity in any situation. But she would laugh later. Right now, it was time to find out why Rob had returned sooner than expected.

Danni turned the handle on the door and opened it just enough to peer into the well-lit hallway, looking in the direction of the elevators. Taking a sleeping pill to forestall another sleepless night had seemed like a great idea two hours ago, but at this point she had to work hard to shake the cobwebs from her head.

None of this made sense. If Rob was in town, why had the alarm gone off?

Caleb tucked his Glock into his waistband and stood out of sight of the peephole, to the right of the door. If he was going to get the upper hand, he would have to catch the occupant of the apartment by surprise. No one who woke up in the middle of the night to a disturbance would give credence to a homeless guy barking instructions at them. They would expect the worse, so he prepared for a fight. The safety of innocents was his first objective.

He would explain his tactics later, after they were secured. And, although he hoped he wouldn't have to tackle a football player or a trigger-happy vigilante, Caleb was confident he could handle whoever appeared at the door. Years of training and street experience—along with the element of surprise—would give him an advantage. Still, he mustered all of his strength as the door opened wider.

The dark-haired woman dressed in a white robe took a tentative step into the hallway, peering to her right. She never saw what, or who, hit her. He lunged forward, pushing her sideways and back across the threshold into the safety of her apartment. With one arm around her waist to keep her from falling, he used the other to close the door behind them.

She screamed. And then a big dog lunged from out of nowhere.

CHAPTER 5

After midnight – March 18

The man who had pushed Danni was now lying in a fetal position on the entry floor and shielding his head from Sophie's snarling teeth. She had to do something. *But what?* There was no way to step around him and run for help.

She spotted a large vase on the hall table and reached to grab it. Securing the heavy object in both hands, Danni raised it high above her head, then hesitated. How could she be sure she wouldn't hit Sophie? The Newfoundland was her sole protector—the only thing between Danni and an unspeakable end, if this stranger should best her.

She would have to deliver a knockout blow. And it had to be accurate.

When Sophie backed off, Danni poised to strike. Then the intruder turned his face upward, pleading for her to call off the dog. *It was the face of the street stalker!*

Fear gripped Danni's throat, muffling her gasp, and then she heard the sound of gunfire down the hall. *He wasn't alone.*

She sent the vase crashing down onto the stranger's head.

An hour later, a uniformed Metro police officer sat perched on the edge of Danni's sofa. He held a notepad in one hand and a pen in the other.

Danni pushed deeper into a armchair halfway across the room. Sophie lay next to her on the floor. Since the attack, the dog hadn't left her side.

"Is that dog secure, ma'am?" The officer eyed Sophie.

"Yes, she's fine." Danni patted Sophie on the head. "I'm not sure what got into her a while ago. She usually loves people."

The officer assessed Danni's grip on the dog's collar and then continued his questioning. "Ms. . . . ?"

"Kemp. Danielle Kemp."

"Can you tell me what happened, Ms. Kemp?"

"I'm not sure." Danni pulled her robe tighter to her waist and thought back to the events of the past hour. "I heard voices shouting in the unit next door. Since it's my boyfriend's condo, and he's out of town, I decided to check it out." She replayed the moment in her head. "Then that obnoxious alarm went off."

"About what time was that?"

"I don't know. I'd been asleep an hour or two. Maybe one thirty?"

The man scribbled on his pad. "What happened next?"

"The sound was deafening. I knew I had to do something." Danni reflected on her decision to enter the hallway. "I guess I did the wrong thing. I probably should have stayed inside my unit."

"That might have been best, ma'am." The officer nodded as he continued to write.

"As soon as I opened the door the homeless man jumped at me. He pushed me back inside, and I thought . . ." An involuntary shiver ran down her spine. "I thought something awful was about to happen to me."

"I understand." The officer looked up.

For the first time, Danni saw compassion in his eyes. "I was scared. I didn't know what to do."

"That's when your dog attacked him?" He glanced toward Sophie, who was now sitting with her head in Danni's lap.

Danni relaxed her hold on the leash. "Yes. Thank God." She bent to give Sophie a kiss on the head. "But I couldn't bear the thought of her being hurt, and I was afraid the attacker was about to get the upper hand. That's why I grabbed the closest thing I could find." She sighed. "Unfortunately, it was an expensive vase. Rob is going to kill me."

"Is Rob your boyfriend?"

"Yes. Actually, we're almost engaged."

"Then I'm sure he'll agree that losing a vase is better than losing you, ma'am." The man studied her face.

"Of course." She was grateful the officer understood her predicament. Perhaps she wouldn't get in trouble for taking matters into her own hands. "I hope I didn't hurt him—you know, the homeless guy—too badly. Do you think he'll be okay?"

The officer returned his notebook to his pocket and stood. "He'll probably have a headache for a few days." The man chuckled. "We'll know more when we see you at the station."

"The police station?" Danni scrambled to her feet, wobbled, and steadied herself with the arm of the chair. The sleeping pill she had taken a few hours ago definitely hadn't been a good idea.

"Are you okay, ma'am?" The officer reached toward her. Sophie growled.

Danni reined in the leash. "Yes. I'm just . . . exhausted. I thought this was over. You know, I don't really want to go to the police station."

"I'm afraid it's necessary if you're going to press charges."

"Press charges? I'm not sure—"

"Ms. Kemp, I'm not trying to tell you what to do. But the guy did assault you in your own home. You could be saving another person from something worse down the road."

Or give him reason to come back for me. Especially now he knew where she lived. Or had he already known where she lived? After all he had found his way to her front door.

Danni's hands trembled as she wrapped her fingers around Sophie's collar and escorted the officer to the door.

"If we haven't heard from you, we'll follow up with you in a few days." He handed her a business card. "We'll also need to talk to your boyfriend. He will need to sign paperwork to press charges for the break-in next door."

Danni tucked the card into the pocket of her robe. "Thank you, officer. I'll have him call you as soon as he can. He's out of town."

"Goodnight, Ms. Kemp." The officer gestured to the deadbolt on her front door. "Lock yourself in and try to get some sleep."

Well, he could count on her locking the door. *But sleep?* That was a different matter. Closing the door and checking the lock twice, Danni took off in search of her phone. She had to talk to Rob now. Even if it was two o'clock in the morning.

Caleb awoke lying flat on his back in a speeding ambulance. The pain in his head dug deep into the left side of his skull, reminding him of the time his brother had whopped him on the head with a croquet mallet. Of course that childhood incident had been an accident. The dark-haired woman had intended to clobber him. Not that he blamed her. She had undoubtedly thought he was the bad guy. Undercover cops dressed as hobos weren't usually welcomed as houseguests.

The last thing Caleb remembered was reaching for his badge and then seeing a large object speeding toward his head. The crash had split his eardrums, and then shards of glass had penetrated his skull.

Ouch! Caleb made an effort to lift his hand, but an EMT sitting next to him grabbed his arm and eased it back to the cot. "Hey, buddy. You don't want to do that. Your hand is bandaged."

Bandaged? "Why—?"

"Dog bites." The tech smiled, a big toothy grin. "Before you got decked by a woman." The man shook his head. "A good-looking one too. What'd you do to deserve that?"

The big guy seemed to be enjoying Caleb's predicament. "Thanks for your sympathy, but I need to—" Caleb reached with his unbandaged hand for his badge.

"Whoa." The EMT grabbed his arm again. "No need to do that. The police took your weapon. Maybe you'll get it back if everything checks out. But for now, just relax and let us take care of you. We're almost to the hospital."

Robert Evans escorted his guest down the long, dimly lit hallway toward the exit of the bus. The soft light emitted by strings of digital LEDs running along the top and bottom of the front lounge sidewalls provided just enough illumination to navigate safely between the sofa on the left and a pair of leather chairs on the right.

He leaned across his guest to flip a switch on the driver's side panel, opening two hydraulic doors into the chilly night.

"I had a good time." The slender young woman, barely twenty years of age, if Rob had judged correctly, teetered on the top step and then planted a kiss on his cheek. "Call me sometime." She smiled.

He brushed his hand against her brow and nodded. She was a beautiful woman, but he didn't need to be tied down with another relationship. He stifled a yawn. He had a full schedule in the morning.

This morning. It was now well past midnight.

The blond hurried down the stairs, then turned and waved before disappearing around the front of the coach.

Rob lingered for just a second before closing the door and retracing his steps to the back of the bus. Picking up his phone, he saw several missed calls from Danni.

It would wait. Right now, he needed his sleep.

He switched the setting on his phone from Do Not Disturb and tossed the smartphone onto the nightstand before climbing into bed.

CHAPTER 6

Rob awoke from a dreamless sleep to the accusatory ring of his cell phone. Reaching across the darkness, he snagged the menacing object from his nightstand, answering without a glance to the caller ID. It was either Danni or one of his tour managers.

If it was Danni, she wouldn't be happy, because he hadn't called her back, but he could smooth it over easily enough. However, dealing with one his tour managers at this time of morning might require a little more finesse. He had learned years ago that the worst problems started at night or in the early morning when tour buses and trucks had stalled between cities. Or when band members had been busted for imbibing too much in a bar.

Rob cleared his head, and his throat, for what would come next. "Hello."

"Robert."

Ramirez? It wasn't the wakeup call he'd expected.

Rob sat up in bed. "Yes, sir."

"We have trouble in Nashville."

"Excuse me, sir?" Rob glanced at his watch. 5 a.m. "What could be—?"

"You've had a break-in at your place, and the word on the street is it was an amateur."

Val Ramirez's voice betrayed his anger, uncharacteristic for a man who could be listed in the dictionary under *stoic*.

43

Rob switched on his bedside lamp and rubbed his eyes. "I don't understand."

"You know as well as I do, Robert, a break-in is like sending an invitation to the cops."

"You're right, sir. I'll take care of it. I don't—"

"This is the last thing we need. I want to know how a street thug heard about your cache."

"I don't know, sir. I'm always careful." Rob swung around, dangling his feet off the side of the bed.

"I don't need to hear how careful you've been, Robert. I need your reassurance that this will be fixed." Ramirez sniped. "If you're incompetent enough to let this happen once, you'll eventually have the cops on your tail. And mine." The man paused long enough for Rob to swallow. "You don't want that to happen, and neither does your girlfriend."

"Danielle? She doesn't know anything about this, sir."

"Spare me the drama, Evans. Just keep her under your thumb, or you're going to wish you had."

"I'll handle it, sir."

"Good. Do it quickly. If you don't . . ." He waited a beat. "I'll have to, and you don't want that to happen."

Rob swallowed again.

"Understood?"

"Yes, sir."

The line went dead, and Rob dropped his phone and slumped forward, supporting his head with his fists.

This couldn't be happening. He had to stop the fallout. And quickly. Ramirez was right. News about his second income must have reached the backstreets of Nashville, and it was only a matter of time before his secret life would be exposed. He had to act fast.

Thankfully, he'd been smart enough to leave the last stash of money with Danni, forestalling an even bigger disaster. But he had to find out how much she knew. If Ramirez made good on his threat, they would both be in danger.

Not long after the first light filtered through her bedroom window, Danni threw back the covers. Staring at the ceiling wasn't accomplishing anything. She would manage to get through the day on adrenaline and caffeine.

After the police officer left, she had dropped into a fitful sleep for what might have been a couple of hours, due only to the sedative she had taken earlier in the night. But the pill hadn't been a perfect elixir. Judging from the looks of the disheveled bed linens, she had fought with the homeless man in her dreams.

Anger settled into the back of her neck, stirring the beginning of a headache. She would have rested easier if she had spoken to Rob. The thought of his sleeping through her phone calls when she needed him most grated on her already-frayed nerves. She had been attacked by a madman inside her own home!

Her heart pounded. Her life had been invaded by something she didn't understand or recognize. And she had the uneasy feeling it was about to get worse. If she pressed charges against her assailant, wouldn't she be inviting more trouble? He knew where she lived—and that she lived alone.

A sudden chill in the room prompted Danni to drape her robe around her shoulders. She slid her feet into her house slippers and headed down the hall to reset the thermostat.

None of this made sense. How did the intruders get past the security guard? And what were the chances the homeless guy would be standing at her door at the same time Rob's condo was burglarized? Were the two men working together?

The police officer had told her the burglar had walked past all of the obvious things, like electronic equipment and artwork, to mine the contents of Rob's closet, and based on what Rob had said before he left town, he had cash in there. A lot of cash. Just as she now had in her clos—

Oh, no! What if someone knew she was keeping Rob's money? Her place could be next. Is that why the homeless man had targeted her?

Panic set in. What should she do? She had always heard that criminals didn't stay in jail for long. He would be back on the street soon, and she would be—

Danni stopped herself mid-thought.

Why was she making up scenarios? There was a good chance Rob's place had been targeted at random. And most likely the Rutherford had already stepped up their security because of last night's break-in.

She forced a breath, willing herself to relax. There was no way the homeless guy or the burglar could know she had a briefcase full of Rob's cash in her closet. And she had survived last night, thanks to Sophie.

Sophie. Where was Sophie?

The big dog was usually at Danni's side the minute she awoke. She had a sixth sense that alerted her to Danni's rousing. But Danni hadn't seen her this morning.

"Sophie?"

Danni wandered back to her bedroom and into the adjoining en suite, where she saw four sets of toes peeking from the dark recess of the closet.

"Get up, lazy girl. It's time for our morning run."

Sophie responded with a *thump, thump, thump* of her tail against the pecan wood floor. Danni switched on the closet light, and the dog stared at her. Her brown eyes pleaded for a few more minutes of rest.

Danni kneeled, folded her body over the Newfie and stroked her back and neck, enjoying her warmth. It would be easy to fall asleep right here on the floor next to her.

"Thanks for being my protector last night, girl. We make a good team." Danni planted a kiss on the dog's muzzle. "It sure would be nice though to have a hero rescue us once in a while."

Sophie responded with another thump of her tail, and Danni jumped to her feet. "Okay. I'm giving you fifteen minutes, missy. But as soon as I'm dressed, and I've had my coffee, I'm leaving. With or without you."

Twice that long, and two cups of caffeine later, Danni snapped a leash onto Sophie's collar, and they set out for their routine Monday morning run to the Bicentennial Mall. The small park, nestled between downtown government buildings and the farmers market, was one of the few remaining patches of grass in a city that had sprouted nothing but skyscrapers in the past five years.

By eight o'clock the sun had transformed the night air into a palpable coolness, pumping enthusiasm into Danni's gait. About the time they turned down Rosa L. Parks Boulevard, her four-legged companion began pulling at the leash.

"We needed this, didn't we, girl?" Danni inhaled the scent of the fresh air. A brisk outdoor run had always been the perfect medicine for her. Jaycee said Danni was trying to run away from her problems and that they would eventually catch up with her. Danni always countered with the idea that, at least by that time, she would have fighting adrenaline running through her veins.

Danni looked both ways as they crossed Charlotte Avenue toward the ceremonial railroad trestle, and a familiar ring shattered the quiet. *Rob.*

She answered her phone and pulled Sophie toward a nearby picnic table.

"Where were you when I called last night?"

"Good morning to you too."

Danni offered no response. Instead she took a seat.

"I must have been in a no-service zone. Are you okay? I just saw I had a message from you."

"I'm fine." Danni's hand trembled as she tugged on Sophie's leash. "But your condo was broken into last night."

There was a beat of silence.

"Why? Who would have—?"

"The cops said he was a young street thug. And he had a gun, Rob. It went off when the police arrested him."

"The police were in my condo?"

That was all he was worried about?

"I'm fine, Rob." Danni stood and pulled the dog forward. "Thank you for asking."

"I didn't mean it that way. I'd assumed you were okay since we're talking." He huffed into the phone. "What's wrong with you today?"

"Are you serious? You have no idea what my night was like."

"Look . . . babe, I'm sorry. You *are* okay, right?"

"Yes. But . . ." She thought about the man who had attacked her.

"What, Danni?"

"It gets worse."

"What happened?" The tone in Rob's voice climbed an octave.

She told him about the homeless man and how Sophie had saved them both. "It was awful."

"Wow. It sounds like it." His voice faded. "So the two guys were working together?"

"There were two men, but I don't know if they were working together. The police are still investigating."

"Hmmm . . ."

Either the connection had been lost, or he was now preoccupied.

"Rob, are you there? I keep losing you."

"I'm here. This is just, just a lot to take in quickly." He cleared his throat and mumbled something indiscernible.

Danni looked at her phone. "What? I can't hear you."

"I said did the first guy damage my place? What about my electronics, the artwork?"

"He walked right past everything. The police said he was digging through the closet in your master suite when they found him."

"Are you serious?" The pitch in his voice rose again. "Did he—did they?—find anything?"

"I don't think so." She directed Sophie around a tree. "The police asked me to have you call them. I have the number at th—"

"Why do they need to talk to me?"

Danni shook her head. "They probably want you to file charges, Rob. Or tell them what might be missing. What else would they want?"

He grew quiet again. "Babe . . . do you think you could take care of this for me?"

"You mean do more than I already have?"

"I know. Really, Danni. I know. And I appreciate it, but I'm on the road." He stumbled through his words. "Just tell the police that I appreciate their offer to help, but that I don't want to file charges."

Well, if you don't, I will. Danni bit her tongue. "Rob, I was attacked. I can't let this drop. And I'm not sure that you—" *I'm not sure that you even care.* The final words not making it past her lips choked her to tears.

"Danielle," Robbed soothed, "you know I appreciate everything you do for me."

"Is that why it took you so long to call me back?"

"I told you, I didn't get your message until this morning."

"Rob!" She turned toward the fountains nearby. "I need to file charges against the man who attacked me."

"I don't think it's a good idea. Let this go." He was clearly aggravated, but so was she.

"Let's call off the wedding . . . At least for now. There's too much—"

"What? Why?"

But she had thought this through. "With you being out of town so much, I need more time. I still have a lot to do."

"Just to mail a few invitations? Danielle?"

"I have to find a church, buy a dress, and before I mail invitations I'll have to put together the guest list."

"Maybe Melissa can help you with the guest list. I'll ask her to start on it. Won't that help?

"I suppose."

"What else can I do to help?"

"Nothing, I suppose."

"Great." He waited a beat. "So when you talk to the police, don't tell them any more than you have to, okay?"

They were back on that subject?

"What do you mean?"

"You know, about the cash we have at our places. They don't need to know about that."

"Of course not."

"Thank you, babe. I'm glad you're okay. I don't know what I would do if something happened to you. I'm sorry you had a bad night."

A bad night? She took a deep breath and bit back her thoughts. Again. "I'm better now."

"Okay. Keep me posted. I want to know about everything, including the police report, and I'll talk to you tomorrow. Okay?"

She didn't answer.

"Or later today if you need me."

"Okay." Danni disconnected the call and slipped the phone into her pocket. Only a few days ago, she had decided to take charge of her life. To make changes. To move beyond her past mistakes. But by all appearances she was going backwards.

She steered the dog back onto the sidewalk. Maybe it would be easier to run away from her problems than to face them head on. The thought was appealing.

Then again, that's what her mother had done. And that hadn't ended well.

CHAPTER 7

One week later – March 25

A portion of the downtown Nashville skyline reflected off the north-facing windows of the Metropolitan Nashville Central Police Precinct building. As she walked closer, Danni took a deep breath to calm her nerves. She had every right to do this, even if Rob had been against it. If she didn't stand up for herself and file charges against her attacker, someone else might fall prey to him. And they might not have a dog or a vase to protect themselves.

She looked both ways before crossing Korean Veterans Boulevard, which ran between the Cumberland River and the Eighth Avenue Roundabout. Pulling open the heavy metal front door, she peered into the small, aseptic reception area, one not unlike the cold antechambers of many other government offices. Although sparsely decorated, it was less intimidating than she had feared.

Danni diverted her attention to the video camera hanging from the ceiling in the corner of the small rectangular space. To her right, a middle-aged African American woman occupied a chair behind a security window. She wore a police officer's uniform that bore the blue and gold seal of the Nashville Davidson

County Metropolitan Police Department—the same emblem hanging on the wall above her.

A row of brochures lined the counter in front of the window. One read *Criminal Warrants Division, Warrants Section, Fugitive Section, US Marshal's Fugitive Task Force.* Another referenced the victim information hotline.

Maybe it was time to rethink the intimidation factor.

"May I help you?" The woman behind the glass broke into Danni's thoughts.

Danni offered an obligatory smile. "I called earlier about signing paperwork."

"Your name?" The woman peered over the top of wire-framed glasses.

"Danielle Kemp, ma'am."

The woman nodded. "And who did you speak with, Ms. Kemp?"

Danni dug for the small scrap of paper she'd stashed inside the Michael Kors satchel Rob had given her for her birthday.

"Sergeant Schlessman. Rick Schlessman."

The female officer pointed toward a single metal chair on the opposite side of the room. "Have a seat. I'll let him know you're here."

Danni pulled her cardigan tighter and took a seat. Based on the comfort, or rather discomfort, of the chair, she shouldn't be waiting long.

She snagged her phone from her handbag and scanned her emails. The first three, all from Jaycee, could wait. And so could the note from her sister in Iowa. But Chamber of Commerce special events manager, Sarah Williams, had marked her correspondence as urgent. Danni read it quickly. The Chamber wanted to add another item to the dessert menu for today's luncheon—a birthday cake for the Chamber vice president.

She glanced at her watch. Not good. Their lunch was less than three hours away. Jaycee wouldn't be happy, but Danni knew the chef would get it done.

Before forwarding the note, she added a frowny face to the top.

In ten minutes she had powered through the remaining stack either answering, rerouting, or flagging each message, then muting her phone and putting it away. She glanced at her watch again. What was keeping him?

Right on cue, the elevator door in the back of the room opened and a uniformed officer stepped forward. He offered his hand and a pleasant smile.

"Good morning, Ms. Kemp."

Danni stood. "Officer Schlessman?"

"Yes. Please follow me."

Danni hesitated. "Will this take long?"

"It shouldn't." He escorted her to the elevator, waved his badge in front of the security portal, and held the door open for her. "I just need to go over everything with you." He smiled again and pressed the second-floor button.

After a quick ascent, the elevator door opened into another sterile-looking environment. Danni followed the officer down a corridor, which appeared to be connected to a spiderweb of hallways, each filled with people. It was controlled chaos, much like the kitchen at Amoré.

Men and women, some dressed in police uniforms, some wearing civilian clothes, milled about. Others rushed past, disappearing around a corner.

In one adjoining hallway, several uniformed officers had gathered in a loose semicircle, chatting, laughing, and whispering. Another group of men were huddled in a corridor and spoke in hushed tones.

Sergeant Schlessman escorted Danni into a small conference room that had been outfitted with a window overlooking the main hallway.

"Please, have a seat. I'll be back in a few minutes. Would you like a cup of coffee?"

"No, thanks. I just need to leave as soon as—"

"This won't take long. Make yourself comfortable." He closed the door as he left.

Danni retrieved her phone from her bag, confirmed that it was muted, stowed it, and then turned her attention to the room. It was clean enough. At least on the surface. But something about it made her want to pull out a bottle of disinfectant spray.

She lowered herself into a chair. Hopefully, this wouldn't take long.

Repositioning her body toward the window that overlooked the hall, she noticed a small group of men had gathered nearby. They talked and laughed as though they didn't have a care in the world.

Our tax dollars at work. They should be out on the streets in search of criminals instead of cavorting inside a police station. Danni frowned and looked closer.

One man, who had his back turned to her, appeared to be the center of attention. Dressed in khakis and a button-down shirt, he looked like he could be the police chief or some other muckety-muck. Perhaps he was an off-duty detective. Or a local news reporter putting in time at the station to chase down the facts for a story.

That was probably it. He did look familiar. If only he would turn his head.

Almost on beat, the man wheeled around to speak to a woman passing in the hallway, and Danni saw his face. It was his big, dark

eyes that took her breath away. They were the eyes of the homeless man who had attacked her.

She blinked and looked again. It couldn't be.

It was. It was him!

But why here? And dressed in normal attire? That's why she
hadn't recognized him at first. He was actually quite handsome.
His dark brown hair was combed in a reasonable style, not greasy
and limp. And his clothes were neat and clean.

Still, she was certain it was him. It was his eyes. She would
never forget his eyes. They terrified her.

She had to leave! But as soon as she stood, he looked her way.
Danni froze.

There was no doubt he recognized her. And this time, instead
of looking away in disgust, as he had done when they met on the
street, he held her gaze.

He leaned toward the man standing next to him and spoke
something in his ear. The second man turned and stared at her
too. She was being viewed through the window like a chimpanzee
in a zoo.

Danni swung the strap of her handbag over her shoulder and
rushed toward the door. If anyone tried to stop her she would say
she had an urgent appointment at the restaurant. That something
had come up, and she would return later for the paperwork.

But as she reached for the handle, Officer Schlessman opened
the door.

"I'm sorry, ma'am. That took longer than I expected. Our
copy machine was down."

"I was just . . ." Danni caught her breath. ". . . leaving. My
office called and—" She had never been good at lying. "I need to
go, so if you will excuse me, I'll . . ."

A gray-haired man in uniform, the one who had been standing next to her attacker, walked into the room behind Schlessman. The older man whispered into the sergeant's ear, glanced at Danni, and then retreated into the hallway.

Schlessman's expression sobered. "Excuse me, Ms. Kemp. I'll be right back."

He pulled the door closed behind him.

What was going on?

CHAPTER 8

Caleb ducked into a side room to call his superior at the Tennessee Bureau of Investigation. It took less than a minute to reach Martin Ridge, the head of the Drug Investigation Division and another thirty seconds to confirm Caleb's suspicions. Ridge wanted to talk to the dark-haired woman and find out what she knew.

They couldn't risk letting her leave and break Caleb's cover. Maybe even cause irreparable damage to the case. They were too close to connecting the dots to let this woman ruin months of hard work.

Caleb stepped back into the hallway, a man on a mission. He would find out if the woman was involved or an unwilling—perhaps even unwitting—accessory.

When he saw Lieutenant Hale, the officer in charge on the floor at Metro today, he motioned for Hale to join him. Hale sauntered toward Caleb, looking somewhat like a kid in a candy shop, wearing a lopsided grin and an eager expression. "What's going on, Samuels?"

"I need your help," Caleb confided. "My boss is on his way over. He should be here in about ten minutes. Can we use one of your rooms to talk with a witness?"

"Ms. Kemp?"

Caleb nodded.

"Of course." Hale checked his watch. "Would you mind filling me in while we wait?"

Caleb clapped the lieutenant on the shoulder. "I hope to be able to tell you everything soon. But I'll need my boss to confirm that we have authorization." He pulled his hand away and winced from the bite marks on his forearm. "This case is much bigger than me."

Hale pressed. "So the Feds are involved?"

"I didn't say that." Caleb flashed a smile.

"You didn't have to." The police supervisor motioned for his officer, a man whose nametag read *Schlessman*. "Rick, the TBI needs to borrow our room for a while. Can you keep an eye on the girl until they're ready for the interview?"

"Yes, sir." Schlessman all but saluted.

Caleb nodded his thanks.

No doubt Hale ran a tight ship, but the TBI would be happy to show them a few tricks of the trade, courtesy of Martin Ridge.

Danni willed herself to try to relax, but her stomach churned as she thought about the possibilities. She was a numbers girl, and nothing about this situation added up.

Was the homeless man actually an undercover police officer? If so, why had he assaulted her? And why had he been watching her on the street? Didn't undercover cops spy on bad guys?

Had he confused her with someone else? And why was no one telling her what was going on? All of this had to be a misunderstanding.

She glanced at the clock on the wall. Ten past ten. There was no way she would make it to Amoré in time for the Chamber luncheon. She had to let Jaycee know she would be dealing with it on her own.

Pulling her phone from her handbag, Danni saw she had missed two calls and a text from Jaycee. The text was cryptic.

Problem! Need to talk ASAP.

Danni groaned. Jaycee had no idea. What she wouldn't give for an ordinary workplace problem this morning. At least Jaycee could be proactive in dealing with whatever situation she had at the restaurant. Danni was sitting here at the mercy of the Metro Nashville Police Department. And it appeared the hands of justice were moving at a snail's pace.

She typed a quick reply.

Still at police station. You'll have to handle the luncheon on your own.

Danni sent the message, and then typed *I'm sorry.* But before she could send it as well, the door opened, and Schlessman walked into the room.

"My apologies, Ms. Kemp. Something urgent came up." He gestured to her phone. "You need to turn that off, ma'am."

Danni frowned, sent the message, and shoved the phone into her purse.

"I was sending a note to my office." She pointed at the clock on the wall. "I've been here longer than I expected, and I need to know—"

"Please, Ms. Kemp." The officer gestured for her to take a seat. "I'll explain while we go over paperwork."

"I keep hearing that, but—"

"This is just routine, ma'am." His expression wavered. "I am sorry. Really. I realize it's inconvenient for you." He appeared to be genuinely contrite. "But we want to be sure we have everything we need so you don't have to deal with this again."

"I would love that." Danni offered a flickering smile. Maybe she would be out of here soon and all of this would be behind her.

He slumped into the chair on the opposite side of the table, a six-top in her business, although this was far from a fine-dining experience. Schlessman stretched his long legs between her and the only exit in the room. Then he placed a short stack of papers on the tabletop.

Danni waited, watching as he meticulously reviewed the first few pages. A minute later, he refocused on her. "Are you sure you wouldn't like to take me up on that cup of coffee before we get started?"

"No!" She huffed. "I'd like to get out of here."

"You have no idea how good our coffee is." He grinned.

"Okay." Danni softened her resolve, sinking a bit into her chair. "That would be great. Thank you."

"How do you like it?" He stood and took two steps to the door, easing it open.

"Black, please. And . . ." She offered a wry smile. "In a to-go cup."

"Got it." He chuckled and walked out, closing the door behind him.

She fought the urge to open the door and leave. But there was no telling who could be roaming the halls. Hadn't she just seen the homeless guy? She shook off a chill. As a matter of fact, hot coffee might be just what she needed right now.

A few minutes later, when the door opened, instead of Schlessman, it was the gray-haired man she had seen through the window. He strolled into the room carrying two cups.

"I believe this is yours." He handed one to Danni and took a sip from the other.

"I'm Lieutenant Jeff Hale." He extended his right hand. "I'm sorry this has taken so long. I'm sure you have a busy schedule, but a new detail about this case has come to our attention." He took a seat. "You appear to be a woman of integrity. May we have a bit more of your time?"

Danni nodded.

"Thank you. We need to ask you a few additional questions about what happened the night of the break-in."

Danni relaxed into her chair. Although the morning hadn't gone as expected, maybe this was routine after all. She glanced again at the clock on the wall.

"Lieutenant, I'll be happy to help. But I would appreciate your assistance in keeping it as brief as possible. I've been here for forty-five minutes, and—"

Before she could finish her sentence, the door opened again. This time two men entered the room.

And one of them was her attacker.

CHAPTER 9

Caleb knew he had made a mistake as soon as he walked into the room. The dark-haired woman stiffened and sat back in her chair, an attempt to put as much space as possible between them.

What had he been thinking? That she would welcome him into the room? He should have asked Ridge to go ahead of him and introduce him. It wouldn't have eliminated her fear, the shock of coming face to face with her attacker. But it might have lessened the impact.

Still there was more than fear in her eyes. There was anger. And questioning. She appeared to be trying to make sense of what was happening around her. It was that confusion—in her eyes and in her body language—that convinced Caleb she was an innocent victim of Evans's. Just like the hundreds, maybe thousands, who stood to be hurt by him. Or already had been.

Caleb prayed to God that he and Ridge could do a good job with this interrogation. If she knew enough, they could be on the verge of a major break in the Evans case. Danielle Kemp had only to provide them with a few important details, and they would be well on their way to a warrant.

Maybe even prosecution.

The latter thought was so appealing it didn't matter to him at the moment whether Danielle Kemp was guilty or innocent.

One woman's temporary discomfort was a small price to pay. He waited for Ridge to begin.

Danni studied the face of the man who had attacked her. For a moment, he met her gaze, then he turned to the older man who had preceded him into the room. Judging from how the first man carried himself, he was in charge. And the scowl on his face indicated he wasn't happy to be here.

Well, neither was she. She stood to leave.

"Sit, Ms. Kemp!" The unhappy man barked.

"Not until I find out why you're holding me here." She pointed to her attacker. "And why is he here?"

"Danielle . . ."

Her attacker knew her name!

"I'm Caleb Samuels." He spoke softly. "I'm a special agent and undercover officer for the Tennessee Bureau of Investigation."

"The TBI?" Danni looked from the younger man to the older man, and then back again. "I don't understand."

Samuels nodded toward his partner. "This is Martin Ridge, my boss and the head of the Drug Investigation Division."

"But why—? I don't—"

Lieutenant Hale stepped into Danni's peripheral vision. "Ma'am, these gentlemen only want to ask a few questions. I'll be in the hall if you need me." He offered her a reassuring smile. "Please, have a seat."

As the door clicked behind him, Danni lowered herself into a chair. "What's this all about?"

The younger man spoke again. "We're investigating a crime that's related to the break-in last week. As Lieutenant Hale said, we only want to ask you a few questions." He gestured to the older man, who was now occupying the chair at the end of the table, opposite her. "We appreciate your time today. Don't we, sir?"

The older man grunted.

"May I?" Samuels pointed to the chair next to Danni.

She nodded, and he took a seat.

"I want to begin with an apology." He ran his hand through his well-coiffed hair. "What happened last week was unfortunate, but I want you to know I did it with the full intent of keeping you safe. I had to react quickly, and with force, to protect you from what could have been a deadly situation."

Danni considered his face as he spoke. His chiseled features would be somewhat handsome in other circumstances. "I was undercover that evening, and I'm sure my choice of wardrobe added to your misunderstanding." He placed his badge on the table between them.

His credentials looked legitimate, and his explanation seemed reasonable. Perhaps his story was plausible.

"I hope my dog didn't hurt you too badly." Danni apologized.

Samuels rubbed his forehead. "Not as much as your vase."

Heat rushed to Danni's cheeks. "If I'd only known."

He grinned. "Of course. You had no idea."

"But why were you on the street that morn—?"

Ridge interrupted from the end of the table. "Now that we've made small talk, let's move forward with the business at hand." Considering the lines in his face, the older man appeared to wear a permanent scowl. "We need a few answers from you, Ms. Kemp."

Danni tilted her chin upwards. "I hope it won't take long. I'm already late for work."

Ridge shook his head and grunted. "That will depend on how forthcoming you are."

"Ms. Kemp." It was Samuels again. He hesitated. "May I call you Danielle?"

"Yes, that's fine."

He flashed a near perfect smile. "How well do you know Robert Evans?"

"What do you mean? Rob is . . . my fiancé." She rethought her reply. "Well, actually, we're about to become engaged."

"So you know him very well." Ridge asked, making it sound like an allegation.

"Of course. I wouldn't marry someone I didn't know. Would you?"

"That's unfortunate." The older man shook his head and set his coffee cup on the table.

Danni glanced to Samuels, but he remained quiet.

She continued. "Rob and I have dated for more than two years. Of course, I don't know everything about him." *Not that it was any of their business.* "We live separately."

"I understand he travels for a living?" Samuels asked.

"He does. He manages entertainers." She glanced toward Ridge. "A long list of them."

"Do you have any idea how much Mr. Evans earns a year?"

Danni leaned back in her chair. "What does all of this have to do with a burglary at Rob's apartment? You're acting as though he's the criminal. It was his place that was burglarized."

She looked from one man to another, but neither responded.

"As I've said, Rob and I aren't married, and I don't expect to know everything about his financial matters." She took a moment to calculate. "I would guess he earns in the mid-six figures."

"Only six?" Ridge sneered. "So can you please explain to me how he maintains an overseas bank account in the millions?"

Danni started.

"Perhaps you weren't aware of that, Ms. Kemp?" Ridge seemed to delight in surprising her.

She folded her hands in her lap and chose to remain silent, wondering what these men were after.

"Danielle," Agent Samuels's voice soothed, "this may be a surprise to you, but we believe Robert Evans is involved in the international distribution of drugs."

Danni choked out a laugh. "You are kidding, right? Rob?" She glanced from one man to the other, and then shook her head. "You heard that from someone in the music industry, didn't you?"

All of this was becoming perfectly clear.

"Rob is not well-liked among his peers. They're jealous because of his success."

Samuels's dark eyes softened. "So you believe what we're suggesting is rumor?"

"Where else would something like that come from?" She searched the agent's face for a connection. He must understand peer rivalry. He looked to be about Rob's age, perhaps in his early thirties, although he was much rougher around the edges. Attractive, but not handsome like Rob.

She took in a long breath, exhaled, and forced a smile. "Look . . . Rob is a genteel kind of a guy. He would rather play tennis or travel on that bus of his than to get his hands dirty." She looked directly at Ridge, not trying to hide her dismay. "Much less deal in a petty street crime."

"Petty street crime?" The older man mocked her with a heavy sigh.

Samuels nodded. Thankfully, one of them understood.

"Rob isn't the kind of person who would go out looking for trouble, no matter what gossip you might have heard about him."

"Our sources are not gossip, Ms. Kemp." The older man stood and crossed the room. "We've been watching your boyfriend for weeks. You may not know him as well as you think you do." He stood over her, his face contorting in anger. "Or is this your attempt to distance yourself from him?"

"Are we finished now?" Danni struggled to get to her feet, but her knees buckled, and she fell backwards into her chair. She looked from Ridge to Samuels.

"We're not finished, Ms. Kemp." Ridge turned to walk back to his seat. "And you won't leave until we say you can leave."

"I don't understand."

Ridge pivoted and pointed his finger at her. "Let me make myself clear then. If you don't give us the information we need about Robert Evans, we will charge you as an accessory to the crime."

"Crime? What crime?" None of this made sense. It was Rob's condo that had been broken into. Her stomach began to churn.

The corners of Ridge's lips tightened, and his already pasty skin turned whiter. "Transporting illegal drugs across state lines for the purpose of resale. Money laundering. And conspiracy to commit fraud against the US government."

CHAPTER 10

"Are you okay?"

Danni heard TBI Agent Samuels's words before she saw his face, and when she opened her eyes, he was right above her. The last thing she remembered was the room spinning.

"Did I faint?"

"Yes." He grinned.

She reached for the pain in her head and realized she was lying on the floor in Caleb Samuels's arms. Not good timing for one of her spells.

"Did you hurt your head?"

"Not really. Just my pride." Danni winced.

"Are you sure you're okay?"

"Yes." Danni pushed the agent away and scrambled to her feet. Faster than she should have.

Samuels steadied her as she settled into the chair she had occupied before her fall.

"We're calling for medical assistance." Ridge had his hand on the phone.

"No, please don't. I'm fine. Really. I just need a few minutes to—" To remember where their conversation had left off. Seeing Ridge's scowling face reminded her.

"Are we finished with this little love fest?" The older man groaned from across the room and then tossed his phone onto the table. "I'd like to get through this interrogation before lunchtime."

"*Interrogation*? Is that what this is?" Danni huffed. "Perhaps I should call my attorney."

"You're welcome to call your attorney, Ms. Kemp." Ridge straightened in his chair and shoved his phone further across the table in her direction. "But I will tell you that we're not prepared to charge you with anything today. We're only trying to learn more about Mr. Evans. And, if you will calm down and answer a few more questions, we will be done soon."

"How am I supposed to calm down when I have no idea what's going on?" She stared at the phone and then back at him. "I'm innocent of whatever you seem to be alleging and . . . and so is Rob."

"Is that so?" Ridge chuckled. "Well, you'll need to prove that to me."

Caleb, who had retaken his seat a few feet from Danni, intervened. "Of course, we'd like to believe that's the case." He reviewed his notes and then looked back at her. "Let me make sure I understand something we discussed earlier. Are you engaged to marry Robert Evans?"

Danni hesitated. How did you explain being *engaged* to be engaged?

"Not officially," she said.

"What's that supposed to mean? Are you or not?" Ridge's cheeks burned red. "Frankly, Ms. Kemp, I'm almost as confused as you are."

"I don't have a ring, but we've set a date." That was the truth, the whole truth, and nothing but the truth.

Samuels cleared his throat, drawing her attention back to him. "Okay, so you're dating Mr. Evans. How long have you known him?"

"Two . . . almost three years."

Ridge set his coffee cup down hard, and Danni jumped.

"Do you use illicit drugs, Ms. Kemp?"

"Of course not!"

"Does Mr. Evans use illicit drugs?"

"No!" She looked from Ridge to Samuels, hoping to find support in the face of the latter. When he didn't respond, she added, "Well, not that I'm aware."

"Do you have a key to Mr. Evans's home, Danielle?" It was Samuels this time.

"Yes. Do I need to call my attorney?"

"That's up to you, Ms. Kemp." Ridge pointed to the phone.

"Danielle," Samuels intervened again, "I'm sure this has been a difficult week for you. Your life was endangered by an intruder at the Rutherford. You've been told there's a drug ring operating out of the condominium next door. And, unfortunately, that condominium is owned by your boyfriend."

Danni nodded.

"We only have a few more questions." He paused, presumably giving her time to object. When she didn't, he continued. "Do you know if Mr. Evans keeps large sums of money in his home?"

Danni swallowed. How did she respond to that? Did a money-filled briefcase count?

"Sometimes."

Samuels and Ridge exchanged glances.

"How much money?" Samuels leaned toward her.

"I don't know." She looked away and then back to him. "I only know what Rob has told me, that he has some cash at his place. And . . ." She shifted her focus to the floor and steepled her hands. "And before he went out of town last week, he gave me a briefcase filled with cash to keep for him. He said it was money from one of his artist's merchandise sales. And other things."

"Do you know how much money?" Samuels's jaw tightened.

"No." She searched his dark eyes hoping to find reassurance. "I don't, I'm sorry." *Why did she want so badly for him to believe her?*

"Aren't you an accountant, Ms. Kemp?" Ridge asked.

"I have a degree in accounting. I'm a restaurant manager."

"But you didn't count the money that came into your possession?" He arched an eyebrow.

"I didn't bother to open the briefcase. Rob told me it was cash. I simply stored it in my closet for his return. Just as he'd asked."

The older agent guffawed. "Do you really expect us to believe you're so naïve? Why are you hiding drug money if you aren't involved?"

"It's not drug money. It's money from Rob's business." She looked to Samuels. "That's what he told me."

"Danielle," the younger agent said, sitting back in his chair, "I'm concerned for your safety. By now every thug in Nashville may know you're hiding money in your home." He shot a glance toward his boss, then back to her. "You need us on your side, not against you."

"But Rob isn't—"

Samuels held up his hand. "If we're wrong, you'll be helping prove his innocence."

Her resolve was beginning to fade, and her stomach began to churn. Why did everything with Rob have to be so complicated? She had no doubt he was innocent, but she wouldn't be in this situation if it weren't for him.

Ridge stood and walked toward her. "Ms. Kemp, there is only one way we can be sure you aren't involved with this." He placed his hand on the back of Samuels's chair. "You need to agree to help us."

"How?" She looked from Ridge to Samuels and then back to Ridge. "What could I possibly do?"

Ridge pulled a small box from the pocket of his jacket and placed it on the table in front of Samuels. "The thug who broke into Robert Evans's condo told us he was sent to retrieve this. Most likely, he was also hoping to find money Evans had stashed."

"What is it?" Danni studied the box, which wasn't much bigger than the one her necklace had come in.

Ridge slid a small bag from the box. "Methamphetamine. Also known on the street as crystal meth, ice, and poor man's cocaine. Its value is about $1,500."

"But how can you be sure it came from Rob's place?"

"We can't." Samuels admitted. "But we have good reason to think Evans's drug ring boss believes he's withholding from him."

The younger man gestured toward the bag. "And this corroborates that theory."

Danni sat silently, not sure what to believe. Everything they were alleging was theory. Samuels had just said so.

"Your help could give us important information that may save lives, including Rob's." Samuels seemed determined to sway her. "As well as your own."

Danni settled back into her chair. "Do you really think I'm in danger?"

"We hope not." Ridge appeared to be sympathetic. "But your relationship with Mr. Evans, not to mention your proximity to him, puts you in a precarious position."

"The TBI will protect you." Samuels leaned forward again. "And you can help us learn the truth about Rob."

"I don't see that I have much choice. I'm not a criminal." She glanced from one man to the other, hoping they believed her.

Samuels nodded.

"Okay," she said. "I'll do it. I'll help you. But I want you to understand, both of you." She looked from Samuels to Ridge. "I'm only helping so I can clear Rob's name. And my own." She toyed with the pendant on the chain around her neck. "You will soon owe me—and him—a very big apology."

Ridge gritted his teeth. "Ms. Kemp, you have it all wrong." He nodded to her necklace. "The money that bought you that was dirty. You're the one who needs to understand . . . and to get your priorities straight. Too many innocent lives depend on it."

CHAPTER 11

Pushing through the glass and steel door, Danni hurried from the lobby of the central precinct police building into the fresh air. Freedom at last. At least for the moment, until she could fully assess what had just happened.

The noonday sun had chased away the morning chill, so she shrugged out of her sweater, threaded it through the handles of her handbag, and stopped to catch her breath. Why was it suddenly so hard to breathe?

Because more than the weather had changed in the last three hours?

Everything she had counted on or believed to be true—her faith in the judicial system, the trust she'd had for Rob, and her ability to read people—had been hijacked by an unseemly stalker who had turned out to be a cop.

None of that made any sense, even if Danni dared believe it, but enough rang true that it took her breath away. She already had doubts about Rob. But those were more about his ability to commit, not about his character. There was no way the man she had known for close to three years could do what those men had alleged.

She straightened her shoulders and turned to the right, the closest route to Amoré and the normalcy she now craved. Her perspective would be better there. This place was skewed toward the criminal elements of life. And while law enforcement was a good thing, these people had no idea who Rob was.

He was a consummate professional. And he didn't like to get his hands dirty, period. Much less deal in something like illicit drugs. If Rob had a fault, it was his dedication to his work. And, while that might be frustrating, it wasn't a crime.

And to accuse her of being involved? She half coughed, half laughed. Samuels and his superior were operating off a ridiculous notion. They were operating on half-truths. Miscommunication. And, unfortunately, probably rumors. She shook her head. But how long would it take to straighten it all out?

In the meantime, she had too much to do, starting with the Chamber lunch at the restaurant today. Jaycee had to be frantic by now.

She checked her watch again. Half-past twelve o'clock. Jaycee would be beyond frantic. She would be furious.

Danni's pulse quickened. The panic—and doubt—was trying to return. *Please God, not another fainting spell.* They always came at the worst time, when she needed her wits about her the most.

She inhaled a ragged breath. Then another. Breathing and exhaling deeper each time. She had learned how to fight this, at least when she knew it was coming on. Back in the interrogation room, she had been blindsided by Ridge's accusations. But here, she could win.

She grew stronger with every breath until she could finally move forward again. Halfway between the police building and Sixth Avenue South, the cityscape began to spin around her, and she reached out. But she had nothing to hold on to. Not a pillar, not a sign post, and certainly not Rob. He had put her in this place, and all she had to lean on was her own determination. And the belief instilled in her by her father that she could do anything she set out to do. That she was strong enough.

She picked her way to the corner. Moving forward, despite her anxiety about what was ahead. The tiny spring buds and delicate green leaves on the trees to her left were proof life remained.

Reaching the street, she hesitated, then turned to look back at the concrete and glass edifice where she had spent the last few hours. She drew in another breath and started across Korean Veterans Boulevard. She would prove to Caleb Samuels and Martin Ridge that she and Rob had been wrongfully accused.

A car horn blared, bringing Danni back to the moment, and she jumped backwards onto the curb, motioning for the vehicle to pass. It might be better if she stopped thinking about the injustices of the judicial system and concentrated on what she was doing.

Looking both ways, Danni hurried across the busy throughway into the shadow of the Music City Center. She had to decide what to tell Jaycee.

Agent Ridge had warned her not to say anything about their conversation, even suggesting she could be charged with obstruction. He had also said telling someone might jeopardize their safety. The last thing she wanted was to drag Jaycee, or anyone else, into this mess. If only Rob had been concerned about the same thing. Of course if he had been in town, she might not have had this encounter with the TBI.

She reached into her handbag for her phone. She would let Jaycee know she was on her way. But before she could send a text, the phone rang. It was the chef.

"Where are you?" Jaycee had an edge to her voice.

"I'm just leaving—"

"I need you here as soon as possible. Michael didn't show up for work. I've called and called him, but I can't get an answer."

"Isn't this the second time in a few weeks?"

"Yes. And today of all days! You need to talk to him, Danni. It isn't like Michael to let us down like this." Jaycee's voice drifted off. "Hold on, I'll be right there." She returned to the phone. "But right now, I have to finish serving the Chamber luncheon. How soon can you be here?"

"I'm fifteen minutes away."

"See you then."

Jaycee hung up, and Danni quickened her pace. Jaycee would be lost without Michael's help. The young man, almost ten years their junior and fresh out of tech school, had worked his way to lead server and "chief motivator" at Amoré. Michael inspired his team members like no one else. And his smile won over even the most dissatisfied customer.

Thinking about her employees—and knowing Jaycee needed her help—was good medicine. Danni hurried down the sidewalk toward the Omni, leaving the morning's problems behind her. She would think about them later.

Right now the restaurant needed her more.

"So what happened?" Jaycee blotted perspiration from her forehead and then tucked the dish towel into her apron strings, the luncheon now behind them.

"You mean this morning?" Danni set another stockpot on the counter.

Her friend rolled her eyes. "Yes, at the police station. What took so long? I thought you were just signing paperwork."

"It's a mess." Danni tucked a strand of hair behind her ear, buying time for her reply. "The man who broke into Rob's condo has a history of drug problems, and they want to know why he chose that particular unit."

"You mean they think Rob is connected to drugs?" Jaycee continued to wash dishes.

"Why would you even ask that?" Danni gasped. "You know that's not true."

"I don't know. I've always thought that man was up to something." Jaycee glanced Danni's way.

"That's not fair, Jay. They're just concerned that word may have gotten out that he keeps money at his condo. And that he's out of town a lot."

"What about the man who attacked you? Have you found out how he entered the building?"

Danni could feel heat rushing to her cheeks. "Well, we didn't talk much about that, but I've heard that our entry code somehow made it to the street. And the guard was in another part of the building when at least one of the men entered. That's been corrected now."

"Are you comfortable with that?" Jaycee looked concerned.

"I wouldn't use the word *comfortable*, but I'm hopeful it could never happen again." She folded her hands and changed the subject. "So how do you think the luncheon went?"

Before the chef could respond, a server interrupted.

"Ms. Kemp. A police officer is here to see you."

Danni froze. What could they possibly want now?

"Ms. Kemp?" The young girl repeated.

"D-did he say why he was here?" Danni stuttered.

"He didn't say, ma'am. He's at the front door." The server nodded toward the dining room and walked away.

Jaycee arched her brow. "Aren't you the popular one?"

"This is starting to get ridiculous." Danni glared at the chef and took off for the front.

When she arrived, she was relieved to see a uniformed officer she hadn't met. Hopefully that meant his visit was unrelated. "How may I help you, officer?"

"Does Michael Ryan work here?"

"Yes." Danni glanced to her right and saw Jaycee had joined them. "However, he's not working today. Is there a problem?"

"I'm sorry to have to inform you, ma'am." The man removed his hat. "But Mr. Ryan was found dead this morning. He was outside his apartment building."

Danni gasped. "How? What happened?"

The officer pointed to a nearby table. "Please. Have a seat. I need to ask you a few questions."

CHAPTER 12

aleb settled onto a bench at a table near the back of the crowded restaurant. Von Elrod's was Ridge's favorite place for lunch and, even though German food didn't set well with Caleb, he had agreed to meet his boss here.

The parking was scarce, but the prices were reasonable, and most importantly he wanted to keep his boss happy. At least long enough to get his blessing for Caleb to stay on the Evans case.

Because his cover had been broken, Ridge might prefer to relieve him. But for reasons Caleb didn't want to disclose that option was not acceptable. If his gut was telling him correctly—and he could usually rely on it—this case was bigger than anyone at the TBI could even imagine. In fact, Caleb suspected Robert Evans was in deeper than even he realized. Evans was a pawn in a very deadly game.

Danielle Kemp was a pawn too. But unlike Evans she was an innocent one. At least that was Caleb's opinion.

He thought back over the interrogation. Ridge might not agree with him, but Caleb had confidence in his ability to read people. He had studied Danni's body language, the subtleties of her expression. Either she was a great actress or she had no idea who—or what—her boyfriend really was. And she was loyal enough to want to defend him. Perhaps to a fault.

Caleb ran his hand through his hair. No doubt Danielle Kemp had captured his interest, but not just because she was beautiful. She reminded him of his family back home. Small town, hard-working people. Good people with good values.

In the weeks he had been undercover, he had seen how she treated others. Better yet, he had seen how they responded to her. It was obvious her staff at the restaurant respected her. And she went out of her way to be courteous to every-one, from the concierge to the security guards at her high-end condominium.

Danielle Kemp may live and work among the elite in town, but beneath the fancy façade of designer clothes and high society, Caleb believed she was a woman with strong values. She was of a different ilk from that boyfriend of hers.

There were givers, and there were takers. Caleb had seen both kinds in his business. And he trusted his intuition to know the difference.

In Abernathy, Mississippi, his family and friends held blue-collar jobs. Through the years, a few had migrated to larger cities, just as Caleb had. A few of those had started "to act above their raising," as his grandmother would have said. But—although they put on airs from time to time, like Danielle Kemp—beneath their insecurities were people who were content to earn an honest day's wage and who would do anything to help each other.

Anytime Caleb reminisced about home, his thoughts always turned to Jonathan. If his brother had lived, he would be thirty and might have a family of his own. He would be working on the medical degree he'd always said he would earn, and they would have had a doctor in their family. But now . . .

Caleb bowed his head. He had been down this road too many times, and he couldn't seem to get beyond the *if only's*. Life had no do-overs. Only course corrections. Mistakes with fatal consequences can't be taken back. Life lost is gone forever.

But life that remains can be redeemed.

That was the tenet of Caleb's faith that kept that him going through the difficult times. He swiped at his eye, his lips curving into an almost smile. If Jonathan were here now, he would never believe his older brother, the one who had always been in trouble for one reason or another, had pursued a law enforcement career. Then again, it was because of Jonathan's untimely death that Caleb had chosen this path. Only God knew where he'd be otherwise.

Special Agent Ridge settled unto the bench opposite Caleb and brought him back to the moment. "Did you order?" Ridge snatched up a menu.

"No. Waiting on you."

Ridge arched a brow. "Know what you want?"

"Same thing I always get. Most of the food in this place is too spicy for me." Caleb held a hand to his stomach.

His boss, who had been born and reared on the East Coast, grinned. "A little bratwurst won't hurt you. Don't they raise Southern boys on sausage too?"

Caleb chose a knife and fork from the condiment box on the table and placed the utensils on his napkin. "Smoked and sugar cured." He assured Ridge. "And we like our potatoes mashed instead of finessed into little pancakes."

Ridge guffawed, putting his menu aside. "So what do you think about the Kemp woman? What part does she play in this?"

"I think she's being used by that scumbag, Evans. But . . ." Caleb chose his words carefully. "We need to keep a close watch on her. No one can be trusted in a deal this big. Or this dirty. There's a lot at stake."

Ridge eyed him for a second, and then nodded in agreement. He leaned back. "I'm glad you think she needs to be watched. You had me concerned back there. You were playing good cop a little too convincingly." Ridge signaled for the waiter. "I thought you might be falling for her. Not that she isn't a looker." He grinned.

"She's a looker all right." Caleb chewed on his lip. If he was right, this conversation was about to go the way he wanted it to go. "But trustworthy is another thing. I'd like to keep close tabs on her. To make certain she doesn't tip Evans's hand. And if she does, we need to know about that too. We're close to breaking this wide open."

"So you think you should stay on the case?" Ridge lowered his voice as the waiter approached. "I'm not so sure—"

"Why not?" Caleb protested. "No one but the girl knows who I am." He glanced toward the approaching server and then back to Ridge. "I can use it to my advantage. I just have to play my cards right."

Ridge's face lit with understanding, and a slow grin spread across his face. He nodded. "You Southerners and your charm."

"Are you ready to order, sir?" the waiter asked Ridge.

Caleb leaned back in his seat, knowing he had won.

"Please, let's sit over here. It's more private." Danni led the police officer to a four-top near the wall. She lowered herself into a chair as the man took a seat across the table.

"This is almost too much. Please tell me what happened."

"We can't be sure, Ms. Kemp. Not until toxicology comes back. But it appears to have been a drug overdose." He pulled a notepad from his pocket and laid it on the table. "I need to ask you a few questions about the people Michael Ryan hung out with, his schedule, and his habits. Anything you can tell me may be helpful."

Danni mentally cycled through her employee roster. "I can't believe that anyone here would have been a party to this. Or a bad influence." She gestured around the room. "We have a good bunch of kids here. At least to my knowledge."

"Did you ever suspect Ryan was involved in drugs?"

"No! Not at all." She thought back to the last few weeks. She knew personally what drugs could do to someone, and Michael's behavior didn't even come close to her mother's. "He has been a bit reclusive lately. And he was late for work a few days, which isn't like him. But drugs? I would never suspect that." She hesitated. "And I've seen the toll prescription medicine can take on someone."

The police officer scribbled a few notes, and Danni turned to Jaycee.

"Officer, my coworker, our chef here at Amoré, knows—" Danni stopped to process that Michael was actually gone. "Jaycee knew Michael and his family from church. Why don't you talk with her, and I'll get us some coffee?"

A smile spread across the officer's face. "Yes, please. Just sugar."

"You got it. I'll be right back."

A few minutes later, as the three of them sipped coffee, Jaycee shared stories about Michael. "I've known him for years." She wiped the corner of her eyes. "I knew he was into some extreme music, but the drug thing? I never would have suspected it."

"Of course we can't be certain until reports come back." The officer placed his empty cup on the table. "But our investigation is leading in that direction. We have a couple of witnesses who admitted to attending the same party last night."

Jaycee shook her head. "At one time Michael considered going into ministry."

"Unfortunately, that's not unusual. A lot of unsuspecting kids, along with their families, find that their world has changed overnight. A few manage for a while to live two lives. One sober and responsible. The other an escape from reality—with narcotics providing a quick fix from their problems. But that quick fix will lure them in, deeper and deeper, until it's too late." He closed his notebook. "Many times their families don't see, or refuse to see, it coming."

A chill crawled up Danni's spine.

The officer stood. "Ladies, I appreciate your time and the coffee." He pulled two business cards from his pocket and handed one to Danni and one to Jaycee. "If you think of anything else, please give me a call. I can assure you that it will be kept confidential. He looked from one to another. "And that we'll stay on top of this case for Mr. Ryan's sake."

"Thank you," Jaycee whispered.

"Yes, ma'am. Once again, I'm sorry for your loss."

Danni nodded and extended her hand. "Thank you, sir. We're happy to help however we can." She glanced at Jaycee, who appeared to be losing her battle with tears. "For Michael's sake, as you said."

The officer returned her handshake with a firm grip. "It's a shame. The real crime isn't being committed by these kids." He looked directly into her eyes. "It's the people who sell the drugs to them who need to be put away for a long, long time." He stashed his notepad in his pocket. "We need all the help we can to get that done."

"We're here to help, officer." Jaycee stood.

"Thank you, ma'am." He returned his hat to his head, turned, and walked away.

The officer's words hung in the air as they watched him walk toward the door. Finally Jaycee broke the silence. "I feel like I've been punched in the gut."

Danni steadied herself with a hand on the back of her chair, as she silently replayed her day. "I know what you mean, Jay. I know what you mean."

CHAPTER 13

Caleb had been hoping, praying for a break. And now he had it.

This case meant more to him than any he had worked during his eight-year tenure at the TBI, and he wouldn't stop until Evans and his cronies were behind bars. *All of them.*

If that included Danielle Kemp, so be it.

Caleb's gut told him she wasn't involved. That she was as much a victim of Robert Evans as the hundreds of kids on the streets and their families whose lives had been ruined because of him.

But Caleb would not be distracted by his feelings.

The dark-haired woman wouldn't be happy about what he had to do, but tomorrow he would file a warrant to seize and examine Robert Evans's money-filled briefcase. The one she told them about. It might put her in danger. More danger. But he had to take that chance, while putting the proper precautions in place, and stepping up the security on her condo. They would monitor her every move, and her response could help prove her innocence. Or her guilt.

The concierge waved Danni toward him as soon as she walked into the lobby of the Rutherford. *What now?* All she wanted was a hot bath and a long run. Or maybe just a bowl of cereal and a good cry.

The young man smiled as Danni approached the desk, which was manned during the day by the concierge and at night by a security guard. Obviously he had no idea how bad her day had been. Or that Michael Ryan's days had ended.

"Good evening, Ms. Kemp." He turned to pick something up, producing a huge vase of flowers when he swiveled back around. "These arrived for you today."

Rob. He always knew how to win back her favor, and he never spared expense. There had to be two—or maybe three—dozen roses in the bouquet.

"May I help you carry these to your place, Ms. Kemp?"

"That's not necessary, Hunter." Danni adjusted her handbag and prepared to take the vase from his hands.

"Then let me at least help you to the elevator." He emerged from behind the desk carrying the flowers. "How has your day been?"

Danni sighed. "You don't want to know."

They walked across the lobby to a marble-lined alcove that held a bank of four elevators. The concierge pushed the elevator call button with his free hand. "Anything I can do to help?"

"No thanks, Hunter. But I appreciate your concern." After she boarded the lift, he handed her the flowers and reached around to punch the seventh-floor button.

"I hope you have a good evening."

"Thanks. You too." She braced herself for the elevator's upward movement. Seven floors later the doors opened. She had barely stepped into the corridor when her phone rang.

Cradling the vase against her body with her left arm, she pulled the phone and her keys from her bag with the other. Walking quickly toward her door, she glanced at the caller ID: *Tennessee Bureau.*

Danni inserted her key and turned the lock. "This is Danielle."

"Ms. Kemp, it's Agent Samuels with the TBI. I apologize if I'm calling at an inconvenient time."

"No. It's fine." She tossed her keys into the teakwood bowl on her entry table, secured her door, and carried the flowers down the hall toward her bedroom.

"How can I help you, Mr. Samuels?"

"Are you home for the evening?"

Was that supposed to be a rhetorical question? Hadn't he followed her around for weeks? He should know her schedule better than she did.

"Yes. Why do you ask?"

"I would like to send an agent to your home to pick up Mr. Evans's briefcase. The one you told us about this morning."

"Oh . . ." She paced across the room and set the flowers on her nightstand.

"Ms. Kemp, let me make this easier for you. That wasn't a question. I have a warrant."

Danni lowered herself into a nearby chair. "O . . . kay. When?"

He cleared his throat. "My agent is standing outside your door right now."

Glancing beyond the flowers reflected in her bathroom mirror, Danni scrubbed makeup from her face. She had relocated the long-stemmed roses to her vanity before letting the TBI agent inside.

Thankfully he came and went without much pomp and circumstance. He showed her the warrant and gave her a receipt for the briefcase. He had also cautioned her not to mention the transaction to Rob, just as Caleb Samuels had requested on the phone.

They didn't have to worry about that. Not unless Rob asked. In the meantime, she could only hope this misunderstanding—or whatever it was—would be resolved quickly. Rob was mild-mannered under most circumstances, but taking his hard-earned money wouldn't sit well with him. And why should it? Even if they did have a warrant.

She drummed her fingers on the marble vanity. How did Caleb Samuels manage to get a warrant? Did that mean he had solid evidence?

The exquisite bouquet in her peripheral vision filled her senses with the perfume of rose petals. The flowers were a brilliant shade of orange, the same color as the sunset she had watched a few hours earlier from her window.

With Rob's help, she had purchased a view of Nashville's western skyline. Standing seven stories above the concrete and craziness, she could look beyond the day-to-day mundane to the promise of possibilities.

But what were those possibilities?

This evening's sunset had been one of those especially beautiful ones you wanted to walk into while holding the hand of the man you loved. Was Rob that man?

Danni reread the handwritten note on the card that had been attached to the flowers. It was Rob's assistant Melissa's handwriting. She had seen it many times. On birthday cards. Gift tags. And attached to countless vases of flowers. Maybe the words were Rob's, but the sentiment was always diluted because he wouldn't take the time to do it himself.

Danielle,

I know I'm not always there for you. Like right now. But that will change one day. We will one day have the rest of our lives to spend together. I remember the first time we met three years ago today. You were the most beautiful girl in the room.

Rob had caught her eye that evening too. She couldn't believe he would notice her, much less ask her out.

You're still the most beautiful girl in the room.

Happy anniversary, babe.

Love,

Rob

P.S. I hope you've made progress with our wedding plans.

Danni pulled her hair into a loose ponytail. The reasons not to sleep were mounting. For the first time since they had started dating, she dreaded seeing Rob. He had changed his plans and would be home in a few days. He would pull her back into his life again. She would become comfortable, and then he would leave for another week. Or more.

Her soon-to-be fiancé, a man who spent nearly two hundred days a year on the road and kept in touch with her by texts and phone calls, had now managed to put her in the middle of a criminal investigation. Right or wrong. Guilty or innocent. Her worries were no longer about how little she saw Rob—or that he left her out of a big part of his life—but about whether or not he was involved in something that could hurt people. If there was even a chance of that, she could never make a commitment to him.

Marriage was forever. *Forever.* Despite what she had experienced as a child.

And because of what she had experienced as a child, she knew how harmful drugs—legal or illegal—could be when misused. They destroyed lives. And families. Michael Ryan's family would no longer have him in their present. Or their future. Just as she and Chloe no longer had their mom.

She fingered the diamond pendant around her neck and stared at the roses that had been delivered a few hours before. Would that picture-perfect sunset she had dreamed about ever become a reality?

Dimming the bathroom lights, Danni turned toward the bedroom for what would likely be another sleepless night. Halfway there, her phone rang. It was her sister.

"Hey, baby girl—"

"Danni, I have terrible news."

"What's wrong?" *Please, God. I can't deal with anything else.*

"Daddy's had a heart attack. He's at Midtown in Cedar Rapids. If the doctors can stabilize him, he'll have surgery tomorrow. You need to come as soon as you can." Chloe's words drifted in and out of sobs.

Searching her memory for something, anything, to make sense of her sister's words, Danni sifted through the emotions of her childhood. Her dad had always been there for them. He was the strong one. He couldn't be fighting for his life.

"What happened?" She paced toward the front of the condominium, almost tripping over Sophie.

"He was driving home from work when it hit him. He said he was nauseous, and then he couldn't breathe. Thank God he turned the truck around when he did. He drove himself to the hospital." Chloe blubbered. "Doesn't that sound like Dad? Who else would drive himself to the hospital in the middle of a heart attack?"

"He's paying the price for working too hard."

"I know. That's all he's ever done. Work hard, so we could have more." Chloe sniffed.

"What are the doctors saying? Is he going to be okay, Chloe?"

"They don't know." Her sister's voice trembled. "Please, Danni. Come home as soon as you can. I need you. We need you."

CHAPTER 14

The next day – March 26

Early the following morning Danni left the Rutherford on the way to the Nashville airport. *Luggage. Laptop. Dog.* She scanned her mental checklist. She had everything she needed for a quick trip to Iowa. The bag and laptop would get her through the next few days, and Jaycee had everything she needed to keep Sophie.

Danni took a right on Murphy Road, and five minutes later pulled into Jaycee's drive on Colorado Avenue. The small brick home was as warm and inviting as her friend's generous personality.

"Godspeed." Jaycee said as she took Sophie's leash. "I'll be praying for him—and for you."

"Thanks, Jay. You know I appreciate it. I'll give you a call when I know more." Danni leaned toward the Newfoundland to give her a final pat. "You be good and mind Jaycee."

The dog responded with sad eyes, taking a step toward her.

"It'll be okay, girl." Danni fought back tears. "I hope."

Jaycee grabbed Danni and hugged her. "It will be, Dan. It will be."

Danni nodded, turned, and walked to her car. If she looked back, she would break down. She had to be strong for her daddy. And for Chloe.

Danni pulled into the long access road that encircled the Nashville International Airport. Glancing toward the terminal she saw a line of planes waiting to be pulled into action. The landscape, temporarily lit by the post-dawn sun and streetlamps, took on an ethereal glow.

Her hands trembled as she pulled her bags from the trunk. She would have been a wreck—well, more of a wreck—if a direct, early morning flight to Cedar Rapids hadn't been available. The combination of stress and little sleep hadn't left her a lot of stamina. It also had a sedative effect.

Danni's check-in process and time spent waiting passed quickly, and once she found her seat and stowed her bag, she settled in for a nap. Curled up against the window on the right side of the plane, she stared into the clouds.

The sound of the engines and the gentle swaying of the aircraft took her back to the front seat of her dad's Ford sedan when he and the girls were on their way home from church. Or an out of town softball game. Or a camping trip. On the longer trips she would try to stay awake and keep her dad company while Chloe slept in the backseat. But Danni would almost inevitably doze off. And when she did, it always felt like she had let her father down.

Much like she felt right now. She wished she could have been there sooner to provide backup for Chloe. It was what she had always done.

As far back as Danni could remember, she had tried to compensate for Chloe's loss. But replacing a mom's love was never possible, even when you had the best dad in the world. Dan Kemp had raised his two girls on his own. And he had sacrificed a lot to give them everything they needed.

Now he needed them.

The strength of their family was lying in a hospital room fighting for his life. It didn't seem real. But nothing seemed real right now. Michael Ryan's memorial would be held in Nashville this afternoon. And because Danni couldn't be there to help encourage the Amoré staff, Jaycee would carry the load.

Danni braced against the window of the plane. At least she wouldn't have to see Rob when he came through town. He couldn't ask her about the briefcase. And her time away would give her a chance to assess everything that had happened since last week. The break-in. Her meeting with the TBI.

And her engagement.

When Danni told her dad about Rob asking her to marry him, he had been polite. But she had heard the hesitation in his voice. Although Dan Kemp had met Rob on a few occasions, they hadn't spent much time together. Typical of Rob, he always managed to be busy beyond a polite meal or two when Dan Kemp was in town.

Danni shifted her seating position and noticed the man across the aisle. She had seen him somewhere before, but where? She met hundreds of people each week at the restaurant and business functions. Most were just nameless faces that appeared and sometimes reappeared in her life.

The man across the aisle glanced toward her. She smiled, and he looked away. Where had she seen him? She would remember eventually. But right now, she should try to nap. It would be hours before she had the chance to relax again. She pulled her blanket tightly around her body and repositioned her neck pillow.

Sleep wouldn't come in the first leg of the flight, but after the plane landed, unloaded, and reloaded at Chicago O'Hare, Danni fell into a dreamless repose. Two hours later she woke to the sound of landing gears grinding into position and the bump of wheels touching down.

Iowa. It had been too long.

Danni grabbed her purse, her carry-on bag, and her goose-down parka. The sooner she reached baggage claim and found her brother-in-law Brian, the sooner she would have an update on her dad.

Stretching as she stood, Danni noticed the seat across the aisle was empty. The man who had been sitting there when they left Nashville, the one who looked familiar, must have deplaned in Chicago.

She made the short walk to baggage claim and found her luggage already on the rotating belt. After snagging it, she scrolled through her text messages.

She had a message from Jaycee. But nothing from Chloe.

"Hey, pretty girl." A tall, slender man with curly red hair pulled her into a sideways embrace while taking the suitcase from her hand. "You're looking great. The air in Tennessee must be good for you."

Danni smiled. Brian Jackson always made her feel welcome. Chloe had found a good man, one not unlike their dad. He was a good-hearted, hard-working guy who loved his family more than anything.

He was handsome too. But he appeared to have aged a few years since she'd seen him less than six months ago at Christmas. No doubt the strain of her dad's sickness was weighing on him too.

"How's dad?"

Her brother-in-law grimaced. "We're worried about him, Danni. Chloe can't wait to see you." He pointed toward the rotating belt behind her. "Do you have everything?"

"Yes." She nodded. "Is it cold outside?"

He grinned. "If we're lucky, we'll break into the double digits today."

"I don't miss that about Iowa." Danni zipped her parka, pulled gloves from her pockets, and started walking toward the double doors that led outside. "You look tired. I'm guessing neither of you have slept since yesterday."

"Not a lot." He allowed her to walk through the door in front of him. "It's okay. We'll sleep later. Our concern right now is for your dad."

Danni startled when a gust of cold air greeted her. "I'm glad I'm here."

"We just wish it weren't under these circumstances." He pointed in the direction of his car. "Chloe and the kids will be thrilled to see you."

"Are we going straight to the hospital?"

"Yes. You can see the kids tonight."

Brian Jackson stopped next to a white minivan. He opened the passenger side door for her, and Danni hopped inside while he stowed her bags.

"So, you traded your GTO for a family van?" She teased when he joined her inside the car.

"No, actually, Chloe has the GTO today." He laughed. "You know how much I love that car."

"A remnant from life as a single man?" She laughed.

He nodded. "Yes, but Chloe loves it too. We traded her old Beetle for this van."

"The two of you are so practical." Danni fastened her seat-belt. "I want to be like you when I grow up."

"Is that ever going to happen?" Her brother-in-law grinned and backed the minivan from the parking spot. He turned to look at her. "So when are you going to settle down? You must have left a long trail of broken hearts behind you by now."

Danni forced a smile. Brian meant well, but romance wasn't her favorite topic. She hadn't dated much before Rob. Taking care of Chloe and helping their dad had changed her priorities as a teenager. At a time when most girls her age were dreaming about boys, Danni had been helping her dad cook and clean. Not because he had insisted but because she had wanted to do it.

Soon after Chloe was twelve, Danni had gone off to college, forever losing her chance to be a teenager.

"Did I say something wrong?" He grimaced.

"No. Sorry." She shook her head. "I was just lost in my thoughts." She checked her lipstick in the visor mirror. "I'm seeing someone right now, but . . ."

He waited for her to finish her sentence.

"I'm not sure how it's going to end."

Brian looked her way. "That guy you've been dating for a while?"

"Yes."

"Well, he'll be a lucky man if you decide to keep him."

"Thanks." Danni smiled, genuinely this time. Her brother-in-law always knew how to encourage her.

Not unlike Rob did. No matter how her relationship with him ended, there was a positive side. He was the first man to pursue her with enough confidence to get past the insecurities that had lingered since her childhood. And in many ways, he had helped build her confidence. Not only because he was charming but because he was the most handsome guy in the room—and he had chosen her.

"Do me a favor and check your messages." Brian interrupted her thoughts for the second time. "Anything from Chloe?"

Danni grabbed her phone and scrolled through her texts and emails. "Nothing here. What time is the surgery?"

"It will depend on the availability of the surgeon." He turned the van onto the main highway. "His doctors also want to wait until he's stable."

"It needs to be done soon, doesn't it?"

"Yes. But his chances are better if he's stabilized going in."

Danni turned to look out the window, the brown roadside vegetation and gray asphalt providing no solace.

Sensing her worry, her brother-in-law reached across the console to lay his hand on her arm. "We have a lot of people praying for him, Danni."

"He's all I have." She scrubbed a tear from her cheek. "Chloe has you . . . and the kids, but—"

"You have us too. We're family."

Danni nodded. "I know . . ."

"This is hard for me too, Danni. I love your dad. He's been a big influence on my life. Even before Chloe and I were married, he helped me through some tough things."

"He's an amazing guy." Her voice trailed off, and memories of her childhood flooded back. *Please, God. Let him be okay.*

Ten minutes later Brian pulled into the circular drive in front of the hospital. He stopped to let Danni out before parking. "Chloe is in the fourth floor waiting room. I'll meet you there."

Danni hurried into the hospital lobby and took the first open elevator. She gathered her courage as she approached the fourth floor. She had to be strong for her sister.

When the doors opened, she saw Chloe sitting in a chair in the corner. Her hands were folded in her lap, and her head was bowed.

"Chlo—" Danni half-breathed, half-shouted as she sprinted across the room.

"Danielle!" Chloe jumped to her feet and pulled Danni into a hug.

"I'm so glad you're here. I'm so glad you're here." She sobbed. "They've just taken him to surgery."

Danni paced the long hallway between the waiting area and the outpatient wing on the far side of the hospital. If her mind couldn't rest, her feet might as well move. By the second round, she decided to count her steps.

One-ninety-five. One-ninety-six. One-ninety-seven . . .

Making an about-face, she started again.

The doctor had told Chloe it would be five or six hours before they knew the outcome of the procedure. The waiting would have been easier if Danni had been here in time for a hug and a few encouraging words to her dad before he had been taken away.

She should have made time in her busy schedule to come home more often. But somehow work had seemed more important than family.

Ironically, her dad had always made time for her.

Please, God, let us keep him.

It had been a long time since she had whispered a prayer. Had she been too busy for that too? Or had she grown self-sufficient? Hardly. She was about to fall apart because her father's life was in peril.

At that moment Brahms's "Lullaby" streamed through the speakers in the hallway. New life had come into the world. But would her father's remain?

An onslaught of shivers traipsed down her spine. Their dad's presence had been a constant in her and her sister's lives. And, although they were young women now, it was impossible to imagine life without him.

Moisture gathered in Danni's eyes, blurring the stretch of hallway in front of her. The only sound in the sterile passageway was the steady fall of her footsteps. She amped up her pace with the inexplicable urge to run.

Out the door. Down the street. Even back to Nashville. To get away—

But she couldn't.

She couldn't do what her mother had done. Even if she shared part of her name. Danielle Grace Kemp was the spitting image of her mother in her younger photos. But following in Grace Kemp's path had always been Danni's worst fear.

You didn't leave the people you loved. They were the ones who needed you most. A commitment was a commitment even during bad times. It wasn't just for when it was convenient. It was forever.

The thought stopped her in her tracks. *That was her answer.*

She couldn't leave Rob, not now when things were bad for him. Not when the authorities were accusing him of a ridiculous crime. She had to stick with him. And support him. He might not be perfect, but he was willing to commit himself to her. Shouldn't she do the same?

Danni pulled her cell phone from her pocket to give Rob a call. She had to let him know she cared. But before she could dial his number, her phone rang. It was Jaycee.

"I just wanted to check on you and your dad."

Danni switched the phone to her other ear as she neared the waiting room. "No news yet. I'm hoping that's good—"

A man sitting in the corner near the vending machines took Danni's attention. It was the same man she had seen on the airplane. The one who looked familiar. What were the chances he would be here?

Danni's stomach churned. Who was he? Her thoughts swirled in a thousand different directions, finally landing on one. *TBI?*

Was that even possible? Would Caleb or his boss send someone to spy on her in Iowa? How dare they! The idea of that made her furious. This was not the time or the place. She took a step toward the man, to confront him, and then stopped.

What if he wasn't TBI but from the other side? What if Rob really was involved in an international drug ring, and she had somehow become involved? What if this was one of the bad guys?

Suddenly the possibility that Caleb had sent someone to watch her—to look after her— didn't seem so bad.

"Danni?" Jaycee brought her back to the call.

"Oh . . . sorry." She collected her thoughts. She couldn't tell Jaycee about the investigation.

"Are you okay?"

Danni saw Chloe waving from across the room.

"Jay, it looks like Chloe has news. I need to let you go."

"Call me when you know more."

"Will do." Danni stuffed the phone into her pocket and rushed toward her sister. Chloe's eyes were red.

The news must be bad.

She reached to embrace Chloe, pulling her into her arms, and they both began sobbing.

CHAPTER 15

Caleb wheeled his 1989 midnight blue Chevrolet pickup into the driveway beside Zach's house and turned off the engine. He hadn't seen the boy in weeks. That wasn't the way to build a relationship. Caleb stepped out of the truck onto the ragged remains of deteriorating asphalt. Zach was already nine, and Caleb had promised himself that he would make a difference in the kid's life before it was too late. It was past time to make good on that promise.

Of course it would be easy to justify his absence. He had been walking the streets day and night trying to crack the Evans case. But work was an excuse too many people used when they didn't want to spend time with their kids. Caleb's own father could have used it many times. But he hadn't. No matter when or where Will Samuels's sons needed him, he had always been there for them.

Caleb slammed the truck door. Unfortunately it hadn't been enough in his case. But it would for Zach. He would see to it, because the alternative was unthinkable. Caleb couldn't imagine the intrusion of narcotics upon Zach's innocence. Despite the boy's family history, he had kept his naivete. And Caleb would do everything he could to keep it that way. Zach was more than a little buddy. He was the absolution of Caleb's past.

Walking toward the small gray bungalow, Caleb noticed the faded, moldy siding. Once the weather warmed, he would pick up a few cans of paint, and he and Zach would spend an afternoon or two working together. It would be good for both of them. And it would help Zach and his mom hold their heads a little higher.

Caleb pulled a dead branch from a shrub adjacent to the sidewalk. There was a lot that needed to be done around here. But elbow grease and a little bit of pocket change could get it in shape. Caleb's parents hadn't had a lot of money either. But they had taught him and Jonathan the value of taking care of what you had. And that included each other. They had taught him that family was the most important thing in life.

That thought punched Caleb in the gut as he stepped onto the sagging floorboards of Zach's front porch. All he had ever done was let his family down. If it hadn't been for his bad decisions, his younger brother would still be alive. Jonathan had been an innocent bystander. His only crime was wanting to be with his big brother. But Caleb had chosen to hang out with the wrong crowd.

Just as Danielle Kemp had.

What she saw in Robert Evans was inexplicable. The man was a scumbag. Poor company to be keeping, much less to consider marrying. If he didn't get her killed first.

Caleb knocked on Zach's front door. He shouldn't be thinking about Danielle Kemp on a day off. He should be focusing on Zach. But the dark-haired woman needed him too. If he didn't help keep her safe, she would become another innocent casualty. And if he had anything to do about it, she wouldn't meet the fate Jonathan had.

When the door opened, a blond-haired boy greeted Caleb with a bounce. Zach's eyes were as wide as his big toothy grin.

"You're here!"

The nine-year-old rushed forward, thrusting his arms around Caleb's waist, and hugged him.

Oh, God. Please help me protect this young man.

Danni pulled Chloe closer, waiting for her to stop shaking. Waiting for her to deliver the bad news. Life for their family had just changed forever. It was impossible to think that—

She couldn't complete the thought. Maybe it wasn't as bad as she feared. Maybe there was a chance. She had to know what the doctor had told her sister. Pushing Chloe gently away, Danni searched her sister's eyes.

Chloe hiccupped and brushed away tears, then broke into a wide smile. "He made it." She grabbed Danni's arm and shook it, jumping up and down. "He made it, Danni! The doctor said the surgery went better than expected."

Danni stared at her. "He's okay? But . . ."

"Yes! Can you believe it? The doctor said it went perfectly."

Brian, who had been on the phone across the room, rushed to his wife and wrapped his arm around her shoulders.

"He's okay?"

Chloe nodded.

"You scared us half to death."

"I'm sorry." She nestled farther into her husband's side. "I was just so relieved."

Danni slumped into the chair beside her.

"God is good!" Brian pulled away from his wife. "I'll call the church office and ask them to share the good news with everyone who has been praying."

"Would you call your mom too?" Chloe acknowledged the approaching doctor. "I'll call grandma as soon as Danni and I talk to Dr. Madison."

A few minutes later, after they had talked to the surgeon, Brian rejoined Chloe and Danni. He glanced at his watch.

"I'm taking Chloe to the cafeteria for something to eat." He clutched his wife's hand. "Why don't you join us? It will likely be an hour or two before we can visit your dad."

"I'll meet you there," Danni said. "Let me make a phone call first.

She dialed Jaycee's number and waited for the ring as she watched her sister and brother-in-law stroll away, laughing and talking, the scene reminiscent of her parents the day they had all taken Chloe home from the hospital.

Years of memories, and regrets, came flooding back.

Jaycee's voicemail picked up. "Jay, my dad's doing better. Thanks for your prayers. I'll call you when I know more."

Danni stowed the phone in her pocket and walked down the corridor toward the elevator. Waiting for the lift to arrive, she looked around. This old building had been through a lot in its days. The paint color looked fresh and new, but she could see the old, familiar cracks in the walls.

That was the problem with rough places. They couldn't be patched. They had to be completely mended or they would eventually work their way to the top again.

She too had a lot of rough places in her past that needed to be mended. She had a lot to think about.

CHAPTER 16

Three days later – March 29

W hen can I get out of here?"

Three days after his surgery, Dan Kemp was asking to go home.

Danni tried not to laugh as she watched him negotiating with the nurse who had just come on duty.

"Give us a week." The woman caught his wrist and watched the clock on the wall beside the bed.

"But that's seven days." He turned to Danni and winked. "Once they get you in this place, they won't let you leave."

Danni smiled. It was easy to see he was feeling better. "Maybe they'll give you credit for time already served," she teased.

"I'm afraid that won't happen." The nurse, whose nametag identified her as *JoAnn*, delivered the punchline. "That would require good behavior." She released her patient's hand and grinned at him.

Dan Kemp flashed a smile in return.

Danni sat back and watched the two of them banter back and forth while the nurse checked the connections to a stockpile of drip bags hanging from a rack next to the bed. After she finished, she looked to Danni and then back to her patient. "Actually, what

I said a minute ago wasn't completely true. We are letting you go this afternoon."

Dan Kemp sat up straight. "Really?"

The nurse held up her right hand, to settle him down. "To a regular floor." She smiled. "You're doing so well you're wasting our time in ICU."

"See, you've made a pest of yourself, Dad." Danni took a seat at the foot of the bed after the nurse had left. "They'll soon be getting rid of you downstairs too."

"Sometimes it pays to be difficult." He chuckled.

She patted his leg. "You scared us half to death. I'm glad you're better."

His expression sobered. "I have to admit; I was concerned too. Especially when I saw you here."

Danni frowned. "Am I that bad of a daughter?" She tucked his blanket around him. "I'll try to do better in the future."

"It's always good to see you, beautiful girl, no matter what the circumstance." He covered her hand with his unencumbered one. "It's just that I feel like I've lost touch. I don't ever want to do that." He shook his head. "What's going on in your life?"

She stood to walk around the room. "Just work, Dad. Lots of work. But you know me; I love it."

"And?" He nodded toward her restlessness.

"And I'm working on my wedding plans."

"Is that what you want?"

"I think so." She forced a smile.

He opened his mouth to speak, then stopped.

"What's wrong, Daddy?"

"Just be sure he's the right one. You don't want to change your mind after it's too late."

She sat down again, this time in the chair beside the bed. "You know that better than anyone."

"I don't regret anything, Danielle. I have you and Chloe, and I'm a blessed man."

"Why didn't you marry again? Chloe and I would have understood."

"Hey, we're talking about you; don't change the subject," he sidestepped. "How do you feel about marrying Rob?"

"The truth?"

"Always."

"I'm ambivalent." Had she really said that out loud? Somehow, he always got to the bottom of things. "Of course I love him. I enjoy his company. He's devastatingly handsome and charming. And he's a hard worker."

Her dad remained silent.

"But I guess I'm not sure."

"Keep your mind open, and pray about it. I know you'll make the right decision."

"Your confidence in me means a lot, Daddy." She stood, walked to the side of the bed, and kissed him on the cheek. "I remember how much that confidence helped me make it through childhood."

"I was proud of my daughter then, and I'm proud of who she has become," he said. "I've always been proud of you." He teared up. "Never forget that."

"Thank you." She wiped tears from her own eyes. "Is there anything I can do for you today?' I'll be leaving for Tennessee tomorrow."

"Just come back and see me when you can."

"I promise," she said. "I promise." She glanced toward the nurse's station. "And I'll see you again during visitor hours this afternoon. Right now, I need to get out of here before that nurse runs me out."

"They do have a lot of rules around here, don't they?" He yawned and settled deeper into his pillow. "I suppose I could use a good nap."

"Take it easy now. It won't be long before you're back at work."

He frowned. "You're right. I'd better milk it while I can."

She laughed. "Do that, and I'll see you in a few hours."

The next day Danni took an early afternoon flight to Nashville with a connection in Atlanta. Her carry-on bag thrown over her shoulder, she strolled through Hartsfield-Jackson Atlanta International Airport and considered her best snack options. She had almost two hours to wait for her connection.

Spotting a coffee shop ahead, she wound her way past business people, families with small children, and a kiosk in the center of the main hallway.

A few yards beyond, Danni settled into a cozy little two-top inside the café. As she waited for her laptop to boot, she thought about the conversation she'd had the day before with her dad. He had always maintained a balance between work and his daughters, giving Chloe and her a great start in life. Not every child had it that good.

She watched as new messages downloaded into her inbox.

With the financial security that Rob would bring to a marriage, she could afford to quit her job if—no, *when*—they had children. But is that what she wanted, children whose dad was never around?

Danni's gaze wandered across the corridor beyond the kiosk to a sandy-haired man who was talking on a cell phone. He looked her way. It was the same man who had been on the airplane to Iowa. And in the hospital waiting room.

He had to be following her!

With shaking hands, she packed up her gear, left a five-dollar bill for the drink she had ordered, and hurried in the direction of the departure gate. As she rushed past the man in the kiosk, he called out to her. "Ma'am, please come and sit down. You look like you need a stress test."

He didn't know the half of it.

Once she'd reached the gate, Danni surveilled the area around her. There was no sign of the man. At least not yet. If he followed her, she would take a later flight. Or rent a car and drive home. She could be in Nashville in less than four hours if she drove.

One thing was certain. She wouldn't be getting on a plane with him.

At the final boarding call, she scanned 360 degrees around her. Not seeing the stranger, she rushed onto the jet bridge and inside the 737. After stowing her bag, she dropped into a window seat, relieved to be on the final leg of her journey.

It had been an exhausting three days that had started with the fear of losing her father. Dealing with that had been enough. She didn't need the stress of another stalker. Even if he was from the Tennessee Bureau of Investigation.

The thought of confronting Ridge brought as much angst as it did relief. She couldn't wait to give those people a piece of her mind. They had intruded on her life one time too many. Wasn't it enough that they had raised doubts about Rob? It was time to go home and prove his innocence.

She watched out the window as the plane took off, ultimately heading northwest. The changing cabin pressure reminded her to breathe. Looking through the clouds, the details on the ground became harder and harder to discern.

Viewing the world from far above always offered a different perspective. It was a small world, after all. Perhaps there was a possibility that seeing the sandy-haired man three times had been a coincidence. Still, the crime Rob had been accused of committing was all-too real. Real enough that Michael Ryan had died from it. Real enough that it had contributed to her mother's death more than twenty years ago.

She didn't want to be a part of that dark world. Coincidences didn't exist there. And if they did, they might get you killed.

An hour later, Danni ran by baggage claim to pick up her suitcase, flagged down a trolley driver, and rode to long-term parking. After throwing her luggage into the trunk of her Escape, she called Jaycee.

"I'm home! Can you meet me at your house so I can pick up Sophie?"

"It'll be about thirty minutes before I can get away."

"Perfect. I'm just leaving the airport."

"How was your flight?"

"No problems." Except for a stalker. "How are things at the restaurant?"

"We're good, Danielle. Everything went fine without you." Jaycee had a smile in her voice.

"It's nice to know I was missed."

"Of course you were missed. We can't wait to have you back." Jaycee laughed. "Oh, and before I forget. Do you know a man by the name of Valentino Ramirez? He stopped by to see you. He said he was a friend of Rob's."

CHAPTER 17

The next day – March 30

The following morning Danni walked into the restaurant dining room and saw a small group of servers gathered in the back corner. The half dozen or so young men and women whispered, laughed, and slapped each other on the back. It would have been the perfect picture of workplace camaraderie but something—someone—was missing.

Michael Ryan.

He had always been in the middle of everything, laughing the loudest, provoking and encouraging his coworkers, and yet always watching their backs and helping them out. He had stood out in every crowd.

It wasn't just Michael's life and dreams that were missing. Losing him had affected each of them. Their lives had been forever changed. A family had lost a son, a brother, a nephew. And coworkers had lost a mentor, a helper, and a friend.

Danni settled into a chair. Michael's life had been extinguished by someone who cared more about money than the welfare of his or her nameless, faceless clientele. Jaycee told her yesterday that Michael's death was likely the result of a tainted batch of street drugs. If that was the case, some dealer, somewhere, had increased his profit by cutting the original substance with a less expensive but lethal one.

Of course Michael wasn't a completely innocent victim. He had agreed to play the deadly game, one that amounted to nothing more than Russian roulette, and it had taken his life. He had hung out with the wrong crowd, and experimenting with one thing had led to another until the loaded chamber had eventually found its target.

Still it didn't seem fair. How she wished she could put her hands around the neck of the person who had done this to him. The drug dealer who had—

Her cell phone rang. Pulling it from her pocket she checked the caller ID.

Rob Evans.

"So are you back at work this morning?" he teased.

"Who is this?"

"What do you mean?" Rob asked.

"You've been scarce for three days. They do have cell service in Iowa, you know."

"I'm sorry, sugar. We've spent a lot of time out of cell range. And I knew you would call me if something was wrong." He stopped. "Everything is okay . . . Your dad is okay. Right?"

"Yes, better. And I'm back at work today." She might as well give in to his good mood. "What has you in such a great mood? Especially this early. Don't music business people always sleep late?"

"Ouch. That hurt." He laughed. "I wanted to tell you I was sorry I missed you when I came through town."

Danni found a seat in a nearby booth. "I wish you could have rerouted to Iowa. I could have used the support. I spent his surgery day pacing the floor."

"You know I had meetings."

"Yes, Rob. I know." He would never change. "Don't worry about it. Thankfully Dad is a strong man."

"I hope he continues to do well." He cleared his throat. "Have you made any progress with our wedding plans? Invitations? Flowers? Dress? You know, all those things I know nothing about."

She planted her elbow on the table and cradled her forehead in her hand. "Rob? When would I have had time to do that? I've been out of town . . . like you always are."

"Wow, it's a tough room today."

She sighed, but not loud enough for him to hear. It wouldn't make any difference.

"I did check on your condo while I was home. Everything seemed to be in order."

"I appreciate it."

"I'm curious where you stowed the briefcase."

Danni's heart dropped to her stomach. "You couldn't find it?"

"Well, I didn't look *everywhere*." He sounded a bit sheepish.

"I would hope not! You know, Mr. Evans, there are some drawers in a girl's house that are off-limits. And well hidden." She was blushing . . . and bluffing.

"Oh, I didn't think about that." He chuckled. "Good girl."

"Thanks." She quietly exhaled a breath.

"It didn't seem right, though, for you to be away. And I missed Sophia. Where did she stay?"

"At Jaycee's house. They had a great time." Thinking of the dog brought a smile to Danni's face. "I picked her up yesterday. She seemed happy to see me, even if Jaycee did fix gourmet doggie meals for her."

"The two of you are inseparable." Rob sounded almost jealous of her relationship with the dog. "A few extra treats aren't going to sway her away from you."

Movement in the front of the room caught Danni's attention. Caleb Samuels had walked in the front door, and he was just the man she needed to talk to.

"Rob, I have someone walking in the door for a meeting. Can I call you back?"

"No need. I only wanted to check in."

"Okay . . . oh, wait. I almost forgot." She fidgeted in her pocket for the business card Jaycee had passed along to her. "Do you know a man named Valentino Ramirez?"

"Wh-who?" The tone of Rob's voice took a nosedive.

"*Valentino Ramirez.* I've never heard you mention him, but Jaycee told me yesterday that he stopped by the restaurant while I was out of town. He said he was a friend of yours."

"He stopped by th-the restaurant?" Rob stuttered. "Maybe . . . no, no. I'm not sure I know who he is."

"Isn't that odd?" She stood to walk toward Samuels. "Whatever. I'll not worry about it unless he comes back in, and then I'll find out how he knows you."

"Yeah, babe. I wouldn't worry about him. He may know one of my acts. Might even be a crazy fan. I'd stay clear of him." Rob coughed. "Okay, I'll let you run. Hank is calling me on the other line."

"Talk to you late—" But he'd already left the conversation. The story of their relationship.

Now, it was time to do battle with the other man in her life.

Caleb caught himself staring at Danielle Kemp as she walked across the room. Why did he do that? Something about her always caught him off guard. And not just in passing. It wasn't her stylish clothes. She would look even better in a pair of blue jeans and a flannel shirt. It was more about who she was.

She met him halfway across the room, and judging from the frown on her face, she wasn't happy to see him.

"To what do I owe the pleasure of your visit, Mr. Samuels?"

With a shake of her head, she dismissed the attending hostess.

"Let's have a seat over there." She gestured toward a booth near the bistro bar in the front corner of the room. "You saved me a phone call."

"I did?" He took a seat.

"Can I get you a cup of coffee before we talk?"

"Is it safe? It appears you're upset with me." Did he dare smile? "I think I'd better pass."

"Then I'll get right to it. I want to know why you had one of your men follow me to Iowa. Or is that a question for your supervisor?"

"What? We didn't—"

"Agent Samuels, I may be a civilian, or whatever you call us common people, but I'm not stupid. I just returned from a trip to visit my father in the hospital, and a man followed me the entire trip. I saw him on the plane, at the hospital, and in the Atlanta airport on my way home."

Caleb sat back in his chair. "I think I will have that coffee, Ms. Kemp. And, yes, we do need to talk, because I can assure you the TBI didn't put a tail on you during your trip to Iowa."

She stared at him in disbelief. "So you knew about my trip, but you didn't have me followed?"

She prepared to stand, but he stopped her. "Please stay for a minute."

He glanced around the room. A few of the wait staff were gathered nearby, watching them. "You're going to call more attention to me than we need."

Apparently she had noticed their audience too, because she made a visible effort to calm herself.

He continued. "Let's just say my office was aware of your father's health problems. And I hope, by the way, he's doing better."

He waited for a reply. She nodded, so he resumed. "We knew you had a legitimate reason to fly to Cedar Rapids." He glanced to the dispersing staff and then back to her. "And I knew where you were because we spoke to the local authorities and to the administrator of the hospital."

A spark in her chameleon-colored eyes ignited. Today they were more of a bluish gray than the green or brown he had seen before. She opened her mouth to protest.

"Hold on. Let me explain." He waited a beat for her to relax. She leaned forward, placed her chin on her hands, and glared. "We had no reason to follow you because we knew Evans was in another state."

"You had no right—"

"I will respectfully disagree with you on that, but let's move on to the most important point, and that would be who followed you."

"Isn't that what I asked you?" Her complexion paled.

"I can assure you that I don't know. But I'm as curious as you are to find out."

"If the man on the plane, and at the hospital, and at the Atlanta airport, wasn't from the TBI," she clasped her hands in front of her, "then who . . . ?"

"That's what we need to find out."

"Agent Samuels . . ." She swallowed hard.

"Caleb, please."

"Caleb." She studied him momentarily. "I want to tell you about something else that happened. But first, let me get you—and me—that cup of coffee. I think we're going to need it."

Danni returned with two coffees. Caffeine was the last thing she should be consuming right now. Her hands were already shaking. But if the Tennessee Bureau of Investigation hadn't followed her to Iowa and back, it must have been someone from the drug ring.

How was that even possible? Still, it appeared that Caleb Samuels was telling the truth. And if the TBI hadn't followed her, it had to have been someone from the other side.

She was repeating herself.

None of this made sense, except that she was too deep into something she didn't understand to consider going it alone. Which meant she had to trust someone.

But who?

She settled back into the booth, watching Caleb prepare his drink. Two sugars and one long pour of cream. She had pictured him as a man who would prefer his coffee strong and black. Maybe there was a softer side to this street-stalker-turned-agent-of-the-law.

Once she had his full attention, she told him everything she could remember about the sandy-haired man who had been on the plane, at the hospital, and in Atlanta.

"Do you think you could pick him out in a lineup? Or, better yet, help a sketch artist draw a composite?"

She assured him she could. The image of the stranger staring at her in the airport had been seared into her memory.

"There's one more thing I think you should know." She calmed herself, taking a deep breath, then another, before continuing. "When I returned to Nashville yesterday one of my coworkers told me I'd had a visitor here at the restaurant while I was gone."

He nodded for her to go on.

"I wouldn't have thought a lot about it. Potential clients and sales people come by every day. But this man told Jaycee he was a friend of Rob's and that he had dropped by to see me since he was in town."

Caleb extracted a smartphone from his pocket, presumably to take notes, as she reached for the business card in her pocket.

"Did you get his name?" he asked.

"Yes." She tossed the card across the table and recited from memory. "Valentino Ramirez."

The agent's jaw twitched, and he locked eyes with her. "Have you ever heard his name before?"

"No. But when I mentioned him to Rob a few minutes ago, his response was less than forthcoming. I could tell it bothered him. Just like it did you now." She waited a beat. "What's going on? Who is he?"

He ignored her questions. "What did Evans say?"

"He stuttered and stammered, so I dropped the subject."

"That was probably a good move." Caleb tucked his phone away without making a note. It was obvious he knew the name, and he had no need to write it down.

Danni took a sip of her coffee and shrugged. "I was uncomfortable making a big deal about it. I didn't want to create something out of nothing."

He waited for her to continue.

"And, well, since you've told me the stalker wasn't from the TBI, I'm not sure what—or who—to believe anymore."

He extended his arms across the four-top, shortening the distance between them, physically reaching out to her. "I can understand why you would be confused and afraid." His expression softened, and for the first time she noticed the scars on his forehead. The ones she had put there. Thankfully they appeared to be fading.

"You have every right not to trust anyone. Including me." He clasped his hands on the tabletop. "But I hope you will. I promise not to let you down."

Danni toyed with her spoon, aligning the tip of its handle with the edge of the table, silently considering his request.

"I am who I say I am." He sought her gaze. "And I will protect you. But I need your help to do that."

She lifted her chin and considered his dark brown eyes. They were the same eyes that had frightened her that first day on the street. But now . . .

She nodded her agreement.

"Thank you." His words were barely audible, but the set of his jaw spoke volumes. This man was strong enough to take care of her.

Danni straightened in her chair. "I realize I have to trust someone. And quite honestly, Rob isn't that man right now."

That had been easier to say than she had ever imagined.

"Good. I need to start with a very important question."

She stiffened. *What now?*

A smile slowly softened his face. "Do commercial kitchens use sandwich bags?"

"Of course, but . . ."

He pointed to the business card on the table. "We need to find out if your chef met the real Valentino Ramirez."

CHAPTER 18

She left because she loved you.

They were the only words Danni remembered from the day of her mother's funeral. Although he had intended them for comfort, decades later her father's sentiments still stung. Why would someone willingly leave when they loved you? That idea had never made sense. Nor had it brought peace.

Few things from her past, as related to her mother, made sense. Or brought peace. Including the fainting spells she'd had for as long as she could remember. Even before.

According to stories her dad told, she had occasionally passed out as a baby in her mother's or father's arms. Each such event had sent her parents scrambling to a doctor's office. Actually, a multitude of doctor's offices through the course of years. But no one could fully explain it.

When she was a baby, her parents were told she was holding her breath. When she was a teen, she was told she was borderline anemic. Or that she might occasionally suffer brief fluctuations in blood pressure. But nothing was confirmed. And in the end, everyone, including a nurse who claimed to have had the same problem as a child, shrugged it off, suggesting Danni would grow out of it.

That hadn't happened either.

"Apparently you haven't grown up yet," Jaycee would tell her, trying to make light of a frustrating situation. But even her good friend's teasing didn't alleviate Danni's embarrassment, particularly when it happened in front of a business associate or in public. So Danni stayed on guard.

She knew her triggers. One of her spells was most likely to happen when she was tired. Or in an especially stressful situation. Like hearing that your fiancé was involved in an international drug ring. Or seeing the look on Caleb Samuels's face at the mention of Valentino Ramirez.

After Caleb left, Danni did her best to put his visit behind her. And to not faint. She had too much work to do. Two upcoming catering events, a corporate party and an art show, vied for her undivided attention. None of it would get done if she continued to dwell on her personal life.

Just as she reached her office door, she came face to face with Jaycee.

"What's going on?" The chef asked before following her into the room. "And who was that guy you just saw for coffee?"

Danni dropped into the chair behind her desk, thankful she didn't have to lie.

"A narcotics agent."

"Oh." Jaycee's mischief turned to concern. She anchored herself against the doorframe. "Does he have new information about Michael?"

"No—" Danni stopped in mid-sentence. *Or did he? Could Ramirez be linked to Michael's death?* The thought terrified her, but she wasn't about to share it with her friend. "They're still investigating."

Jaycee stepped into the room and closed the door behind her. "You're not telling me something. I know you too well." She took a seat on the edge of the chair nearest to Danni. "What are you not telling me?"

Danni shook her head. "What I know is confidential."

"So you do know more!" Jaycee gasped.

"Agent Samuels asked for specific information about the restaurant, okay? That's all I can tell you."

Jaycee contemplated the floor, then lifted her gaze. "I understand. But will you do me a favor?"

"That depends. What is it?" Danni shuffled the paperwork on her desk.

"Be careful." Jaycee leaned forward in her chair. "I don't like the way this is going."

"I don't either, Jay. Feel free to pray for me. For all of us."

The color left Jaycee's cheeks. "Now you're really scaring me. You're rarely serious about that."

"I almost lost my dad last week, remember? I've been saying a few prayers lately myself."

"Of course. I'm thankful he's better." A light bulb seemed to go off in Jaycee's head. "Maybe now's the time to ask you to come to church with me." She smiled. "You're still looking for a venue for the wedding, right?"

Was she?

"You'd love my church. And it's big enough for your guest list."

Danni was happy to change the subject. "Now I'm worried about you. Since when are you supporting my marriage to Rob?"

Jaycee's eyes twinkled. "I'm not, but if it will get you to church . . ."

Danni suppressed a grin. "I'll take you up on that invitation."

"Really?" Jaycee squealed. "When?"

"Next Sunday?"

"Deal!" The petite chef jumped from her chair and gave Danni an air-five.

"It's just one Sunday, Jay." Danni cautioned. "Not a commitment to sing in the choir."

"I know." Jaycee's enthusiasm wasn't deterred. "But you're going to *love* it!"

Rob settled into his chair in the front of the bus. It wasn't quite noon, and he had already put in a full day's work.

Still, the most important job remained.

He straightened the wrinkle in his long-sleeve button down, then pushed up his sleeves. If his colleagues in Nashville had any idea what his sideline job entailed, they would run the other way. Of course managing entertainers had its risks too. But nothing compared to what he and Hank would do this afternoon.

His heart poked at his chest. The risk he took with every trip to Phoenix, or Houston, or Seattle paid big dividends. Much bigger than artist management.

It had taken years for his management company to earn what his sideline operation brought in regularly. In fact, his secondary job had supported his fledgling music business efforts. It had taken nearly half a decade to build a stable of artists who could consistently produce the cash flow he could make in a single week of trafficking.

But now that it did, now that things in Nashville were heating up and Ramirez was becoming more and more difficult, it was time to make a change. Hopefully Valentino wouldn't renege on his original deal that Rob could walk away at any time. As temperamental as entertainers and musicians could be, they weren't even close to being as difficult as the shady characters he had met on the dark side. A few situations had left him scrambling for his life, and it was then he appreciated Hank the most.

Hank Porter was not only a good bus driver, he was a former Army sniper. He had also trained in the martial arts. They'd had a gun pointed at them on several occasions, usually by a street thug who thought he could take the big boys down.

That wasn't about to happen with Hank on duty. His driver was especially helpful on pick-up days like today. They had a one o'clock appointment at the arena, right under the noses of security. A tour bus drew too much attention in a hotel parking lot, so Rob would arrange to meet his contacts backstage where coaches and motorhomes were a part of the regular scenery.

It was not only exhilarating to make a pick up in the presence of security guards, who were usually off-duty cops, it was also safer. Only an idiot would cause trouble when the cops had the place surrounded.

To avoid video capture of the deal, Hank would park the bus with the bay doors opening away from the cameras, about five feet from the venue wall and leaving very little room for a stray passerby.

"That looks good." Rob pointed to the back wall of the massive arena.

"You got it, boss." His driver had mastered the art of pithy conversation.

The big brute of a man was also low maintenance. A shower, a change of clothes, and a couple of good meals a day were all he required.

Hank switched the bus into idle and vaulted down the steps to begin his preparation. Their connection would be arriving in half an hour, and Hank would be ready.

In the next thirty minutes, he would run a site inspection, assessing where all cameras and security personnel were located. Then he would meticulously rearrange the right front bay, offloading a half dozen T-shirt cases and setting them beside the coach.

After the product arrived—and the delivery men had left— Hank would remove the false bottoms in the cases, stow the new "merchandise," and cover it with stacks of souvenir shirts. He could pack six cases in less than twenty minutes, concealing at least ten pounds of drugs per case. He would then store the repacked cartons in a specially-designed bay area that ran straight down the middle of the belly of the bus, secure the false back wall of the bay, and close and lock the bay doors. Ideally, those doors would not be opened again until the driver exchanged the pickup for cash in Atlanta—and Rob would already be home in Nashville, his fingerprints never touching the actual product.

At exactly one o'clock, Rob watched his computer screen as what appeared to be a local courier van pulled behind the bus and stopped. Two men, both looking a lot like roadies, exited the dark-colored vehicle and started walking toward the coach door.

Hank bolted down the steps to greet them. A few minutes later, Rob saw the men pull a dozen cartons from the back of the van. According to the bill of sale he had been emailed in advance, each carton contained two dozen baseball caps, plus two-and-a-half pounds of un-inventoried merchandise.

Hank quickly scanned the products, nodded, and sent the men on their way. By the time they had left the parking lot, the bus driver had completed his work of packing and stowing.

Within minutes Hank boarded the bus and closed the door behind him. "The merchandise is stored, Mr. Evans."

"Good job." Rob exhaled before he spoke. "I've called for your runner."

Hank nodded and grabbed his duffel bag from behind the driver's seat. Five minutes later a car pulled in front of the bus. It would take Hank to the hotel, where he could sleep in preparation for tonight's drive to their next tour stop.

Most days, when there was no delivery, Hank had twelve hours to sleep, eat two or three good meals, relax, and shower at the hotel before they left for the next show. It was only on pick-up days his schedule was rushed. But Rob made it worth his time. Hank was no doubt the wealthiest music coach driver in the state of Tennessee.

Now their connection had been made, Rob could also relax. He poured a glass of ginger ale over light ice, added a twist of lime, and settled back into his chair to tidy up loose ends before tonight's show.

CHAPTER 19

Two days later – April 2

Caleb tapped on Martin Ridge's open door.

"Yes, Samuels." The older man never looked up. "Come in and have a seat." He nodded to one of two antique wooden ladder-backs in front of his desk.

"When are you going to get some better chairs in here?" Comfortable was not Ridge's style. Not for furniture or conversations.

"I like to keep my meetings short."

Caleb chuckled, lowering himself into one of the rickety chairs, and surveyed the clutter on his boss's desk. "Think you'll ever find the bottom of that thing?"

Ridge frowned. "I know you didn't come in here to reorganize my office. What's on your mind?" He popped his knuckles. "It's about the Kemp woman, isn't it?"

"We have a new development. I saw her this morning."

A quick retort almost escaped the older man's lips, but he hesitated, frowning instead. "Well, go ahead."

"Someone followed her to—and from—Iowa last week."

Ridge's interest peaked. "Who?"

"She didn't recognize him."

His supervisor studied the top of his desk as though the answer was written there.

"And there's more."

Ridge looked up.

"She's been contacted by Valentino Ramirez."

A slow smile spread across Ridge's face. "Well, well. It appears we have awakened the sleeping giant."

Caleb nodded and settled back into his chair. "Apparently he paid a visit to the restaurant when she was out of town."

"So . . . she didn't see him?"

"No." Caleb pulled the plastic bag from his pocket and dangled it midair. "But he left his card."

"With . . . ?"

"Her associate."

Ridge smiled again. Something Caleb didn't usually see twice in one day, much less in the same meeting.

"It looks like that break-in at Evans's place shook some people loose." Ridge cocked his head. "But Ramirez in Nashville? That's unexpected."

"Yes, if it was Ramirez." Caleb countered. "It could have been someone calling himself by that name."

"Exactly." Ridge scowled, rapping his knuckles on the arm of his chair. "I have a hard time believing the big boss would actually show up in Nashville."

Caleb returned the bag to his pocket and prepared to leave. "I'll run prints."

Ridge leaned back into his chair. "For what it's worth, I'm hearing that the FBI now has someone on the inside. Your hunch has been spot-on since the beginning of this, Samuels.

"Thank you, sir." Caleb stood.

"We'll know more when we meet with them this afternoon."

"Great. In the meantime, I'll set a meeting with the Kemp woman, her associate, and our sketch artist. We'll get to work on a composite for both men."

The main floor receptionist called Caleb at ten till two. The team from the FBI had arrived early. He grabbed a notebook and stood, apparently too quickly, setting off a cramp in his leg.

"Man, that hurts." He mumbled to himself as he limped across the room. It was time to get back on the street. Sitting at a desk every day, as he had done since his encounter with a dog and a vase, had left him with stiff joints and lungs that ached for fresh air.

He massaged his calf and hurried from his office, slamming the door behind him. This meeting had to go well. His place in the fight for justice was on the street, not pushing paperwork in a stuffy office building.

Ridge greeted him at the conference room door. "Come in, Samuels." Apparently, he was the last to arrive. The rest of the party was seated. "Gentlemen, let's get started."

Martin Ridge lowered his husky frame into the chair at the end of the mahogany table. Caleb took the chair next to him.

"Samuels, this is Mack Brown and Danny Parker of the DEA. And you know Sam Wiley from the FBI."

Caleb acknowledged each of the men, and then turned back to Ridge.

"Samuels's been our lead agent on the Evans case." Ridge patted Caleb on the shoulder. "And he's done some good work. Some very good work."

Ridge didn't often compliment him, especially in a group setting, but Caleb knew his boss took great delight in the competition between agencies. So far, the TBI had bragging rights on this case. They had brought it to the Fed's attention early on, and if it proved to be successful, they would be looking even better.

Caleb's seat faced the window that overlooked the Tennessee countryside, but the importance of today's meeting assured him he would not get lost in the view.

"I understand you're good at what you do." Wiley spoke first. "At least that's what Captain Ridge here alleges." He paused a beat, and then smiled. "I'll have to agree with him. The information you've supplied—along with names—has opened up some very interesting leads for us."

Caleb nodded his thanks to Wiley and glanced at Ridge, who was beaming like the father of a winning high school star quarterback.

"I've asked Mack and Danny to bring all of you up to speed."

The two DEA men took turns explaining to everyone on the TBI team how Caleb's suspicions about Robert Evans had been substantiated. In fact they believed the entertainment manager was involved in something even bigger than what the TBI had suspected.

"We're waiting for key information before we make a significant move." Wiley spoke directly to Caleb. "It's my understanding you now have an informant."

Caleb exchanged glances with Ridge, who nodded.

"She's the girlfriend." The thought made Caleb's stomach turn. "We're fairly certain she's not involved. In fact, she's willing to help us prove her boyfriend's innocence."

Brown snickered. "That woman is either stupid or naive."

Caleb bit his lip.

"But can we trust her?" Wiley didn't appear to be convinced.

"Yes." Caleb scanned the faces on the far side of the table. "So far she's handled herself very well. She's willing to wear a wire, if needed, but we have been waiting for the right time and the word from you."

Caleb looked from Wiley to Ridge to make sure he should continue. "In fact she gave us some new information today."

Everyone locked focus on him.

"She has apparently been approached by Valentino Ramirez."

"In person?" Wiley asked.

"Yes." Caleb shifted in his chair, leaning forward. "She was out of state last week to visit her father who was in the hospital, and when she returned she had a message that Mr. Ramirez had dropped by the restaurant where she works. He asked for her by name." Caleb pulled the card, now encased in a plastic evidence bag, from his pocket and tossed it on the table. It landed in front of Brown. "Here's the card he left for her. It has been tested for prints. They're running them now, and we'll let you know if the prints come back with anything."

Brown picked up the bag. "Do we know for sure it was Ramirez?"

"I'm not sure how we could." Caleb answered. "I've never seen a photo of him, have you?"

The men across the table shifted in their seats.

"Can we talk to the person Ramirez spoke to at the restaurant?" Wiley asked.

"If you want to bring another person into the circle." Caleb wasn't so sure that was a good idea.

Brown picked up the card and read out loud what was written on it. "*Valentino Ramirez. Importing/Exporting 24 hours a day, 7 days a week.* And there's a phone number?" He looked to Caleb and then to Ridge "Do you mind if we check this out?"

"Take it. It's yours." Ridge broke his silence. "But we want to know who you have on the inside."

The men across the table looked from one to the other. Wiley finally spoke.

"Let's just say this. We have someone close to being on the inside, someone who will be there soon if I know Evans like I think I do. He appears to have an ego the size of his bus."

Everyone in the room laughed.

Wiley continued. "We have a young woman, actually an agent, who will be posing as a magazine reporter. She will contact Evans this week, asking for an interview." He grinned. "And, if we're right about him, he'll agree to it in a heartbeat. Our gal is quite the looker, and Evans seems to love the ladies. I expect Cassia to help fill in some of the blanks we need."

Parker nodded in agreement. "We also have knowledge of a big shipment being planned. Our people are still gathering details, but when the time comes, it will be helpful if your informant will wear a wire. Once this thing starts falling together, it may be a landslide."

"More like a mudslide," Brown snickered.

Caleb could feel his jaw muscles tighten. Wearing a wire would put Danni Kemp's life in jeopardy. Even more than it already was. But it had to be done.

"We'll get it done," he agreed. "Whenever you need it."

Wiley nodded. "In the meantime, can we move quickly to get that artist sketch of Ramirez?"

"Or the man who's purported to be Ramirez." Brown reminded them.

Ridge looked to Caleb for a response.

"The woman who saw him is an employee of Ms. Kemp's. Right now, she has no idea what's going. Or at least that's my understanding. We will have to trust her."

"Whoever it is, she just happened to be in the right place at the right time. Let's take that risk." Wiley said.

Ridge grunted his agreement, and the wheels in Caleb's head started to turn.

They would have to bring Jaycee Alexander up to speed with what was going on. He would first check with Danni to make sure her coworker was a woman of integrity, someone who could keep her mouth shut. And that would require another meeting with Danni Kemp tomorrow.

That thought pleased him.

CHAPTER 20

The next day – April 3

Rob's phone rang as he stared out the bus window, bored with the monotonous geography rolling past. He answered without noting the caller ID.

"Robert Evans?"

"Yes."

"This is Cassia Noelle of *Celebrity Lifestyles* magazine. How are you today?"

"I believe that question is better answered with a question. How did you get my number?"

A beat of silence.

"Oh, I'm sorry, Mr. Evans. I didn't mean to bother you, but your assistant, Melissa James, gave me your number. She said you would be happy to speak with me."

Melissa should know better than that. And for what it was worth, this Cassia Noelle woman didn't sound very sorry.

"Ms. Noelle, I don't usually handle publicity for my artists. You will need to speak with our pub—"

"Mr. Evans, I—I . . . may I call you Robert?"

This woman was aggressive. He had to admit he liked that. And her voice was quite appealing.

When he didn't respond, she continued. "I'm not calling for a story on one of your artists. I'm calling because I would like to do a story on you."

Really?

"Ms. Noelle, I believe I owe you an apology. Let's start this conversation over." He exhaled a long, obvious breath. "Hello . . . and how are you today?"

She laughed. "Please call me Cassia."

The woman had a provocative laugh.

"And please call me Rob."

"It's a beautiful day in Los Angeles, Rob. What's the weather like where you are?"

"I'm in Arkansas, and we're enjoying an invigorating forty degrees." He checked his phone for the current temp and her caller ID. "Although I'm riding in a very cozy bus, rolling along the highway."

"I understand you're on tour with several of your acts?" It was more of a question than a statement. She appeared to be referring to notes.

"What else do you know about me, Cassia? That's a beautiful name, by the way."

"Thank you. It's biblical, actually." Her voice smiled. "And I know just enough about you to be intrigued. That's why I'd like to interview you."

"Well, as I said. I'm in the middle of the country. Quite a long way from you. And unfortunately I don't expect to be in Southern California anytime soon, so I'm not sure—"

"That's an easy fix. I'll come to you." She offered the statement so matter-of-factly she must have some clout. Or a significant travel budget. A good indication the magazine had credibility—not that he read the rags. He preferred *Business Week* or the *Wall Street Journal.*

He initiated an Internet search of *Celebrity Lifestyles* magazine.

"Just how much of a budget does your publication have?"

He found the listing before she could answer. *Circulation, one million. Published monthly since 2002.*

She laughed. "Our editors travel all the time for our bigger features. And . . . oh, I wasn't going to say anything about it yet, but this will likely be a cover story. Most likely for our August issue."

Rob allowed his mind to drift for a bit, enjoying the idea of a magazine cover featuring his face on display at newsstands and airport coffee shops across the country.

"Mr. Evans?"

"Sorry . . . I was just thinking. If you're doing a cover story, I assume you will have a photographer with you?"

"Yes, I will. You're reading my mind." She had that smile in her voice again. "When and where do you suggest we meet up?"

"I'm in the Arkansas right now. But I will be in Idaho, Oregon, and then Montana in two weeks. Does the Big Sky country work for you?"

"That's perfect! We can do some great location shots there."

Rob ran through the possibilities . . . "Would you please work the details out with Melissa?"

"That sounds lovely! I'll give her a call."

"I look forward to meeting you, Cassia."

"It's mutual, Rob! Our audience loves unusual lifestyle stories like yours. In fact I'm a bit jealous of your being able to wake up each morning in a different city. It sounds like such fun."

"It can be. It's something I've worked toward for a long time."

"There's nothing like living your dream, is there?" She sighed. "I also understand you operate using a new model for artist management. Everything we've heard about you is fascinating, and I know our readers will enjoy the story."

"I do things a bit uniquely. I have artists in all stages of their career, and I like to think my hands-on approach is why they do so well." He leaned back in his chair and recited his roster of entertainers. "Ask Melissa to send you a press kit on each act. When we talk, I can explain how I've gotten them to each stage in their careers."

"That sounds great. I'll see you soon, then."

If Cassia Noelle was as attractive as her voice, he would enjoy that indeed.

Danni pulled her Ford Escape into an empty loading zone near the back entrance of the restaurant. The sun had yet to come out from behind the clouds this morning, and a few snowflakes swirled about the cityscape, the crystals disintegrating upon impact with the hood of her car.

The southernmost portion of First Avenue North in front of her disappeared into the horizon beyond Lower Broadway, its thin strip of pavement cutting a path between the Cumberland River, with Fort Nashboro clinging to its banks, and the aging red brick façades of eighteenth-century warehouse buildings turned twenty-first century restaurants, bars, offices, and retails stores. Amoré sat squarely in the midst of them in Nashville's Second Avenue Historic District, surrounded by two streets and an alleyway running along one side.

Danni pulled her jacket closer as she stepped out of the car. It was cool, not cold, like the freezing temps her home state was still experiencing. She'd heard on the news this morning that Cedar Rapids had received a foot of snow, with more expected tomorrow.

Tennessee was looking better all the time.

She had been thrilled with the opportunity to move south shortly after graduating from Iowa State in business accounting and hospitality management five years ago, and now, like all seasoned Nashville residents, she had come to expect unusual weather in early- to mid-April. But today the wind was stirring up warmer temps for later this week.

Danni popped her trunk and slung her handbag over her shoulder before bending forward to lift a box of cocktail napkins out of the car. Jaycee had asked her to reroute by way of the restaurant supply store this morning so she could pick them up. Her chef had said it was because they were running low on inventory, but Danni suspected it was more of a ploy to make sure Danni drove her car to work. Her friend hadn't stopped pestering her about the dangers of the five-block walk to and from the restaurant, especially during late nights.

Although the box was heavy, it rested much lighter on Danni's shoulders than her concern about a man she'd never met. Valentino Ramirez. She hadn't stopped thinking about him since witnessing Caleb's reaction yesterday.

Who was Ramirez? And why had he paid her a visit?

If the mention of his name made Rob stutter and Caleb go silent, she wasn't certain she wanted to know the answer to those questions. But not knowing what she was up against was the least appealing of her options. She couldn't fight the battle until she understood who the enemy was. Nor could she move on with Rob until she understood which side he was on.

Propping the backdoor of the restaurant with her foot, she shimmied inside with the heavy carton swaddled in her arms.

Judging from the way her shoulders ached, it might be time to add weight lifting to her morning cardiac routine. At this point in life, her upper body workouts consisted of pushing a pencil and trying to keep a 150-pound dog from chasing squirrels. The former with much more success than the latter.

Stepping inside Amoré brought memories of the young man who had been taken away from them. Michael's death still haunted her. If it had anything to do with Ramirez—or Rob, God forbid—she had to know.

That thought brought to mind an image of the man on the plane and at the airport. She had awakened last night with his face intruding on her dreams, adding to her sleep deficit. Operating on five and six hours a day wasn't helping her skin tone or soothing the dark circles that had formed under her eyes. Hopefully it hadn't yet affected her mental acuity at work. She had way too much to do. They had several special catering events coming up, and she didn't need to let her mind linger on boogeymen who might never materialize.

"Hey, let me help you with that." Jaycee grabbed one corner of the box and walked backwards toward a large steel table in the center of the kitchen. "Let's put it here for now."

"Are you sure? I can help you carry it to the storage room."

"One of the servers can do that. Besides, you have a guest to entertain."

"What? I'm not expecting anyone."

"Really? He seems to have become a regular around here." Jaycee's mouth twisted into a cat-like grin. "It's that detective who was here yesterday. I think he's infatuated with you, girlfriend."

"He is not!" Danni snapped back. But, as an afterthought, she took the time to check her face in her office mirror before sauntering out to the dining room. She needed to look present-able out on the floor anyway. Right?

She approached Caleb Samuels's table, giving her jacket a final tug just before he looked up.

"Hi . . ." His greeting faded into the back of his throat. "I'm here on official business again." He rose from his seat to pull out her chair.

"Okay." She took a seat. Were those butterflies in her stom-ach? No. She was hungry. She hadn't taken time for breakfast this morning. "How about coffee . . . or something to eat?"

"Maybe in a while, but let's talk first." He reclaimed his chair.

Danni searched his face for a clue as to the nature of his visit. "So . . . this will be a lengthy discussion?"

"It may take a while. Do you have time?" He stumbled over the last sentence.

A chuckle escaped her lips. "Well, I'm guessing I don't have a choice, Agent Samuels, considering you're on official business, and I'm the suspect in a criminal case."

"Call me Caleb." He hesitated. "And let me say off the record, you're not really a suspect. At least, not in my opinion." He looked around the room and then back to her. "But you have managed to land yourself in a position that's dead center of a major drug trafficking operation."

"Ouch." She cringed. "Not a good choice of words. I prefer to remain alive. I'm thinking I definitely need coffee before we talk."

"Make that two."

Was he blushing?

"You're the most interesting TBI agent I've ever met." Her turn to blush.

He smiled. "How many others do you know?"

She stood. "Well, actually, none . . . I'll get the coffee."

A few minutes later, with a pen and pencil in her hand, Danni followed one of her servers carrying a tray to the table. "Thanks, Meg. That's all we need."

"Yes, ma'am." The server placed the coffee and pastries in front of them and started to leave.

"Wait." Caleb reached into his pocket and pulled out two bills. He held the money out to the server. "Just because I'm a guest, doesn't mean I don't tip."

"Thank you!" The server grabbed the cash and turned on her heels to rush away.

"Oh, no . . ." Danni deadpanned.

Caleb frowned. "Did I do something wrong?"

"No. It's just that now you're also the nicest TBI agent I know."

His shoulders relaxed. "I realize how hard it is to make a living in her business."

"You're right. Thank you for doing that." She glanced over her shoulder. "And I'd like to share something with you before we talk business."

"Okay." He stirred his coffee.

"This isn't easy to say, but my chef thinks she's on to you."

He refocused on her, concern in his expression. "You didn't tell her about the investigation?"

"No . . . no. It's not that." She waved off the thought. "It's just that, well . . . she saw you in the restaurant yesterday. And . . . how do I say this delicately? She thinks you're here because you have a crush on me. How funny is that?"

The muscles in his jaws twitched. "You're right. As if that was even possible."

He said it so softly, Danni wasn't certain she was supposed to hear the last sentence, but it confirmed what she had thought.

The last thing he wanted was to fraternize with the girlfriend of a suspect in a major case.

No. This was all business. Just like he had said. Jaycee had it all wrong. "We both realize it's not, but I thought you might like to know that our secret is safe. She has no idea about your investigation."

"Good." He avoided her eyes. "So let me tell you why I'm here. In fact, I need to talk to her."

"Oh? What about?"

Caleb looked over her shoulder. "Is she here now?"

"Yes." Danni nodded.

"I had a meeting with my boss yesterday, and we decided that since Ms. Alexander is the only person who has seen Ramirez, we need to have her help us with a sketch."

"So it's like I thought. You know more about Valentino Ramirez than you're telling me, don't you?"

"Some." He made eye contact. "But I'm not at liberty to talk about it."

Danni squirmed in her seat. "But you're going to tell Jaycee about the investigation you're doing of Rob?" She would never hear the end of this from her friend. "She already doesn't like him."

Caleb's interest piqued. "Really? And why is that?"

Danni could feel the heat rise to her face again. She had said too much. That's what she got for feeling comfortable with Caleb Samuels. *Reminder to self: Talk less and listen more.*

"She never has. Actually, I think the feeling is mutual. You know, water and oil. They're just clashing personalities." Danni did her best to stop there, but her mouth stayed activated even when her brain told it to shut down. "And she thinks he's shallow, selfish, and narcissistic."

The corners of Caleb's lips twitched, as though he were trying to hide his amusement.

"You agree with her, don't you?"

He hesitated.

"That's really none of my business. And I *am* here on business, remember?" He smiled and gulped his coffee.

"Agent Samuels, I'm not sure why I feel so comfortable with you—maybe that's part of your TBI training—or just my vulnerability right now. And, yes, I do feel vulnerable because there's so much happening around me that I don't understand. Quite frankly it scares me." *Why am I rambling? Hush, Danni!* "I'm going to shut up now."

"May I interrupt your monologue?"

"Please."

"First of all, it's my Southern charm. Women can't resist it." He grinned, and then his face grew serious. "Secondly, and more importantly, you can trust me. I meant that when I said it yesterday." He waited for her to digest the thought. "Keep trusting me. I'm going to get you through this."

She nodded. For some inexplicable reason, she believed him.

"And to answer your first question, here's what we're going to tell your coworker . . ."

Caleb went on to explain that he would not mention Rob in his conversation with Jaycee. He would let her know that he was investigating a major drug operation and that he had learned about Ramirez's visit through Danni. Because Jaycee was the only one who could identify him, and that information was crucial to his case, he needed to talk with her.

Unfortunately, Jaycee's well-being would now be in jeopardy, just like her own. It didn't seem fair that her friend had been drawn into this mess. But she had been the moment she met Valentino Ramirez.

What had happened to their ordinary lives?

Danni wished they could go back to the days when their biggest worry had been catering an event for the governor. She silently prayed God would help them get through this . . . alive.

Caleb wanted to kick himself. Why had he addressed out loud what he shouldn't have been thinking? He didn't need—or want—a relationship with anyone, much less a confidential informant. A very attractive confidential informant, nonetheless.

He finished off his coffee and made a few notes while waiting for Danni to bring Jaycee Alexander to the table. Hopefully they could keep the conversation brief. The less she knew, the better. For her, as well as for the case.

Ten minutes later, Danni made the introductions.

"Agent Samuels, I'd like you to meet Amoré's executive chef, and the best chef in Nashville, Jaycee Alexander."

Jaycee extended her hand and smiled, "Nice to finally meet you." She gave a sideways look to Danni, who immediately blushed.

"Ms. Alexander, if your food is as good as your coffee, it's top-notch." Caleb pulled out a chair.

"Thank you! Lunch is my treat any time you want to try it. But please call me Jaycee." She lowered herself into the chair he offered.

It was obvious this woman wasn't easily rattled. Caleb liked that. Not to mention that she agreed with his assessment of Robert Evans. Danielle Kemp had found a good friend. One she might need in the difficult times ahead.

"I'll take you up on that, Jaycee. And feel free to call me Caleb." He held a chair for Danni and then settled into his own across the table. "In the meantime, I need your help."

The chef nodded.

"I'm not sure what Danielle has told you." He acknowledged Danni who sat quietly, her hands in her lap.

Jaycee shook her head. "Not much."

He gave the chef his full attention. "I work for the drug enforcement division of the Tennessee Bureau of Investigation. We have reason to believe a major player in narcotics trafficking may have come into your restaurant last week, and I understand you met him. I'm hoping you will remember a few things about him. His name is Valentino Ramirez."

The chef looked to Danni and then back to him. Her eyes widened. "Well, yes. He did. Or at least a man by that name was here." She turned to Danni again. "And he asked for Danni."

"That's what I was told." Caleb cleared his throat. "The TBI is asking for your help. We have no visual record on file for Ramirez. You're the only known person purported to have seen him."

Jaycee gasped. Danni reached out to her, laying her hand on her friend's arm. Both women paled.

"Do you remember enough about what he looks like to work with a sketch artist? We'd like to have a composite."

"Yes, I think so, Agent Samuels. But I have a question."

"I'll do my best to answer it," Caleb said. "But I will tell you now that I'm not at liberty to talk a lot about this case."

"I—I understand." Jaycee nodded. "I'm just wondering, though. And I'm sorry if I'm asking more than you can tell me. Does this have anything to do with the recent death of one of our employees?"

Caleb hesitated before answering. He wasn't certain how Danni would respond to his conjecture. "We don't know for sure," he finally said. "We're well aware of Mr. Ryan's death, but we haven't yet connected the dots."

"I see," Jaycee nodded again. "I'd be more than happy to help you. And I'm sure Danni will be too." She acknowledged her coworker who was sitting beside her with a terrified look on her face. Danni had both hands on the table now, one clasped around the other, no doubt trying to keep them from shaking.

Caleb wanted to reach out to her but knew he couldn't.

"As you know, I've already been talking to Ms. Kemp. And she has been very helpful. She volunteered the information about Ramirez."

Danni remained silent, but Jaycee ventured another question. "Just so I understand then. If Danni hadn't reported Ramirez, if I hadn't seen him, the TBI wouldn't have known he was in town?"

"Yes, I'm afraid that's true. We weren't aware of his presence in town, as troubling as that may be."

The two women looked at each other, and the expression on Danielle Kemp's face turned to panic.

"How did this happen?" Jaycee asked as Danni took a seat at her desk.

"Jay, I don't understand everything that's going on." Danni reminded herself to tell her friend as little as possible. "I have suspicions, but they're just that. Even Agent Samuels said the TBI isn't sure."

"That's reassuring, isn't it?" Jaycee plopped into a chair.

"I agree. But if it makes you feel better, I have confidence in Caleb Samuels."

Jaycee stared at her.

"I can't tell you why. Not because I won't, but because I don't really know. He just seems to be a man who can take care of himself. And us."

Jaycee focused on her hands, which were gathered in her lap. She shook her head. "I hope you're right, my friend, because all of this is scaring the dishwater out of me."

Leave it to Jaycee to add levity to a frightening situation.

CHAPTER 21

The following Sunday – April 7

From a distance Danni recognized Jaycee waiting at the front doors of the church. She quickened her pace as she made her way across the parking lot to join her friend.

Seeing all of the cars parked in front of the church reminded her of the many Sundays and Wednesday nights she and Chloe had attended their little community church with their dad. She wondered now why she had stayed away for so long.

Jaycee gave her a hug when she reached the top landing. "I wasn't sure if you'd really be here," she teased with a bright smile on her face.

"Do I look okay?" Danni straightened her skirt and smoothed her jacket.

"You look great. Let's go inside before the service begins. I don't want to miss the music."

Jaycee led her to a seat, three rows from the back.

"Do you always sit here?" Danni asked. "Or are you trying to hide your heathen friend?"

Jaycee stifled a laugh. "Yes . . . and no! Of course, I always sit here." She handed Danni a worship guide and a songbook. "Here, you may need these."

Danni gave her an I-have-been-to-church-before look and harrumphed, and then she settled comfortably into the padded pew. She looked around the large auditorium with its twenty- or thirty-foot ceilings held in place with massive wooden beams. Each arched stained-glass window along the sidewalls had been pieced together in a random mosaic pattern reminiscent of the European cathedrals Danni had seen on her senior class trip.

It could be a beautiful setting for a wedding.

Casting her gaze to the floor, she noted the neutral beige carpet. She could picture her bridesmaids—Jaycee, Chloe, and an old friend from college—wearing simple turquoise chiffon halter dresses as they walked down the aisle carrying white lilies. She would be following in an off-white, dropped waist gown with a wrapped bodice. Her veil would stream from a beaded tiara on top of her head, and—

Jaycee punched Danni and whispered, "Stand up for the prelude."

Within seconds dozens of choir members, wearing sapphire blue robes topped with gold-colored stoles, filed into the loft from doors on either side of the stage. Danni stood in awe of the pageantry, bracing herself with her hands on the back of the pickled oak-colored pew in front of her.

The pipe organ blared a gothic intro that emerged into a hymn she had sung for years in her hometown church in Iowa. When the congregation began to sing the words to "How Great Thou Art," Danni averted her eyes to the ceiling. The beauty of this grand chamber almost took away her breath.

The light mahogany beams running across the ceiling, parallel to the choir loft, began at the front of the church and continued all the way to the vestibule behind her. The narrow, arched windows along each wall filtered a kaleidoscope of colors onto rows of benches filled with worshippers, who were standing to worship with the choir. Danni marveled at the intricacy and detail of the voices as they blended together and remembered the vow she had taken as a young girl to follow her faith no matter the cost.

When had she let that slip away?

A few minutes later, the choir director led the congregation in prayer and asked everyone to take a seat and turn to the first song in their program. Jaycee opened her hymnal and began to sing, an enraptured look on her face.

Yes, this church was perfect for a wedding. Now, if only she was as certain about the groom.

After the service, Jaycee invited Danni to lunch, but she declined so she could take Sophie to the park for a run. Hurrying back to her condo, she changed into shorts and a T-shirt while Sophie romped through the house in anticipation. As soon as Danni grabbed the leash, the big dog pounced, landing at Danni's feet with a bow.

"We're going to have fun, Soph." Danni snapped the leash onto the Newfie's collar. "I'm taking you to the big park today."

Within ten minutes Danni had secured the Newfoundland in the rear cargo area of her Escape. Then, buckling herself in, she rolled down her windows and opened the sunroof. It was a beautiful spring afternoon for driving the short distance to Centennial Park. After their run, they would eat lunch on the patio of M. L. Rose, a dog-friendly establishment on Charlotte Pike. It was tempting to bypass their run and head straight to lunch, but a three-mile jog around Centennial Park would give her a chance to clear her head. And maybe do some soul-searching about church today, as well as the events of the last few weeks.

God had brought her here, to Nashville, for a purpose. She was sure of that. But somehow in the messiness, and the busyness, of everyday life she had managed to leave Him out of her decisions.

She was now facing one of the biggest decisions she would ever have to make. She needed to pray about it. Isn't that what her dad had told her less than two weeks ago?

Help me, God.

She exhaled the words, and then slammed on her brakes to avoid a car merging on the right from 25th Avenue. The driver of the other vehicle honked his horn and sped away. Danni regained her composure, looked twice—and then one more time—to be sure there was no other oncoming traffic before easing into the far right lane. A few seconds later she turned right into the West End Avenue entrance of the park.

That had been close. Her heart still palpitated in her chest. She watched carefully as she navigated between parked cars and pedestrians, finally wedging her Escape into a small parking spot on the west side of the Parthenon.

When Danni opened the door, Sophie bounded from the car, leaping with enthusiasm.

"Let's go, Soph."

Following a few minutes of walking to warm up their muscles, Danni signaled the dog it was time to run. Sophie took off in a slow lope, increasing to full speed as they approached the front of the giant pavilion. From there, they took a right to continue their run around the park's perimeter.

En route to the dog park near Thirty-First Avenue, they jogged passed flowering cherry and dogwood trees, a fountain, and a water bridge. Then a rustle of activity caught Danni's attention. A man jumped up from a blanket on the ground and waved to her.

"Hey, what are you two doing here?"

Caleb Samuels.

He seemed happy to see her, but he cautiously eyed Sophie.

The dog growled, and Danni averted her attention to a young, red-haired boy still sitting on the blanket. Danni pulled back on the leash and signaled for Sophie to sit.

"Why is that dog growling at you, Caleb?"

Danni tightened her grip on the leash, remembering the first time Caleb and Sophie had met. "She's just cautious about who to trust," she told the boy, then turned the question on Caleb, "What are you doing here?"

"I asked you first." Was it his lazy smile or the shock of stopping so quickly that caused her heart to palpitate?

Another low growl emulated from deep within the Newfoundland's chest. "That's enough, Soph." The dog settled onto the ground, still watching the TBI agent.

He switched his attention to the boy, who was now standing behind him. "Zachary, I want you to meet someone." The boy jumped up and stuck out his hand.

"Danielle, this is Zachary."

She gave the boy's hand a firm shake, a sense of illogical disappointment rushing through her. Could this be Caleb's son? That was something she hadn't seen coming. And all along she'd thought he was single because he didn't wear a wedding ring.

"So what are the two of you doing here?"

Danni felt her cheeks flush when she realized she had repeated her opening question. Not to mention that it was obvious they were having a picnic.

Caleb placed his arm around the boy's shoulders and drew him close. "Actually, we were just about to have lunch. Would you like to join us for barbecue sandwiches from Hog Heaven?" He motioned toward the blanket on the ground behind them. "I think we even have enough for Sophie, don't we, Zach?"

"Sure!" Zach smiled up at Caleb and then turned his attention to Danni. "Could I take your dog for a walk?"

"Do you think you can handle her? She's a big girl."

"I can. I used to have a big dog."

Danni looked to Caleb, and he nodded his approval. "Okay. But how about this . . . why don't you play together inside the dog park?"

"Okay!" Zach reached for the leash.

Danni turned to Sophie. "Sophie, you mind your manners. Zach's in charge."

The Newfie wiggled her tail as if she completely understood. What dog didn't love little boys? In fact, Sophie loved all children, as most Newfoundlands did.

"Call me if you need me, okay?" Danni reminded the boy.

"I will, but we'll be fine!" He took off running, whisking Sophie away with him.

After a few seconds of awkward silence, Caleb offered Danni a cold drink.

She fluffed her T-shirt. "That would be great. I'm a bit overheated."

"We have bottled water."

"Water sounds great."

He escorted her to the blanket, and she eased herself to the ground, positioning her body so she could watch Zach and Sophie playing inside the dog park.

"He'll be fine with her. He's good with animals." Caleb pulled a bottle of water from a small cooler of ice, wiped it with a napkin, and handed it to her.

"What kind of dog do you have?" Danni took a sip.

"Me? I don't have a dog. They don't like me, remember?" He laughed. "Zach and his mom used to have a lab."

"Oh." She was now more confused than before.

"I'm Zach's big brother from our volunteer program at church."

"Oh . . . church." Danni could tell she was blushing again. Had she forgotten how to speak in complete sentences? Church? Another side of Caleb she hadn't seen coming.

"Does that surprise you?"

"Oh, no . . . no. Not at all." She took a long drink of water. "Where?"

"Mt. Zion on Ebenezer Road." He studied her, his face unreadable, a reminder he made a living doing interrogations. "Where do you go to church?"

"Agent Samuels, I have the feeling you know everything I do, so I'm guessing a reply isn't necessary."

His lips curved into a warm smile.

"Would you please call me Caleb? And no, I don't know everything about you. But it will be interesting learning more." He gestured toward Zach and Sophie playing together.

Danni watched as the boy chased the dog, and then the dog chased the boy. Sophie had found a new friend, so she settled into a more comfortable position on the blanket. Perhaps she had too.

"This sandwich is good. Do you think I could give Sophie a bite?" Zach asked.

"It's up to Danni." Caleb deferred to their guest, who looked even more striking in her casual clothes than he'd ever seen her when she was outfitted in her fancy business suits.

"Sure. If it's only the chicken and not the sauce." In less than an hour Danni and Zach had become best buddies.

The boy wasted no time in giving the dog a portion of his sandwich. "You need to eat up, Sophie, because we have more to do after we're done eating."

Sophie was lying on her side stretched out between Danni and Zach, convenient to the food, as well as the fun, and opposite Caleb. He wasn't certain if the dog trusted him yet. Although she hadn't growled again, she had kept her eyes on him.

After his sandwich was completely gone, Zach started pulling bites of meat from the Styrofoam to-go container and giving them to the dog. Sophie took them eagerly but gently from his hand. It was obvious she understood kids. Now . . . if she would only warm up to him.

"You're a good girl. I hope I get to see you again," Zach announced.

Caleb smiled and leaned back on his hands. He was curious how Danni would react to such an overt invitation. She threw him a puzzled look and then turned to Zach. "I'm sure she would like that. Hopefully you'll see her again sometime."

"When?" The boy asked.

Ah. The innocence of youth. Caleb bit his lip, watching Danni.

"Well, I don't know." She seemed uneasy. Much more so than the dog. "Sophie and I don't come to this park very often."

"But you would come if Caleb and I invited you, right?" Zach turned to Caleb with pleading eyes.

Caleb ruffled the hair on the boy's head and grinned. "You ask too many questions, Zach. We don't want Danni to think we're pushing her into anything." He hesitated and then turned to Danni. "We want you to know that you're welcome anytime."

Danni wasn't quick to reply. She watched Zach as he scratched the wavy hair behind the big dog's ears. He was unaware of the implications of his request. "Well," she finally said. "I believe I can speak for both Sophie and me." She smiled. "We would be honored to take you up on the invitation some time, Zach."

"How about next Sunday?" The kid was determined to pin her down. He turned to Caleb. "We'll be here next week, right?"

Caleb nodded.

Zach quickly turned back to Danni. "Would you bring Sophie and meet us here then?"

Danni leaned back on her hands, mirroring Caleb's position, her face glowing. Caleb wasn't sure if it was from embarrassment or the early afternoon sun they had soaked up in the last hour.

She sat up and pulled her phone from her pocket. "Let me see. I need to check Sophie's calendar to be sure."

Zach grinned as he watched Danni search her phone. Finally, she looked at the boy and said. "Looks like she's available. Want me to pencil you in?"

"Yes, please. If Caleb is okay with it."

Zach and Danni both turned to face him. He threw his hands up in the air, palms outward, as if he had just been talked into the idea.

"Next Sunday works for me. Same time, same place. Zach and I'll bring Kentucky Fried Chicken."

"I'll bring dessert." Danni volunteered. "If that's okay?"

"We'd be happy for Danni to do that, wouldn't we, Zachary?"

"Yes, sir!" The boy jumped to his feet. "It's a date! C'mon, Sophie." He grabbed the dog's leash. "I'll race you to the gate."

"Be back in a few minutes." Danni shouted after them. "Sophie and I need to leave soon."

"Okay!" Zach's response trailed behind him. The youngster appeared to be having more fun than he'd had in a long while.

"To say the least, Zach has enjoyed this afternoon. I have too." Caleb hoped he wasn't overstepping his bounds.

"I'm certain that's because of Sophie, but I'll try not to let it hurt my feelings." She tucked her phone back into her pocket and prepared to stand.

"Are you really okay with meeting us next weekend?" he asked. "We don't want to push. And I know you have a lot of other commitments."

"No, I'm good with it, if you are."

The woman blushed more often than anyone he'd ever met. There was an awkward moment of silence, and Caleb wondered if his attraction to Danielle Kemp could be mutual. If that was the case, he had a whole lot of thinking to do.

"I'm great with it," he said. "In fact, I'll look forward to it."

CHAPTER 22

The next day – April 8

Monday morning Jaycee stepped inside Danni's office door. "Thanks for meeting me at church yesterday. I hope I haven't beaten you up too badly in the past about going. I have to admit, I never thought you would go."

"I enjoyed it a lot." Danni returned her focus to her paperwork.

"Does that mean you'll visit again?"

Why not? "Sometime. It's a beautiful church."

"This Sunday?"

Jaycee could be relentless. *As relentless as Zach had been.* "Maybe." Danni grinned.

"Really?" Jaycee squealed. "Great!"

Danni laid her pencil on her desk, put her paperwork aside, and looked up. "Jay, why do you keep asking when you don't think I'll do it?"

"Just hoping, I guess." Her smile reminded Danni of the Cheshire cat. "Want to go to lunch afterward?"

"I can't. I have a date."

"Is Rob in town?"

"No. I have a date with a ten-year-old boy." She might as well have some fun with her friend.

"What?"

"Go ahead and have a seat, Jay."

Jaycee sat tentatively. "This should be interesting."

"It is. But it's not what you think." Danni leaned back in her chair. "I took Sophie for a run in the park after church yesterday and . . . well, we ran into Caleb Samuels."

"The TBI agent?"

"Uh-huh."

"And his son?" Jaycee's expression dropped. "He's married, and you're meeting him at the park with his ten-year-old son? I don't get it."

"First of all, the boy is not his son. Zach is from Caleb's church. Caleb is his mentor. Sort of a big brother."

"Oh . . . kay" From the look on Jaycee's face, it was evident she liked what she was hearing. "And?"

"Zach fell totally in love with Sophie, and it was Zach who asked us to meet them at the park next weekend."

Jaycee nearly tumbled off her seat. "Are you going? Please tell me you're going."

"Relax. It's not a *date* date. It's just a play date for Zach and Sophie."

"Right . . ."

"I'm serious."

"I hope so." Jaycee had that catlike expression again.

"You're bad." Danni didn't try to hide her amusement.

"I'm not only bad, I'm happy!" The chef stood and pumped her fists in the air.

"You will be disappointed when this turns out to be just a play date, like I'm trying to tell you." Danni picked up her pencil and made an attempt to return to her work.

"What are you planning to wear?"

"Oh, Jay, don't be silly. I'm going to wear shorts and a T-shirt, just like I did yesterday."

Her friend rested one elbow on her hand and placed her other hand beneath her chin mimicking Auguste Rodin's *The Thinker*.

Finally, she shared. "Here's what I'd suggest . . . You look great in running shorts and a T-shirt, but since this won't be a chance meeting, why not dress up a bit more? You know, jeans and a plain white blouse with a sweater. Or cute shorts and a white top would look—"

"Jay, you're making too much out of this. He doesn't care what I wear. The boy just wants to play with my dog, and Sophie needs more opportunities to play with kids, so I accepted."

"Okay. One question, and I want you to tell me the whole truth and nothing but the truth." Jaycee tapped her foot. "Absolutely, without a doubt, you have no interest in Caleb; is that correct?"

"I know he's not interested in me. That's the same thing. He's working with me on a case. Just like he's working with you."

"Yes, but he didn't invite *me* to a picnic at the park."

"How many times do I have to tell you that I ran into him yesterday? Sophie is the connection between the boy and me, which naturally makes a connection between Caleb and me. Don't you see it? It's innocent."

"What I see is you going through a whole lot of grammatical calisthenics, trying to keep from admitting this guy likes you." A knowing smile spread across the chef's face. "Stop making excuses. You have the perfect opportunity here to get to know a nice guy, play the field, and date somebody without getting serious. Maybe it will help you see that Rob is not your only option in life."

"May I say something now?" Danni looked up from her paperwork.

"Sure."

"Dating around is not a bad thing when you're unattached, but I've been dating Rob for almost three years. I don't want to date someone else just for variety. After all, he thinks we're getting married in January."

"What did you just say?"

"What do you mean?"

"You just said you didn't want to hurt Rob because *he thinks* you're getting married in January."

"Yes, and your point is?"

"Evidently that means you're already convinced, or never were fully committed to the fact, that you won't be getting married to Rob in January." Jaycee stepped back and studied her. "What are you not telling me? I have the feeling you're leaving out important information."

Danni stared at her friend. She had to be careful or she would tell Jaycee too much. But what to say . . . where to stop? And how did she really feel? Had she made up her mind that she wasn't marrying Rob in ten months?

"I'm going to come clean, Jay." She nodded to the chair. "Sit back down."

Jaycee flopped into the chair in front of Danni's desk.

"I believe Agent Samuels does have a special interest in me. But it's not what you think. He's working on a case, and he thinks I have information. Apparently he's not the only one."

Danni explained about the man who had followed her to her fathers. "He says the man isn't TBI, but I don't know. That's why they want to put us both with an artist. You for Ramirez and me for my stalker. So this is just business. He sees me as someone who can help him with his case—a case he's very committed to solving. Guess what that makes me? It makes me a source and not a date. Do you understand?"

Jaycee lowered her chin. "I hope it's more than that. And I think it is more than that. I've seen him look at you, interact with you. All I know is I don't want you to get hurt."

Danni smiled. "That's why I'm not building any of this up to be something it's not." She leaned across her desk toward her friend. "Now, can we leave this where it is? Just a play date for Sophie?"

"And if something else comes from it?"

"Fine. Then you can say, 'I told you so.'" Danni tried to refocus on her paperwork for the third time. "I'm already almost engaged, so I'm not sure why I would even want to explore other options."

About an hour later, Danni took a call from Caleb. He had made arrangements with a sketch artist to meet her and Jaycee at Danni's condo the following day. He explained he wanted to do it away from the restaurant to avoid alerting the Amoré staff that something was up.

"Your condo is neutral ground for you and Jaycee," he said. "The artist's name is Amy Force, and she works for us here at the TBI. She's great at what she does and will make it as easy as possible for you."

The following morning, Agent Force met Danni and Jaycee at the condo. Danni glanced behind the woman who stood at her front door, hoping to see Caleb. But she had come alone.

Sophie nosed her way to the front to greet the female artist.

"What a beautiful baby. May I pet her?"

"Of course, but step inside." Danni moved out of the way, holding Sophie's collar until the woman walked into the foyer.

Amy Force bent down to rub the Newfie's neck. "Sophie, you're such a pretty girl. I'm so happy to meet you."

Danni cocked her head sideways. "How did you know her name was Sophie?"

"Oh, she's famous down at the Bureau." The woman grinned. "We've had great fun teasing Agent Samuels about his dog bites."

"Oh . . ." Danni had never thought about that possibility. "That's an unfortunate reputation for Sophie to have."

"Don't worry. We know she was protecting you." The woman gave Sophie one last pat. "Isn't that what dogs are for? Especially the big ones. And this girl is certainly big." She looked around the condo. "Where do you want me to set up?"

"Would the dining room be okay?"

"Sounds great." She followed Danni and Sophie through the living room and into the dining room, where Jaycee was waiting.

"Ms. Force, this is Jaycee Alexander. "Jaycee, Amy Force."

"Nice to meet you. Is that all you brought with you?" Jaycee asked as she took a seat.

"Oh, yes." Amy patted her laptop bag. "We travel light these days." She pulled her compact computer from its case, set it on the table, and took a seat.

"May I get you a drink?" Danni asked.

"Perhaps later. I'm fine right now."

"How long will this take?" Jaycee seemed to be intrigued by the process.

"About an hour each. Who would like to go first?"

"Why don't I," Jaycee suggested. "Then I can leave and go on to the restaurant if it's getting too late."

"Sounds like a great idea, Jay." Danni took a seat.

After the artist had booted up her computer program, she turned to Jaycee. "So what can you tell me about how this man looked?"

Jaycee thought for a few seconds and then rattled off several general characteristics. "I would say he was about six feet tall. He had dark hair, dark eyes, and he wore a business suit." She laughed nervously. "Although I suppose it doesn't matter what he was wearing."

"No, that's fine." The artist assured her. "Whatever helps you remember him. Just let your mind go back to that day and place. What else do you remember?"

In about an hour, Jaycee had told Amy Force everything she could remember, and they had gone over possible face profiles, finally coming up with a composite that pleased Jaycee.

"That looks almost exactly like him. How do you do that?"

The artist smiled. "Years of experience and a bit of luck. It helps when people remember unique facial characteristics, like you did. Our worst fear is having someone described as average." She laughed. "You know, 'He was average height, weight, and nothing about him really set him apart.'"

"I can see why that would make it difficult for you," Jaycee agreed.

"Impossible, actually." She turned to Danni. "Are you ready to do yours?"

"Sure. But I'm worried now that my guy looked average." She took a deep breath. "Let me get us a cup of coffee, and I'll try to conjure up the best memories of him I can."

"Sounds great. Two sugars and one cream, please."

"I'll make the coffee, Dan. You go ahead and get started. I'm fascinated with this process, and I'm going to stay for a while longer."

Danni and Amy Force had already started going over basic face and body characteristics when Jaycee returned with steaming mugs of coffee.

"Perfect." Danni stopped to take a sip. "I can think so much better when I have caffeine in my body."

Within the hour, despite Danni's fears that she wouldn't remember enough detail, Amy Force had captured the likeness of her stalker. Seeing his image again sent a chill down Danni's spine. In fact he was an average-looking man, but remembering the way he had looked at her in Atlanta and knowing that he had followed her to three cities and back, still made her skin crawl. She wrapped her arms around her shoulders and rubbed away goose bumps.

A few minutes later Jaycee returned from putting their coffee cups in the kitchen sink. Wiping her hands on a dishtowel she positioned herself behind Agent Force.

The TBI artist tilted the computer screen so Jaycee would have a better view.

"Oh, wow!" The color left Jaycee's face. "I've seen him in the restaurant."

Danni's mouth dropped open, and Amy turned to stare at Jaycee.

"In fact, I saw him there yesterday."

CHAPTER 23

Several days later – **April 12**

D anni saw Caleb every day that week, although she didn't always talk to him. Even when she didn't see him, she knew he was there.

On Monday morning, he loitered at the crosswalk where she had first met him dressed as a homeless stranger. Tuesday, he paid a visit to her condo to return Rob's briefcase full of money, now counted, logged, and marked. On Wednesday, he stood in the shadows of an adjoining building while she parked her car behind Amoré. That same evening, she saw him start up his old Chevy pickup truck and follow her home. He waited until she stepped safely inside the elevator in the lobby of the Rutherford before driving away. The man who had once been her stalker had become her guardian.

Regardless of the security Caleb and others at the TBI now provided, she drove her car to work every day. She didn't want to tempt fate. Plus, Jaycee had no idea about the surveillance, and her friend continued to nag her.

Danni's initial resentment of the TBI's intrusion upon her life had transitioned to gratitude that they had her back. Of course the Bureau's reason for watching her was twofold. Caleb had told her they believed she would be contacted again—and not so benignly the second time. He theorized her next communication would come unexpected, just as the others had been. That meant it could come anywhere, at any time, and it could be anything from a hired street thug to a second visit from Ramirez or an encore appearance of the sandy-haired man.

Caleb had also told her that so far neither of the composites she and Jaycee had helped Amy Force put together had garnered a hit, which led him to believe the two men were either smart enough to maintain a low profile or were hired pawns with no prior arrests. Caleb still believed the man who had presented himself as Ramirez was actually a paid actor, a stand-in who had been hired to scare Danni into apoplexy. If that was the case, the man hadn't achieved his goal. She was scared but determined not to let anything stop her in her search for the truth. Less than a month ago, she had decided to change her life for the better, and if facing down criminals who controlled Rob was part of that effort, she was willing to take it on.

Friday morning, she arrived at Amoré later than usual because of a midmorning meeting at the Tennessee State Museum, where they would soon be catering an event. She spotted Caleb sitting at the bistro bar in the far corner of the room, staring out one of the front windows. After speaking with several of the wait staff, she walked over to his table, catching him off guard.

"And how's your service been today, sir?"

Caleb jumped and then smiled when he realized it was her.

"Wow, some great agent you are," she teased. "The woman you're following just ambushed you."

He pulled out a chair for her. "And I'm not sure how I could have missed her. She looks beautiful today."

Danni felt heat rise to her face. This man was quick to make her blush.

"Thanks." She took a seat. "And in case I haven't said so lately, thank you for keeping an eye on me. I have to admit I sometimes feel like I have a target painted on my back."

"The first part's easy." He grew serious. "And, yes, you do. That's the other reason I've been watching."

She wrapped her arms around her shoulders.

"Is it just me of did it just get chilly in the room?" She tried to laugh. "I've never been targeted for anything before, so you'll have to excuse my discomfort."

"It's something you never get used to, trust me." He studied her as he sipped his coffee. "I doubt you would have been followed or contacted by anyone if you hadn't come under the TBI's scrutiny."

"I'm going to respectfully disagree, Agent Samuels." She forced a tight smile. "The problem, as you call it, would still have existed. I just wouldn't have known about it."

Caleb nodded, and she repositioned herself in her chair.

"I would rather know about it if it's there. You can't fix something if you're not aware the problem exists."

"You're a smart woman." His gaze lingered.

"Thanks . . ." She relaxed into her chair. "Maybe you should withhold your judgment on that until this thing is over."

He smiled. "In the meantime, I want to ask you a favor."

"Sure." She eyed his coffee cup. "More coffee?"

He grinned. "Not right now, thanks. And that's exactly my point. I'd like to buy your lunch today, if you have time. You've bought my coffee for weeks. It's time I repaid you."

Where was he going with this?

"That's not necessary." She studied him.

The normally self-assured man who she knew to be Agent Caleb Samuels disappeared behind a boyish smile. "I'd appreciate it if you would. I also want to show you something before you see Zach again on Sunday."

"Oh . . ." Was she disappointed that this was business? "Okay. I have about an hour's work to do before I'm free. How about 12:30?"

He checked his watch and gestured around the room. "I'm not going anywhere, so take your time."

Danni stood quickly, almost tripping over her chair. Caleb reached out to her, but she managed to regain her balance on her own.

"Are you okay? I didn't mean to run you off."

"No . . . no, you didn't." She backed away. "I'll meet you right here at 12:30." She smiled and turned around, heading for the sanctuary of her office.

Why did she let her guard down like that? How could she even think he was asking her for a date?

"See you then." His reply trailed behind her.

As soon as she took a seat at her desk, Jaycee stepped inside the room. "Do you realize you've seen Caleb Samuels more in the past few weeks than you ever see Rob?"

"Very funny."

"What did he have to say this morning?"

"We talked business."

"Is that all?" Jaycee raised an eyebrow.

"Actually, it's a bit embarrassing. I'm not sure I want to talk about it."

"What do you mean?" Her friend closed the door behind her.

"He asked to take me to lunch."

Jaycee pumped her fist and looked skyward. "Thank You, Lord!"

"It's not a date."

"Are you kidding me? What else would it be?" Jaycee's smile flickered, and she took a seat.

"He wants to show me something relating to Zach. It really is just business."

"I'm not buying that."

"Please don't go there." Danni couldn't believe she was about to admit this. "I'm already concerned he may think I'm interested in him. It's embarrassing."

"And you don't think that feeling is mutual?"

Danni shook her head. Jaycee completely misunderstood the situation. "Jay, this man spends his days protecting damsels in distress. I'm sure he has women falling at his feet all the time."

She almost had, literally, a few minutes ago.

"But how about you?"

"What about me?"

"Are you interested?"

"Not really."

"That means yes." Jaycee leaned across the top of the desk and took Danni's left wrist in her hand. "Do you see a ring on this finger?"

"What's that got to do with anything?"

"It's obvious this guy is attracted to you, Danni. And you're about to blow it because you don't have enough confidence in yourself." She settled back in her seat. "Please give him a chance."

Danni stared at her friend. "Why are you so passionate about this? About him?"

"You don't get it, do you?"

"Get what?"

"God is giving you a second chance to get out of your relationship with Rob. Please don't make a commitment to Rob that you can't undo before you've explored other options."

Danni's mouth opened, but nothing came out.

"You don't have to marry Caleb Samuels, but at least follow your heart."

"I promise. Whatever that means, I'll do it." She picked up a stack of papers. "But you'll see, Jay. This is going nowhere."

Caleb took Danni to his favorite restaurant, a meat and three near the heart of Nashville's downtown. The little red diner located on Eighth Avenue South and handy to Music Row and the Gulch was always packed with locals as well as tourists. Arnold's Country Kitchen wasn't the fine-dining experience his lunch companion was used to, but there was no better way to show her who he was than to bring her to his favorite place. One that reminded him of his childhood.

Hopefully she could find something here to eat that she would enjoy. Even if she was one of those high-society types who preferred their meals to be vegan, Arnold's served a variety of vegetables, as well as a number of entrée options.

Caleb hadn't just memorized the weekday specials, he usually ate them by regimen. Fried chicken on Monday, meatloaf on Tuesday, catfish on Wednesday, country fried steak with gravy on Thursday, and chicken and dumplings on Friday. Unfortunately, the restaurant was closed on the weekend.

Although his mouth was watering for the chicken and dumplings, he would forgo them today. They were a bit messy for a first date.

Not that this was a date.

"Know what you want?" He asked Danni as they approached the serving line.

"Wow . . . I don't know." She scanned the hot bar with its double rows of steaming food pans. "I've always loved my grandmother's chicken and dumplings, but that's messy. I think I'll try the fried shrimp. I've never had that here."

The irony brought a smile to his face. "So you've eaten here before?"

"Are you kidding? They received the James Beard award a few years ago. I have to stay up on my competition. Have you ever had their fried green tomatoes?"

He nodded. "The best in town."

"If you love Southern cooking, you should try Jaycee's family restaurant in Laverne. It's a drive from here, but they have some of the best diner food in Middle Tennessee."

"Your chef's family runs a diner?"

She gave him a knowing smile. "You look surprised."

"I am. I would never have suspected your gourmet chef grew up on Southern cooking."

"Hmmm," she teased. "Someone needs to do his homework."

"That's twice today you've found me out. I'll try to be more careful."

She smiled, and he realized he could get lost in her beautiful eyes, more green than gray-blue today.

After lunch, Caleb turned his old Chevy truck toward East Nashville. It was time Danni saw how others lived. She might enjoy good diner food, but every night she went home to a high-rise luxury condominium with amenities some people couldn't dream of having in a lifetime.

In recent years Nashville had fallen prey to man's cravings for modernization. Demolition and reconstruction had replaced many of the older structures—unfortunately, some rich in history and lost forever—with high rises that reached toward the sky. The Rutherford, not many blocks away from where they were now, was just one of those buildings, physical evidence that today's movers and shakers wanted to live in a manufactured urban paradise rather than commute. That was not Caleb's kind of world.

Conversation languished as he and Danni crossed the Korean War Veterans Memorial Bridge, which spanned the Cumberland River toward East Nashville, toward Zach and his mother's rundown house on a dead-end street.

They too had been victims of man's cravings of a different kind. Ginny Franklin's former husband, Zach's dad, had never made an attempt to support his family. He was far too interested in his next high.

After Wade Franklin went to prison for possession, dealing, and attempted robbery, Ginny had done her best to make a home of their structurally sound but badly neglected frame house. Thankfully, it was situated in a decent neighborhood, and it might one day acquire enough equity to help them build a better life.

Because their home wasn't far from his office, Caleb routinely stopped on his way home to help Ginny and Zach with maintenance. As far as he knew, no other consistent adult male influence existed in their lives.

"Where are we going?" Danni asked, breaking the silence. Caleb had been lost in thought since they left the restaurant.

"It's not much farther." He glanced to her. His dark eyes reassuring, despite her growing discomfort. "I want to tell you a little more about Zach, and to do that, it helps to show you where he lives."

"Do you live out this way too?" she asked, trying to connect the dots, even though Caleb didn't appear to be ready to show her the whole picture.

"No. My place is west of town."

After a few more minutes of silence, she broached the subject again. "I'm fine with doing this, but I can't help but wonder why it matters where Zach lives."

Her words must have broken the spell. Caleb pulled his old truck to a stop in front of a ramshackle cottage on a small lot between two similar homes. The landscaping left a lot to be desired. In fact, there were only a few scraggly evergreens growing near the sidewalk and the house.

What lay in front of her took her back to a place and time she rarely revisited. "Wow . . . this reminds me of my mother's house."

"Really?" It was obvious her words surprised him. "It's Zach's house." He clicked off the ignition. The old motor ceased its roar, and silence overtook them.

Momentarily staring out the window, Danni collected her thoughts and then turned to the man beside her. "You obviously haven't done your homework again, Agent Samuels. My mother left me, my sister, and my dad when I was a kid. Occasionally my father would drive us past the house where she lived, although we never attempted to contact her."

She shook her head. "In my childish dreams, I never understood that, but my dad always said, 'She'll come home when she's ready.'"

"And?"

Danni turned away from him and focused on something in the rearview mirror. "She died trying."

"I'm sorry."

The pity in his voice caught in his throat. But Danni had shed too many tears through the years to bring them back now. Or maybe she had just stuffed her feelings into the deepest, darkest regions of her subconscious.

"She was killed when I was eight. My daddy told my sister Chloe and me that she was on her way home to us when the accident happened. I guess I've always wondered if that was true, but it was comforting to a child."

He nodded.

"So what did you want to tell me about Zach?"

"You have a lot in common." His voice was soft. "More than I knew."

She nodded.

"Zach's dad left him and his mother. He's serving thirty years in the state prison for armed robbery and possession of narcotics with the intent to sell."

"Now I know why you care about him like you do."

A part of who Caleb was had begun to make sense to her.

"That's not exactly the whole story."

CHAPTER 24

aleb knew it was Danni's turn to be surprised. He collected his thoughts before he spoke. Not many people knew his history. At least not to the extent he was about to share with her this afternoon.

"I care about Zach on a personal level," he said. "He's a great kid, despite the hard upbringing he's had. Thankfully, he has a good mother, and he's been raised in church."

Danni settled back into her seat, leaning against the passenger side door of his truck, facing him.

"I do what I can for him because of something that happened years ago, when I was nineteen." He sucked in a long breath, letting it out slowly. "I was raised in a good home. And, unlike Zach and you, I was blessed to have both my father and my mother."

Danni nodded.

"But boys will be boys. Not that I didn't have choices, and I made some bad ones."

For a reason he was not willing to admit—even to himself, he wanted to connect with her. But this was harder than he'd thought it would be.

"I started experimenting with drugs. Just marijuana at first. Then after a while, I developed a habit for cocaine."

Danni was staring at him now.

"It gets worse unfortunately." He cleared his throat, tasting the bitterness of the words he was about to utter. Something inside him offered hope that finally telling his story would exorcize their rancor.

"My younger brother Jonathan went with me to a drug deal." He shook his head as the scene played out in his memory. "It wasn't supposed to happen the way it did. There had never been trouble before, or I wouldn't have taken him. But . . ." Even now that day was his worst nightmare. "He was killed by a stray bullet."

Danni's mouth dropped open, but she didn't speak, so he continued.

"I was devastated. My parents were devastated." He scrubbed his face with his hands. "But there are no do-overs when the stakes are that high. The only thing I could do was turn my life around."

He studied her face and their eyes met again.

"I've spent every minute of my life since that day trying to make up for what I did. Fighting for other kids so they won't become casualties in a culture war that couldn't care less about them."

"Why are you telling me this?" Danni asked, her voice cracking.

Caleb swallowed. "I just want you to know that what we're doing—what you're doing—is really important." He looked beyond her to Zach's house. You can't let down your guard or question if you're doing the right thing . . . not even for a minute. Because it's a battle between life and death."

"I understand," she said. "Zach is the Jonathan you can help today."

"He is." Caleb turned the key and the engine in the old Chevy roared to life. "But so are all of the Zachs out there." He turned the truck around in the driveway and headed back toward town.

"We're fighting a war against a society where drugs are glorified by actors and musicians who send the wrong signal to kids.

Even when one of their role models die, that death is glamorized in the media. And, let's face it, most kids think they're bulletproof. But the odds are stacked against them. Someone in our country dies of drug-related causes every thirteen minutes. And illegal narcotics are often involved in crimes that ruin lives, even if the victims survive. Studies have—"

He glanced to her as he drove. "I'm sorry. I can't stop talking about this when I get started."

"You're passionate about it." She smiled, and then shrugged. "At least you're doing something in your life to help people. I spend my waking hours running a restaurant. It's rewarding, but what you're doing is life-changing, life-saving. I respect you for it."

He was quiet for a few seconds, and then an idea took root in his head. "Would you be willing to spend another afternoon with me?"

She didn't hesitate. "Of course."

"I want to introduce you to some young women who are fighting to regain control over their lives. Some are relatively new to the criminal scene, but many have spent a good portion of their adult lives incarcerated. Most have lost everything—families, homes, wealth, and even the sense of who they are. All are recovering addicts who are trying to make the best of a new opportunity to stay sober."

"Sounds depressing."

"It can be. But you will see the incredible work people are doing on their behalf. If you think my job is rewarding, wait until you meet the staff at Hope and Grace Resource Center."

"Let's do it!" Danni seemed eager. "When can we go?"

"I'll call my friend Angela Tomas at the center, and we'll set it up."

CHAPTER 25

Sunday – April 14

The second time Danni walked into Jaycee's church, she felt at home. Perhaps she had put the possibility of a wedding with Rob out of her mind, because this morning she was able to focus more on the service than on her physical surroundings.

Before the first congregational song was over, she had a working theory as to why few people were sitting immediately in front of them. Just like last week, even though the church was full, there was an obvious gap of two rows directly in front of where she and Jaycee sat. During that first song, Danni figured out why.

Jaycee sang loud. And very much off-key.

Danni smiled to herself. Not only was her friend tone deaf; she didn't know it. Or she didn't care. Either way, it didn't interfere with Jaycee's enjoyment of the music. Danni watched as she sang with an enraptured look on her face. And very little skill. Jaycee even had problems with the rhythm, not that all church music was easily sung, especially when you didn't know the songs well. But Jaycee had worshipped at this church every Sunday for years.

By the third song, Danni was biting her lip to keep from laughing as she listened to Jaycee singing out of sync with the instruments. And, at times, she would switch harmony parts for no apparent reason—and with no real sense of harmony.

Years ago, while in high school, Danni sang in her church praise band. At one time she had considered majoring in music. What a difference it might have made in her life. Maybe, like Caleb, she would now be working to help people instead of managing a restaurant.

But if God could love Jaycee's off-key attempt at worship—and Danni knew He did—He could also accept Danni's feeble attempt to turn her spiritual life around. That thought transformed the smile on her face to a stirring of hope in her heart. And, as she took in the sights and sounds of the service, she sang as loudly as Jaycee, not paying attention to the disparate blend of their voices.

Jaycee turned to her and smiled, and Danni was grateful her friend never gave up on her. No matter that she was tone deaf, Jaycee Alexander was the best friend anyone could have.

After the service, as they strolled back up the aisle toward the church foyer, Jaycee asked. "So where's your handsome TBI agent—and lunch date—this morning?"

"He's at church."

"I knew I liked him." She nodded toward the man sitting in the last row of pews before the door. "That must be why we've had a new guest at church for the last two Sundays." She mouthed a silent hello to him as they passed. "You have some good-looking bodyguards," she whispered to Danni.

Danni laughed nervously. "So you've noticed?"

"Do you think I'm blind? I know there's something going on, girlfriend." Jaycee gave her a knowing look. "But I also know better than to ask."

"His name is Jake Matheson. Caleb told me he would be the one following me around on Saturdays and Sundays." When they reached the veranda outside the church, she repositioned herself so the agent wasn't within earshot. "I don't think he's married. That's why he works on weekends. You might want to brush up on your flirting skills."

Jaycee grinned. "Thanks, but no thanks. I'm thinking about joining the church choir. Have you seen the music minister? He's not only cute; he's single."

The thought of Jaycee singing in the choir brought a smile to Danni's face. But buoying her spirits even more was knowing she and Sophie would soon be meeting Caleb and Zach at Centennial Park for lunch.

As the pastor wrapped up his message, Caleb gave a sideways glance to Zach, who was sitting with his mother across the aisle. Danni had been right about Zach being a surrogate for Jonathan, but Caleb knew the boy was more. He was the son Caleb had always wanted.

With Zach's real dad behind bars for, perhaps, the next twenty years, Caleb could become the father Zach needed, and he had thought many times about asking Zach's mother out. Ginny Franklin was an attractive woman. Her wavy blond hair and delicate features reminded Caleb of a girl he had dated in high school. But, although Ginny was a good person, no sparks flew when he thought about her.

Unlike when he thought about Danni Kemp.

Ginny looked up, catching Caleb's gaze. She smiled and put her arm around Zach's slender shoulders, then returned her focus to the front of the church.

Caleb straightened his tie. Maybe he needed to be more open to a relationship with Ginny. Perhaps he had overlooked the woman God had planned for him all along. With time, he could probably make himself fall in love with her.

But that wouldn't be fair to her or to Zach.

Caleb settled back into the wooden pew and tried to return his attention to the final few minutes of the sermon. The last thing he needed to think about was a relationship with Danielle Kemp. She was all but engaged to another man. A man Caleb was doing all he could to put behind bars.

Sophie was waiting at the door when Danni walked into her condo.

"Are you excited about going to the park, girl?" She patted the Newfie on the head. "Give me a few minutes to change clothes."

Sophie followed her into the bedroom and plopped onto the cool floor of the master bath to wait while Danni re-hung her church clothes and then looked though a stack of T-shirts on the shelf. Maybe she would dress up a little more, just as Jaycee had suggested. Making a one-eighty, she selected a pair of fitted jeans from the lower rack of the closet, and then picked out a cute top.

Sophie watched as Danni freshened her makeup. *Was it too much?* She didn't want to look like she had tried too hard to put herself together. She rationalized that it was okay since she had just come from church.

Not that it really mattered. She and Caleb may have had a personal conversation on Friday, but he was still a cop—and one who was investigating Rob. A man paid to watch her and protect her. His attention would move on as soon as this case was resolved.

Danni grabbed the dog leash and snapped it to Sophie's collar.

"Come on, baby girl." Sophie jumped to her feet, as anxious as Danni to see Zach and Caleb. "Let's go make a little boy happy and have some fun at the park."

Caleb and Zach were sitting in their usual spot on a blanket when Sophie and Danni approached. Zach threw his arms into the air, jumped up, and ran toward them as fast as he could, skidding to a stop at Sophie's feet.

"Can I take her to the dog park?" he asked.

"You remember the rules, right?"

The boy nodded. "I sure do."

"Okay, then go have some fun. Sophie has been looking forward to this."

"She has?" Zach's smile widened, and he grabbed the leash. "C'mon, Sophie. Let's show Ms. Danni how fast we can run to the dog park."

"Be careful." Danni shouted behind them.

Caleb stood, watching with her, and then offered his hand as she settled onto the blanket. "I've been looking forward to this too."

"You have?" Why was she always so attracted to charmers?

"I enjoyed our conversation the other day." He handed her a bottle of water from the cooler. "You look nice today, by the way."

"Thank you." She suddenly felt silly for wearing makeup to the park. "I've been to church this morning." Thankfully, a blush wasn't obvious in the midday sun, because more than the day's heat warmed her cheeks.

He leaned back. "That's what Matheson said."

She laughed. "Sounds like you've done your homework today."

Caleb grew serious. "I talked to Angela Tomas at the Hope and Grace Resource Center. That's the place I was telling you about. If you can do it, I have us set up to visit on Tuesday evening."

She nodded.

"I think you'll enjoy it."

Danni wasn't too sure about that. How could you actually enjoy a visit to a rehabilitation center? "Maybe I'll get an education, but I'm not sure I'll *enjoy* it."

"Trust me," he said.

She laughed.

A mischievous grin spread across his face, and the muscles in his jaw twitched. "I say that a lot, don't I?"

"Yes," she said. "But I do trust you." She found herself staring into his dark eyes a little too long, and the conversation lulled—

"Weeeee're back." Zach and Sophie screeched to a halt right in front of them.

Saved by the boy and the dog.

"Are you ready for lunch, Zach?" Caleb asked.

"Yeah, sure. But first, can we show Sophie and Danni what you've been teaching me?"

"You mean the fold command?"

"Yes!" The boy's voice raised an octave.

"Okay, hand the leash to Ms. Danni."

The boy obeyed.

"And step back a way."

Zach turned and took a giant leap forward.

"Okay . . ." Caleb delayed, as the boy waited impatiently for what would happen next. "Fold!" Caleb finally yelled.

Instantly, the boy hit the ground, lying flat and completely still for a few seconds.

"Good job." Caleb praised him. "You've definitely got a career ahead of you at the Bureau."

Zach scrambled to his feet, dusted himself off, and grinned as he ran toward them.

"Wow." Danni said, looking from Zach to Caleb and then back to Zach. "Are you learning how to be a TBI agent?"

Zach puffed up. "I want to be like Caleb when I grow up."

Caleb shook his head, deflecting his gaze to the blanket.

"Well," Danni told Zach. "I don't think you could do any better than that."

Caleb and Zach packed up the leftovers from lunch while Danni stroked Sophie on the tummy. The dog had passed out, likely from too much playtime with Zach.

"Looks like Sophie will sleep well tonight." He winked at the boy. "You've worn her out."

"Nah. She's just digesting her lunch."

Danni laughed and slowly stood, stretching her slender frame. "Either way, it's time Sophie and I leave the rest of this beautiful weather to the two of you and head on home."

Zach's lower lip sagged. "Could I take Sophie to the park one more time? Just for a few minutes? Please?"

Caleb climbed to his feet, shaking his head. "No way, Zach. Danielle makes the rules for Sophie."

Danni looked from the dog to the boy, contemplating Zach's request. "Okay. Just for a few minutes." She focused on Caleb. "But only if Caleb says you can."

He nodded.

"All right!" Zach jumped up. "How long do we have?" he asked Danni.

"Fifteen minutes?"

"Perfect!" Zach grabbed the leash and urged Sophie forward. The dog lumbered slowly beside him, heading once again toward the dog park.

As soon as the boy and the dog were safely inside the fence, Caleb asked Danni to join him for a walk. "Maybe our food will settle better."

"Sounds good to—" Danni froze, and her complexion paled. She appeared to be focused on something over his left shoulder.

"What's wrong?" His senses heightened, but years of training had taught him to remain calm.

"It's him—"

"Who?" Every inch of Caleb's skin prickled, and his right arm inched toward the Glock in his shoulder holster.

"The man from the Atlanta airport." Danni didn't move as she continued to look behind him.

"How far away is he?"

"Maybe twenty or thirty yards."

"Okay." Caleb's mind raced as fast as his pulse. "I'm going to make a move that will surprise you, but I want you to go with it."

"Okay." She kept her face neutral, but he clearly read fear in her eyes.

Caleb took two steps toward her, hoping she wouldn't resist him. Then, as quickly as he could think it, he threw his arms around her waist, pulled her close to him.

"Work with me," he whispered. And then he kissed her.

She leaned into him, and he slowly repositioned her, so he could get a visual on the man now behind her. The intruder, who had been staring straight at them, jerked his head to the side, pretending not to be watching.

Caleb pulled away from Danni. "Are you sure that's him?"

She nodded.

"Okay." He kept his voice level, hoping to reassure her, while his eyes remained on his target. "On the count of three, I'm going to take off after him. If I'm not successful in bringing him down, call 9-1-1." He squeezed her shoulder.

"Okay," she said. This time the word was barely audible.

"On the count of three, take one step to the left." He took a deep breath. "One, two, *three*."

Danni shifted sideways, and Caleb took off running. The sandy-haired man, who had been trying to look disinterested in them apparently didn't know what, or who, hit him until he was down on the ground.

"TBI." Caleb yelled, then saw the gun tucked in the man's belt. "You're under arrest."

"Don't shoot, please." The man fell limp. Caleb released his hold slightly, grabbed the weapon, and tucked it inside his own belt, well away from the intruder's reach.

Within minutes, Danni, Zach, and Sophie were standing ten feet away.

"Stay back." Caleb motioned to them and then plucked his phone from his pocket. He dialed the TBI switchboard operator. "This is Special Agent Caleb Samuels. I have a suspect under arrest and am requesting backup at Centennial Park. We're about fifty yards from the dog park. Behind the Parthenon."

Caleb stowed the phone back inside his pocket and recited Miranda rights to the man on the ground. "Do you understand?"

The man nodded.

"Yes or no?" Caleb asked.

"Yes! I understand."

"If you promise to mind your manners, I'll help you stand up. Can you do that?"

"Yes." He nodded again.

Caleb assisted the suspect to his knees and then his feet. "Place your hands behind your back and grab one wrist with the other hand."

"Yes, sir." For the first time, Caleb saw his face up close, and he was the spitting image of the composite Agent Force had drawn from Danielle's memory.

He heard Danni gasp behind him.

"Are you okay?" He shouted over his shoulder.

"Yes." Her breathy response wasn't convincing.

"Zach, take care of Danielle."

"Yes, sir!" The boy replied with the enthusiasm and calm deportment of a junior agent.

Satisfied everything was okay behind him, Caleb readdressed the offender. "Why have you been following this woman?"

The man shook his head, not speaking, and kept his eyes focused on his shoes.

"You'll either tell me now or later." Caleb assured him in his gruffest tone.

"I don't understand. Why am I under arrest?" His expression wavered, and then finally looking into Caleb's eyes, he pleaded his case. "This is a public park. I didn't do anything illegal."

"That's where you're wrong." Caleb tried to suppress a smile, knowing he had the man on a technicality. "You're under arrest, my friend, for carrying a firearm inside Centennial Park, a violation of a special ordinance set forth by the city of Nashville."

A look of panic crossed the intruder's face. "I wouldn't have used it. I swear." His ruddy complexion turned a darker shade of red. "Robert Evans hired me to follow her."

Behind him, Caleb heard Danielle cry out, and then the sound of her—or someone—hitting the ground.

CHAPTER 26

Danni swiped her hand across her face. *What was that?* Blood? She pried open her eyes and saw Sophie standing over her, panting.

"Ewww. Soph, back off." Danni pushed the dog away and wiped drool from her cheek.

"Are y-you all right, Ms. Danni?" Zach appeared in her peripheral vision.

She turned in his direction. "I'm okay."

"I think you might have fainted." The boy's blue-green eyes widened. "Sophie and me . . . and the police officer, we've been taking care of you."

Police officer? What police officer?

Danni tilted her head to the right, opposite Zach, and the familiar shape and color of a uniformed Metro police officer emerged. The man was kneeling alongside her, shielding his eyes from the sun.

"Are you hurt?" His voice was gruff.

Danni shook her head and made an attempt to sit up.

With both hands on her shoulders, the officer pushed her back down. "We have EMTs on the way, ma'am. Please let them check you before you get up."

"I'm okay . . . really." Against the officer's wishes, Danni struggled to a sitting position. The world shifted into slow motion, and her vision wavered, so she planted her hands into the thick grass on either side of her and closed her eyes.

"She doesn't look too good." Zach sounded worried.

"Your mom will be okay, son. It's just the heat and the excitement."

Mom? Danni shook off her lethargy. *And what excitement?*

Oh . . . *that* excitement. Caleb had saved her from the sandy-haired stalker. Or was it all a dream? She strained to catch a glimpse of her hero, and then remembered the kiss.

Had that really happened? She brought a hand to her lips and from a few yards away heard Caleb talking. Sophie must have heard him too because she whined.

Danni looked to Zach. "Is Caleb okay?"

"Yup! He's good." The smile on the boy's face stretched from ear to ear. "Did you see him tackle that guy?"

So it wasn't a dream?

"He did good, didn't he, Ms. Danni?"

She mirrored the boy's smile. "Yes, he did, Zach—"

The officer beside her intruded on the conversation. "Ma'am, do you know both of these men?" He asked.

Danni shook her head.

"Only Caleb and Zach. I met them for a picnic at the park today, and then that man—" she raised her right hand toward the stalker, who was now surrounded by a swarm of policemen less than twenty yards away—"was following me. He appeared out of nowhere just before Caleb . . . before Agent Samuels took him down."

"Did he attack you, ma'am?" The officer pulled a notepad from his shirt pocket, poised to write down her every word. *Couldn't these guys remember anything?* They were always taking notes. Her waiters logged multiple orders every day without so much as a scribble.

"Ma'am?"

"No." Her thoughts traveled back to the moment when Caleb bested the stranger. "But he had a gun."

Zach frowned. "Caleb's not in trouble, is he? He saved our lives."

Before Danni could reassure the boy, Zach jumped to his feet. "Didn't you, Caleb!"

"Didn't I what?" Caleb walked up beside them and ruffled Zach's hair.

"You saved our lives." The boy repeated.

"I did the best I could. That's all anyone can do." Caleb's words seemed strained. "You know, Zachary, I think Sophie needs a walk. Would you mind taking her to the dog park again while I talk to Danni and this officer?"

"Sure!" Zach grabbed the leash, and the boy and the dog padded off.

Caleb turned to Danni, "Are you okay?"

"I should be asking you that question. You did all the work. All I did was faint."

He grinned and opened his mouth to respond, but the officer behind him intervened.

"Excuse me." The man pointed to Danni. "Don't let her get up. We're still waiting on the EMT."

"I'm okay." Danni insisted, then looked to Caleb. "I'm just sorry I wasn't much help."

"Actually, I'm proud of you." He had a twinkle in his eye. "You're a good . . . um, actress." He lowered his voice. "I want to apologize for the kiss."

"Oh." Her hand found her lips again. "It was all a part of the ruse, right?"

"Well, you could say that." His smile lingered. "But, of course, some parts of my job are easier than others."

So she had felt it too? He could see it in her eyes. Was it even possible she was attracted to him?

No way. He was only a cop. She had far richer tastes. Besides, the last thing he needed was to lose his heart right now. Especially to an informant in the biggest case of his career.

It wasn't that he doubted her character or that her attachment to Evans was over. If it wasn't now, it would be soon. Evans would see to that with his complete disregard for the one beautiful thing in his life. That alone was enough to define the man as a fool.

No. Danni Kemp would end her relationship with Evans. Of that he was certain. But she wouldn't be looking to Caleb to fill that void in her life. He was nothing more than a temporary hero, if that.

Thankfully, he had been at the right place at the right time to help her out of a bad situation. She might be grateful, even find him somewhat attractive, but she would never have serious affection for him. Not that he even wanted that.

Of course he was attracted to her. A man would have to be blind, deaf, and just plain dumb not to recognize her as something special. And not just physically attractive. He had seen the beauty inside her the day they had talked in front of Zach's house.

Zach?

Caleb refocused on his surroundings. Another good reason to temper his feelings for Danni Kemp. She had a way of taking his mind off his work—and in this business that could get you, and others, killed.

"Zach!" He called to the boy. "Help me carry the picnic supplies. We need to get you home."

Once there, Caleb would explain to Ginny Franklin what had happened. If he didn't, Zach might fill her head with an exaggerated tale about their adventures, and Caleb didn't want her to worry about her son's safety on their outings. The last thing Zach needed was to lose another male role model in his life.

While the paramedics examined Danni, Caleb helped Zach carry the leftover food and drinks to the truck. He would have a busy afternoon after he dropped the boy at home, starting with a stop at the police station for paperwork pertaining to the arrest.

Then it would be time to explain to Martin Ridge why he and Danielle Kemp had been on a picnic. That news wouldn't sit very well. Dread burrowed a hole in Caleb's gut. He prepared his speech while carrying the cooler to the truck.

On his way back to retrieve the food and blankets, Caleb saw the boy laughing and clowning around with Danni and Sophie. It was quite the picture—the beautiful woman, the kid, and the dog. They were oblivious to him as he watched them, so he pulled his phone from his pocket and snapped a few pictures, quickly reviewing them. One was good enough to frame.

He thought for a moment about putting it on his desk, where he could gaze at it whenever he wanted, feeling as if he had accomplished a major goal in life. The one about having a family, giving grandkids to his parents, and actually moving on despite the pain of losing Jonathan.

A rustle of activity ahead caught his attention. The Metro guys were escorting Danni's stalker past her and Zach on their way to the patrol car. Caleb stepped up his pace, quickly inserting himself between them and the man who, according to his driver's license and a preliminary records check, was Edwin Burton, a Nashville area businessman.

Burton, with hands cuffed in front of his body, stared at Danni with disgust. "No wonder Robert asked me to follow you. You're running around on him. You sl—"

A swift tug on the arm by the escorting officer obscured Burton's final word, but he had said enough to make his point.

Danni's mouth dropped open, and Caleb feared she might reach out to slap the man. Instead she laid out a verbal punch. "Things aren't always what they seem. You don't know half the story."

"Then why were you kissing him?" Burton shot Caleb a glance.

Danni recoiled.

"Get him out of here." Caleb ordered, wedging himself between her, Zach, and Sophie.

The big dog growled as the Metro guys whisked Burton toward the police cruiser.

"Are you okay?"

Danni nodded, but her face had taken on every color of red in the rainbow, and she had tears in her eyes.

"It's okay, Ms. Danni." Zach said. "The bad guys don't win in the end"

Danni smiled and wiped her eyes.

Leave it to the kid to save the day.

In the meantime, Caleb had to calculate the long-term cost of the kiss he had used as a momentary ploy in pursuit of Burton. On the one hand, it had been a great way to divert the man's attention. But he hadn't thought enough ahead to realize the deeper implications it would have for Danni. And for himself.

CHAPTER 27

The next day – April 15

Rob opened his hotel room door to a woman more beautiful than he had imagined. Her headshot didn't do her justice. Not even close. Spending this week with Cassia Noelle would be a pleasure.

"You must be Rob." The tall blond glanced flirtatiously from his head to his feet.

Forward too. This should be fun.

"And you must be Cassia." He stepped sideways, pointing her toward the sofa. "May I get you a cup of coffee or tea?"

"Tea would be lovely." She cast a glance around the room before taking a seat, then stroked the sofa cushion with the palm of her hand. "Nice place you've got here."

"Thanks." He tossed the reply over his shoulder on his way to the drink cart. "I'm away from home a lot. Having a nice hotel while I'm away is one of my few perks. "Cream and sugar?"

"Both, please." She pulled a phone from her handbag.

Rob recognized the designer label from having shopped for gifts for Danni. Either *Celebrity Lifestyles* paid very well or designer handbags were one of Cassia's favorite indulgences. He made a mental note. Gifts could be useful for swaying someone to your way of thinking. And he had several days to learn more about

Cassia Noelle's tastes. From the looks of her, despite her playful flirtatiousness, her price was high.

He handed her a cup of tea and retrieved his own refreshed coffee. He would enjoy the challenge. She appeared to be his kind of woman. Although he had to admit he was easily infatuated. Thankfully, he also had some semblance of self-control. He enjoyed the single life far too much to make a mistake that would tie him down. Well, at least on the road.

He took a seat in the wing chair nearby.

"Where do we start?" he asked.

"Let's start at the beginning." Martin Ridge pointed to the chair in front of his desk. "What were you doing at the park yesterday with Danielle Kemp?"

Caleb took a seat on the edge of the rickety old ladder back, half hoping it would break apart and send him tumbling to the floor. It could be more merciful than the dressing down he was about to receive from his supervisor.

He had been summoned into his boss's chambers as soon as he had stepped inside the door this morning, less than twenty-four hours after his confrontation at Centennial Park. He had broken the news to Ridge over the phone yesterday, but it was time to talk about the details, even though much of what had happened was already making its way up and down the grapevine.

Scandalous news traveled fast in the law enforcement community. The TBI now had egg on its face, and it was his fault his department would bear the brunt of nonstop locker room jokes over the next few days.

What does a TBI agent do when he can't get a date? Kiss the confidential informant.

The only good news was that the local paper hadn't run the story, and the kiss was merely hearsay. The angry accusations of an indignant felon.

"Well, Samuels?" Ridge stared at him, waiting for a response.

"Yes, sir. You've always said the best way to get information from a CI is to get close to them. That's all I was doing."

His boss arched an eyebrow. "That's an inappropriate attempt at humor. I'm not in the mood."

"Sorry, sir." Caleb inhaled and started over. "I realize my method was unorthodox, but it was the best way I could think of at the time to position myself to have an advantage over the suspect."

"You've been watching way too much television. We're the laughingstock of the Nashville law enforcement community." Ridge pushed away from his desk. "And I don't have to tell you that a romantic relationship with a CI, even a perceived one, is way over the line."

"Yes, sir, but—"

"I should put you on unpaid leave for a month. In fact, I haven't decided that I won't." He drummed his pen on the desk. "If I don't, it's only because we're shorthanded right now. And you know this case better than anyone else." He turned to stare out the window. "I'm disappointed in you."

Caleb wished for the thousandth time he had thought of another way to take down Burton. Not only for his sake but for Danielle's. And the Bureau's.

"I did the best I knew to do at the time, sir. And in my defense, I did get the job done."

Ridge spun around and drilled him with a stare. "Are you letting this woman get to you? Because if you are, that's dangerous."

He stabbed his finger in Caleb's direction. "Dangerous for you, dangerous for her, and dangerous for the case."

Caleb thought before speaking. "I'll admit she's an attractive woman, Captain. But I'm an agent first and foremost in my life. I would never do anything intentionally that would jeopardize anyone at the Bureau or put my personal integrity in question."

From the expression on his face, Ridge wasn't buying what Caleb had to sell. He threw his pen on his desk, frowning. "I'm not so sure you haven't already—"

"Captain Ridge. I'm sorry to bother you, sir." It was Ridge's secretary on the intercom. "But Lieutenant Hale at Metro asked to speak to you as soon as possible."

"This ought to be good." Ridge grumbled under his breath. "Thanks to you, Samuels."

Caleb sat back in his chair, dreading the verbal beating his superior was about to take on his behalf.

"You might as well hear it firsthand so you will know what you've caused." Ridge engaged his speakerphone.

"Ridge here."

"Martin, it's Jeff Hale. I'm sorry to bother you, but we've had an interesting turn of events. The background check we ran on Edwin Burton's fingerprints just came back with an alias. And an arrest warrant."

Caleb held his breath.

"Don't keep me in suspense, Hale," Ridge huffed.

"Your agent took down a pretty interesting character. His real name is Maximilian Roman. He's an accountant by trade, and he's wanted for conspiracy to commit income tax fraud against the United States government."

Yes! Caleb suppressed an urge to pump his fist in the air.

A smile slowly crawled across the Captain's face. "Interesting."

"Congratulations, Martin. I'll email copies of the paperwork for your files."

Ridge disengaged the phone and leaned back in his chair. "You're one lucky man, Agent Samuels. Now get out of here before I change my mind."

"Yes, sir!"

"And one more thing . . ."

"Yes, sir?"

"Watch your step. I don't want to lose you to some street punk because you've let your heart rule your head."

"Yes, sir. I understand."

Caleb didn't waste time leaving Ridge's office. *Vindicated.* He had been vindicated!

Now to find out how Robert Evans had come to be acquainted with Max Roman, alias Edwin Burton.

CHAPTER 28

The next day – April 16

D anni was disappointed when Caleb called to say he wouldn't be taking her to the Hope and Grace Resource Center this evening, especially after he had told her he had new information to share about Edwin Burton, the man Rob had presumably hired to follow her.

It had taken every ounce of restraint she had to keep from calling Rob and giving him a piece of her mind. But Caleb had warned her not to say anything. He had said it would be harmful to the case, and it could put her in more danger. Another reason she wished Caleb could be with her tonight. His presence brought her comfort. More than any other agent. And certainly more than Rob ever had.

In Caleb's stead, Agent Jamie Wade would be picking her up in the Rutherford lobby at seven o'clock to take her to the resource center, and when Agent Wade arrived exactly at seven, it gave credence to Danni's theory that punctuality was a required gene in law enforcement DNA. Caleb, and every other agent Danni had met so far, had always arrived on time. Not a minute early. Not a minute late.

The slender blond agent drove a white Volvo and asked to be called by her first name. Although Jamie looked to be several years younger than Danni, after Danni heard about the younger woman's career accomplishments, and that she was married and had a newborn baby girl, Danni suspected the young woman had already lived a full life.

She told Danni she had paid for a criminal justice degree while working part time as a cosmetologist. And that she subsequently used her salon skills in undercover work for the TBI.

"You know how clients tell their hairdressers and manicurists everything," Jamie laughed. "That's how I get a lot of my information." The young agent's face grew serious. "Do you have any questions about tonight?"

"I'm not sure what to expect." Danni didn't want to admit that her stomach was in knots. "I've never done anything like this before."

"You'll do great." Jamie stopped at a red light and glanced in her direction. "Just be yourself."

"I guess that's all I can do." Danni relaxed back into her seat as the sun prepared to take its final bow on the horizon. "It's just that I'm usually more analytical than spontaneous."

"My guess is that these girls will bring out your emotional side."

The thought piqued Danni's interest. "Tell me more about them."

"They're all recovering addicts." Jamie maneuvered through the remnants of rush hour traffic, which seemed to be lingering this evening. "Some were transitioned to the center after prison. Others came from directly off the street. A few of the lucky ones are there because their families still cared enough about them to encourage them to seek sobriety."

Danni hesitated. "I'm not sure I understand."

"The majority of the women at HGRC have severed ties with their family. Usually not by their own choice."

"That's sad." Danni thought about her mother, who had cut off all familial ties.

"Let me restate that." A mist of rain obscured their view, and the agent engaged her wiper blades. "Indirectly it was their choice. At one point they gave drugs, alcohol, or both priority over everything else in their lives, including their families."

"I get it. But it's still sad." Danni shook her head.

"You're right. It is. And although the girls you'll meet tonight have moved beyond the initial physical aspects of their addictions, they still have a long way to go toward recovery. At the center, they're being taught life-coping skills, learning how to make new friendships, and establishing self-worth."

"All of that is necessary because they were addicted to drugs or alcohol?" Danni asked.

"Absolutely. It's difficult for us to understand which came first: the lack of social skills or the addiction."

"Makes sense." Danni feared she was in over her head. Or was that her heart? She could somewhat relate. Losing her mother at an early age hadn't exactly instilled confidence in her either, especially when it came to lasting relationships.

"While at the center each of the girls is evaluated by counselors and mental health professionals. If all goes well, they will eventually be reacclimated into society, and that includes helping them find work." Jamie continued. "And some will be reunited with family."

"How did you and Caleb . . . Agent Samuels, learn about the center?"

"Narcotics and crime go hand in hand." Agent Wade pulled the Volvo into the parking lot of a nondescript, three-story brick building. Switching off the engine, she turned to Danni. "Many drug abusers die because of their addiction. But some, who don't, will lose more than that. They will lose their freedom, their mental or physical health, and quite possibly the people they love."

Danni nodded in the near darkness of the evening.

"Their entire support system, including their self-image, may disappear." Jamie opened her car door and the light came on. "A lot of these young women, some younger, some older than us, are fighting for more than their lives. They're fighting for the lives of their children who have been taken away from them."

Danni nodded. "They've lost a lot, haven't they?"

"Yes." Jamie offered a reassuring smile. "Are you ready?"

"As ready as I'll ever be." Danni opened the passenger side door and stepped into a drizzling rain. She pulled her sweater closer to her waist and sprinted toward the front entrance of the resource center.

Jamie rang the doorbell to the left of the double metal doors, and within seconds someone buzzed them inside. A female guard at the entryway desk greeted them and added their names to the visitor sheet. Then they took a seat along the sidewall.

A few minutes later, Danni watched a tall brunette taking long strides toward them. Her enormous smile immediately put Danni at ease.

"Jamie, great to see you!" She said, before reaching to shake Danni's hand. "I'm Angela Tomas, the facility manager. And you're Danielle, right?"

"Yes. It's nice to meet you, Ms. Tomas."

"Please call me Angela. If you're a friend of Caleb and Jamie's, you're welcome here. Caleb is one of our biggest supporters." She smiled at Agent Wade. "We love Jamie too. I wish the good people in law enforcement were commended more by the news media. They've given us a lot of support and shown a lot of compassion for our girls and others like them."

"Thank you." Jamie's face lit up.

"Danielle, are you ready for a tour?" Angela asked.

"Please call me Danni."

"Of course. Danni, we have a night class this evening, and I thought we would sit in for a few minutes."

They followed the facility manager down a long, central hallway, and Danni noticed that the building was immaculately kept and ultramodern.

"We're teaching basic accounting tonight." Angela said, turning to Danni as they walked. "I understand that's your area of expertise."

"It is. I plan budgets in my sleep." She laughed. "No, let me rephrase that, when I *should* be sleeping."

Her companions laughed.

"That's one of the things we teach, how to set up a budget. When the girls are released from here, we don't want them to have to commit a crime to pay their bills. Or to resort to drugs to compensate emotionally when they can't provide for themselves."

"I understand. It's an important skill," Danni agreed.

On their way to the lecture, Angela pointed to various rooms in the building—the library, a cafeteria, and a small chapel.

"We use the main theater for classes as well as Sunday worship." She paused in front of the chapel, with its stained-glass door and windows. "But our little chapel is open all day, every day until room curfew."

Danni couldn't hide her surprise.

"Maybe Caleb and Jamie didn't tell you, but we're a faith-based program. We're partially funded by area churches."

"I had no idea." Danni said, realizing there was a lot about this place she didn't know. "What are the girls' rooms like?"

"Like a college dorm room. Actually, nicer than the ones I had." Angela chuckled and gestured toward the elevators at the end of the hall. "The dorms are on the second and third floors. Two girls share a room and a bathroom, with a central lounge on each floor to facilitate community."

Their tour guide stopped in front of what appeared to be the entrance to the main theater. "We don't allow television or Internet access anywhere in the building. Some people might call that cruel and unusual punishment," her eyes crinkled when she smiled, "but we don't want the world intruding on them at this stage of recovery."

Angela put her fingers to her lips to request silence.

"Let's slip in here and watch some of the class." She opened the door to the theater, and Danni and Jamie followed her inside.

"After class is finished," Angela whispered. "I'll introduce you to a few of the girls. Hopefully you will have a chance to talk with one of them." She gestured toward the back row of seats. "Don't be surprised if they open up to you. It's cathartic for them."

The three women took seats in the back, and for the next forty-five minutes listened to a basic presentation from the instructor, followed by questions from the girls. Danni estimated the class was the equivalent to Accounting 101, which could have put her to sleep except for her fascination with the girls. They were sponges, soaking up the teacher's advice on balancing a checkbook, maintaining a budget, and planning for financial ups and downs. Many of the young women took notes. Some frowned. Others smiled and nodded their heads as though they finally understood a great mystery.

Angela occasionally broke into the teaching to whisper a word of explanation in Danni's ear. Then, after the session was over, when the lights went up and the girls began to file out, she stood and faced Danni, beaming with pride.

"I hope that gave you some idea of the education we provide for our girls. We don't want to send them out into the world unprepared." She held the door so they could step back into the hallway. "Our program is comprehensive. We're all about helping our girls grow not only physically, emotionally, and spiritually but also as future contributors and even leaders in society."

"And they do a great job." Jamie said, returning the compliment Angela offered earlier. "They address the many aspects of drug and alcohol abuse. Some people fall prey to addiction because they're bored. Others use it as a crutch to escape reality. But far too many just want to be like everyone else, which is why building a good self-image is important."

Angela agreed with a nod. "We believe God is big enough and gracious enough to fill all of the empty places inside them. And us." She gave Danni a reassuring smile. "We also believe it's our responsibility as Christians to serve with love and to help our residents understand they aren't alone."

"Everything you do makes sense." Danni said. "I'm impressed."

"Everyone on our full-time staff is certified by one, if not several, agencies to work within their field of rehabilitation. And—"

Angela stopped when she noticed Caleb walking toward them.

"Several of our staff members have law enforcement backgrounds, because most of our women, young and older, have been incarcerated at least once. Many are trying for the second or third time to break free of self-defeating behaviors."

"How are you, ladies?" Caleb asked when he reached them.

Angela extended her hand. "We're better now that you've decided to join us, aren't we?"

Jamie and Danni smiled and nodded.

"Sorry I'm late. I had urgent business at the office." He turned to Danni. "Have you learned anything?"

"A lot. I'm grateful for the opportunity."

"But she hasn't talked to one of our girls yet." Angela looked around. "Oh, here you go. Rachel?" She reached out to a young woman who was walking past them. "I'd like you to meet some people."

The woman, who appeared to be in her midtwenties, looked more poised than the majority of the women Danni had seen so far.

"This is Danni, Jamie, and Caleb. Danni is visiting us for the first time tonight. I would love it if you would show her around . . . the cafeteria, the library, the chapel."

Angela turned back to Danni. "Rachel has been with us for almost eight weeks now, so she knows her way around."

Rachel squared her shoulders. "I'd be happy to give you a tour."

She turned to retrace the route Caleb had just walked. And as soon as Danni had caught up with her, she began walking at a leisurely pace.

"How do you like it here?" Danni asked, hoping she wasn't being too forward.

"It's a great place." She studied Danni before she continued. "Not everyone has a second or third chance in life."

Danni nodded, waiting for Rachel to continue.

"I've made a lot of mistakes." She fixed her gaze on something at the end of the corridor. "And I've lost a lot, but my life is turning around thanks to Angela and her staff."

Rachel opened the door to their immediate left. "This is the cafeteria. We also have activities here that are a lot of fun." She flipped the switch back to her personal life. "No one in my family wants anything to do with me. Not even my daughter."

Danni wasn't sure what to say. A picture of her mother walking out the door came to mind. "I-I'm sorry," she finally said.

"My parents take care of her." Rachel walked quickly from the cafeteria to the chapel. She held the door open for Danni. Once inside, she placed her hands on the back of the last row of pews. "This is our chapel. Isn't it beautiful?"

"Yes, it is." Danni said, stepping up beside her. "Lovely."

Rachel nodded and smiled. "It's so peaceful in here." She paced to the front of the room and took a seat in the first row of pews, directly in front of the altar. "Sometimes I just come here to sit, think, and pray."

Danni took a seat across the aisle, wondering if Rachel would continue to unravel small pieces of her past.

The younger woman remained silent for a minute and then turned to Danni. "I'm grateful to everyone who has done so much to help me. There were times when I didn't appreciate them enough." Her eyes glazed over, but she didn't cry, and her focus drifted to the altar. "They've got a lot of nerve believing I can make it this time. But if they believe I can . . ." She turned back to Danni. "Then I have to believe it too."

"Of course, you can make it." Danni reassured her, not certain if she really meant it.

"Why?" Rachel challenged.

Danni swallowed hard, digging into the depths of herself to find encouragement. "Because you're in a good place. I've heard a lot about it here. And—"

Memories of her childhood rushed back to her. How her own mother had failed, despite the help of those who had loved her.

Really loved her and wanted her to come home. They would have taken her back anytime.

Danni thought about how much Chloe, her dad, and she had needed Grace Kemp. Needed and wanted her to return, yet—

"And?" Rachel seemed to be hanging on her words.

"And . . ." Danni turned to look at her. "You have to make it. Because your daughter needs her mother, despite what you or she might say or think right now."

The younger woman startled, as though not expecting such a direct response.

Danni continued, looking first at the floor and then directly at the hurting young woman. "You also have to make it because, whether you realize it or not, your family really does love you."

Rachel sat back in her seat and looked down, her lower lip trembling. "How do you know that?"

"I know . . ." Danni's words were barely more than a whisper. Could she admit everything to Rachel?

"I wish I believed it." Rachel shifted her gaze. "But you have no idea." Her hands shook despite being anchored to her lap.

"Actually, I do." Danni leaned forward to lessen the distance between them. "I know because my mother was an addict." She took in a deep breath. "I know because my sister and I, as well as my dad . . . we all loved her and would have taken her back any time."

Rachel looked up, her dark brown eyes brimming with tears, and searched Danni's face, hoping to see the truth written there.

"Believe me," Danni breathed a silent prayer that she would make a connection, "it's true. You need to go home to them. To your family. To your daughter. She needs you even more than you can imagine."

Rachel wrung her hands. They were no longer shaking.

Finish your story, Danni. "I know because my mother never made it home to me." Danni fought to control her emotions. "She died in an automobile accident, and I miss her, just like your daughter misses you."

"I'm so sorry—" Rachel wiped moisture from her eyes. "Thank you for giving me hope."

Danni smiled. "Don't ever doubt the bond of family." She knew she was speaking to herself as much as she was speaking to Rachel. "It never goes away."

CHAPTER 29

Jamie and Angela were waiting when Danni and Rachel walked into the lobby.

"Where's Caleb?" Danni glanced toward the seating area.

"He has an early meeting in the morning. He went on home." Jamie gave her a curious look. "You okay riding home with me?"

"Of course." Danni bit her lip and turned to Rachel. "I'll be praying for you and your daughter."

For the first time tonight, the younger woman's smile reached her dark brown eyes. "Thank you."

Angela extended her hand to Danni. "I hope we will see you again."

"I hope so too." Danni said goodnight to the facility manager, waved goodbye to Rachel, and followed Jamie out the front entrance of the building.

The drizzle they'd had on the way over had turned into a downpour, so they waited beneath the small entryway cover for a few minutes, hoping it would subside. When it didn't, Jamie buttoned her jacket and told Danni, "Wait here. I'll get the car."

"Are you sure? I don't mind getting wet." Danni pulled her sweater around her face and head, preparing to make a dash for the vehicle.

"No reason for us both to get wet. I'll be right back." The petite blond took off running, screaming with childish delight when she splashed through a puddle halfway across the parking lot toward the Volvo.

Seconds later the car exploded, and the night sky lit up like a fireworks display gone horribly wrong. Shrapnel and shards of glass flew in every direction. Flames surrounded the car, and Jamie's slender frame, which was silhouetted against the light of the exploded Volvo, folded and then fell backwards.

Danni screamed, twisting her body sideways to avoid a large object speeding toward her. Throwing herself against the building behind her, she bent forward, covering her head with her hands. The debris ricocheted off the wall less than a yard away, falling onto the pavement with a loud clang.

Gulping, Danni went on offense, running into the billowing black smoke to find Jamie. In the now dim light of the fire, which had been somewhat diminished by the pouring rain, Danni saw a body on the ground. It lay twenty feet from the vehicle.

She pushed forward. The heat grew more intense, despite the rain, and the chemical-filled air sliced at her throat. Danni coughed and wheezed, fatigue and the sheer wetness of her shoes and clothing slowing her steps. Time seemed to be standing still. It was as though she were reliving each second over and over.

Reaching the young woman's motionless body, Danni called her name, but there was no response. Danni fell to the ground searching for any sign of life. Thankfully, the smoke was less dense down here, but the sight of the inferno that had once been Jamie's Volvo, along with the popping and cracking of the flames, unnerved her.

She put her finger to Jamie's temple. A slight, but rapid pulse. The smell of gasoline and charred metal mingled with the distant sounds of sirens, but Danni's focus returned to Jamie's motionless body. Could she move her on her own?

Then she felt a firm tug on her shoulders.

"Let me help." It was Angela Tomas.

Angela gently pulled Danni away from Jamie, helped her to stand, and then handed her off to the night guard, who stood nearby. Angela knelt close to Jamie, placed one hand on her shoulder and one hand on her arm. Then Danni saw Angela's lips moving, as if in silent prayer.

Danni wiped rain from her face and bowed her head. *Please, God, don't let her die. Her baby needs her. I remember You said that when two or more pray in Your name, and if it is Your will, You will hear and answer.*

Without warning the darkness descended upon her. Danni tried to tell her companion that she needed to sit down. But the words wouldn't come, and she slipped from the larger woman's grip onto the ground.

Minutes later she awoke to chaos all around her. Men and women shouted back and forth. Unintelligible conversations cut in and out of the static of an emergency radio. Farther away, gushing water struck hot metal, searing it into rancid steam that mingled with the smoke already surrounding her. The acrid smell almost sent Danni's stomach over the edge.

A bevy of emergency workers dressed in rain slickers had gathered around Jamie. Danni watched as they worked with her, shouting instructions back and forth. One technician fitted an oxygen mask over the young woman's mouth and nose and then solicited two others to help lift her onto a stretcher. The bed was quickly raised and rolled into a nearby ambulance.

In a matter of minutes, the vehicle sped away with lights flashing. Its siren faded into the darkness.

At some point, a fireman wrapped a blanket around Danni's shoulders, leading her to a dry spot beneath the cover of the HGRC building entryway, putting more distance between her and the noise and activity that still surrounded the smoldering car.

"Are you hurt?" he asked.

Two EMTs, rain dripping from their slickers, joined him. Following them was Angela, who looked as though she had taken a shower in her street clothes.

"I'm okay." She acknowledged Angela. "But how is Jamie?"

The female EMT squatted beside Danni and reached for her wrist. "We're not sure yet. She's on her way to the hospital."

"I don't understand why her car would explode like that, do you?" Danni asked.

The EMT exchanged glances with the fireman. "Could be lots of reasons." She released Danni's arm and smiled. "It looks like you made it through relatively unscathed." The woman climbed to her feet. "Would you prefer to go to the hospital in the ambulance or by private car?"

"Hospital? Why do I have to go to the hospital?"

"I'll take her." Angela took a step forward. "And while we're there, we'll check on Jamie."

Danni nodded. "Yes, I want to do that." She took the hand extended by the second EMT, who helped her stand.

The hospital staff was expecting Danni when she arrived. She and Angela had hardly warmed their seats in the waiting room when a nurse came to retrieve Danni. She led her through a set of double swinging doors and down a hall to a door labeled with the numeral 14. The room was only large enough for a hospital bed, a row of cabinets, and two folding chairs.

"Have a seat on the bed." The nurse reached for the blood pressure cuff. "You're one of the car bomb victims, aren't you?"

Danni shook her head. "No. The car just explod—"

The nurse stopped what she was doing and waited for Danni to finish her sentence.

"Oh." Now it made sense. Her life had forever changed. Car bombs and drug overdoses were no longer reserved for the news on her television. Or tomorrow's headlines. In fact, she would probably be among tomorrow's headlines in *The Tennessean*.

Danni nodded. "Yes, I guess I am the lucky one. The thought of that just doesn't seem right."

"I understand, sweetie." The woman laid her hand on Danni's arm.

About ten minutes into her preliminary exam, the door opened, and a tall, older man strolled into the room. He introduced himself as Dr. Williams, the physician on call.

"You're very fortunate, Ms. Kemp." He studied her chart and then gave a cursory glance to her face and extremities. "The first young woman who came in tonight wasn't nearly as fortunate." His voice dropped, and Danni's heart took a plunge. Surely Jamie hadn't...

Dear God, please, no.

The doctor must have read her concern. "She's going to be okay. She had a number of first-degree burns, mostly superficial cuts, and smoke inhalation, but her worst injuries were a gash on her arm that required stitches and a concussion from being thrown to the ground."

"Thank God." Danni whispered.

The doctor studied her over the top of the rim of his glasses. "Are you ready to go home?"

"Yes, sir."

"Give me ten minutes to prepare the paperwork."

He stopped on his way out the door and turned around, "I want you to take it easy for the next twenty-four hours. You've been through a lot tonight."

"I will."

"Do you have someone who can take you home?"

"Yes, sir. A friend brought me to the hospital."

He nodded and left.

True to his words, Dr. Williams released her within ten minutes. Hopefully Angela wouldn't mind driving her home. But when the large sliding doors opened into the waiting room, Angela wasn't there. Instead Caleb was sitting in her place, fidgeting with a magazine. As soon as he saw her, he jumped to his feet and rushed toward her. He pulled her close to him and cradled her in his arms.

Feeling his strength, Danni's pent-up emotions broke through the dam of defenses she had built around herself. Not just those required to get through the past few hours but also those that had built up since her childhood.

Her mother's drugs of choice may or may not have been prescription, but her family had suffered the same loss as those of the young women at the rehabilitation center and the family and friends of Michael Ryan.

Rachel had gotten to her tonight. And then Jamie had almost lost her life. How did people live with themselves knowing they caused such pain? How could they put greed and dishonesty before the lives of those they were hurting?

Please, God. Don't let me be a part of hurting someone by turning a blind eye to the problem. By turning a blind eye to Rob.

As she held tightly to Caleb, tears she had needed to shed for a long time finally poured down her cheeks. Silently. And without fanfare. The cleansing came. And Danni made her decision. She would fight until every last drug dealer was taken off the street. And if that meant Rob Evans was going to jail, so be it.

CHAPTER 30

She felt so right in his arms. Caleb's heart ached as he held her. She could have been killed tonight. Only by God's grace did she, and Agent Wade, survive.

But his heart had not.

In his hurry to compare Danielle Kemp to his brother Jonathan, wanting to keep her safe, he had failed to protect himself. Without trying—because he had little doubt that she would never reciprocate those feelings—she had slipped through the wall he had built around himself.

She pulled away and wiped the corners of her eyes, their color an extravagant green, despite the things she had endured tonight. He reached to rub a smudge from her cheek.

This wasn't the well-kempt and confident woman he first met. Her fashionable clothing had been saturated with smoke and rain, her hair was straight and limp, but he had never seen her more beautiful.

Angela had told him, while they waited for news about Jamie, how Danni's words had made an impact on one of the girls at the center. Angela had seen what Caleb had always known was there. A strong woman. And one with enough wisdom to eventually see her way around Robert Evans.

"Why are you looking at me like that?" Danni took a second step backwards and straightened her disheveled sweater. "I look terrible, don't I? I'm dirty and smelly and—"

"You're alive and well."

She stared at him, her expression softening. "Yes, I am. Miraculously. And did you hear the good news about Jamie?"

He nodded. "Angela and I were in the waiting room when we got the word. I sent her home after we found out. Although I'm sure she'll return to the center." He scrubbed his brow. "And it looks like I'll be up for most of the night. Are you ready for me to take you home?" He gestured toward the door, but she didn't move.

"Will you tell me about the explosion?"

"When I can." He caught her by the elbow and started to walk her toward the exit.

She stopped, and he jerked to a halt. "Does that mean you can't tell me what you already know?" She asked.

He set his jaw and turned to look at her. "No. It means I don't know enough to tell you. Everything is subjective until we finish our investigation." He started her walking again. "It also means we don't know if it was related to the Evans case."

She nodded. "Fair enough. But what else could it be connected to?"

Once outside the exit, he stopped her this time. "Danielle."

She turned to him.

"Jamie works a lot of dangerous jobs. The explosion could be related to any one of them." The emergency room doors closed behind them. "Don't beat yourself up, okay?"

She bit her lip and nodded.

"Wait here, and I'll get my truck so you don't have to walk in the rain." He zipped his jacket.

"Are you kidding? I'm not doing this again." She smiled for the first time tonight. "Look at me."

He resisted the urge to kiss her. "Okay, let's go. Let's get out of here, before—"

"Before what?" She stared at him suspiciously.

Before something else happens.

This case was about to escalate. He could feel it in his bones. The timing of the car bomb was too suspicious. Word had just hit the street that Maximilian Roman had been arrested.

"Caleb?"

"Before I fall asleep." He glanced at his watch. "Would you be up for a cup of coffee before I take you home?"

"Sure. But let's just go to my place. I make better coffee than we can buy anywhere this time of night." She gestured to herself. "And besides, I'm not really dressed to go out."

"You look beautiful. I'd be seen with you anywhere." He grabbed her arm and guided her through the downpour toward his truck. The rain didn't appear to be letting up anytime soon.

They kept the conversation light on the way to her condo. It was always safe to talk about the weather. Although it was also easy to let her mind wander when talking about life's trivialities. Danni had to rein in her thoughts more than once.

Had Caleb really told her she was beautiful? She glanced in the side mirror when they stopped at a red light. You would have to be half blind to call *this* beautiful. She pushed her stringy hair behind her ears. *Unless you had feelings for someone.*

Did Caleb Samuels really care for her?

Within fifteen minutes, he had parked in the multilevel lot beneath the Rutherford and escorted her up the elevator. When they reached the door, Danni inserted her key in the lock.

"Do you think Sophie will let me in?" Caleb's expression showed genuine concern. "Remember what happened last time I came in."

"After all of the chicken you fed her on Sunday?" She reassured him.

"I'd feel a lot better if I had a drumstick on me right now." He eyed the big Newfoundland that greeted them when the door opened. "Once bitten . . ." He laughed nervously.

Danni tugged on the dog's collar to get her attention. "Hey, Soph. Be a good girl and welcome Caleb into our home."

Sophie sniffed the hand Caleb offered, licked it, and then looked behind him.

"She thinks Zach is with me." Caleb pulled the door closed and stepped farther into the foyer. "What'cha think, Sophie? Am I trustworthy?"

"She associates you with Zach now."

Caleb visibly relaxed. "Saved by the boy."

Danni laughed. "Zach's not here, girl. But you remember Caleb."

The dog wagged her tail and led them toward the living room. After Caleb took a seat on the sofa, Sophie plopped on the floor in front of him.

"She's got me cornered." He laughed.

"Stop it. She likes you. I'll be back with coffee." Danni left the two of them to get reacquainted.

After setting the coffee to brew, she retreated to her bedroom to scrub her face and try to wrangle her hair. Applying makeup would have helped, but she'd already reasoned that her houseguest was farsighted.

Returning to the living room with two cups of coffee, she set a creamed and sugared version on the table beside Caleb, settling into the chair a few feet away with her undiluted brew.

"It looks like you're not only friends but good friends at this point."

Caleb glanced up from scratching the dog behind the ears. "Either that or she's keeping me here until the police show up."

Danni almost spewed her first sip. What a difference a few weeks made. Just over a month ago, she had been a wreck when Caleb broke into her life. Now, just having him in her home made her happy.

"I like this relationship much better." He picked up his cup. "To Agent Wade's good health."

Danni returned his toast with a nod.

After a long draw from the cup, his expression grew serious. "How much do you want to know about Ramirez?"

Danni cradled her hands around the steaming mug. "As much as you can tell me."

Ten minutes later, as Caleb continued his lengthy exposition on Ramirez's connection to a well-documented global narcotics operation, Danni set her drink aside, curled up in her chair, and folded her arms over her stomach.

"We're not sure how involved he is in the international operation," Caleb confided. "But we know he's key to US distribution."

"And you think Rob works for him?"

Caleb took another long sip from his cup, set it on the side table next to him, and looked squarely at her. "You tell me. Is there another reason Ramirez would suddenly take interest in your life?"

A chill crawled up Danni's spine. "More coffee?"

Caleb accepted her offer, and after she had refreshed their cups, she answered his question.

"I don't understand why, or how, Rob could ever get involved with something like this." She shook her head. "It doesn't make sense. It's not like he's some kind of macho man."

Caleb remained silent.

"Rob is, well, you know, a pretty boy. He doesn't like getting his hands dirty. He studied business in college. Just as I did." She blew air from her lungs. "Maybe his love for money drove him to it."

She retreated to her thoughts, studying her hands, which were folded in her lap. She could make excuses all day long, but there was no other explanation.

She looked up at Caleb. "He has to be involved, doesn't he?"

Caleb nodded. "We're sure of it."

"So how is Edwin Burton involved?"

"He's not who we thought he was. Not exactly anyway."

Danni's heart took a dive to her stomach.

Caleb continued. "His name's not Edwin Burton. It's Maximilian Roman. Ever heard of him?"

"No." Danni sifted through her memory. "Never."

"He's wanted on a felony for treason against the US government. It's how we're holding him without bail."

She swallowed hard.

"You'll be interested to know he's also an accountant." Caleb continued. "He tried to scam the fed for millions of dollars."

Danni relaxed a bit. *How dangerous could an accountant be?*

"He works for Valentino Ramirez."

"Oh." Her heart took another plunge. "That's not good, is it?"

"Not really, no. It means you're definitely being watched by Ramirez."

After Caleb left, Danni took a long, hot bath, reset her alarm for an extra hour of sleep, and went to bed. Before turning out the light, she paused to say a prayer of thanksgiving for Jamie's—and her own—protection in the explosion. Then she added a prayer for Rachel, as she had promised she would. And a prayer for

Angela, who was responsible for helping turn around so many lives.

Finally, she prayed for Caleb. That he would have the wisdom and the strength to see his case to the end. Whatever that meant for Rob. And whatever that meant for her.

I just want the best for those who are doing the right thing, God. Please help me to do the right thing too.

As soon as she turned out the light, Sophie jumped into bed. The dog rarely cuddled with her. She usually slept on one side of the bed while Danni slept on the other, presumably to stay cooler.

But tonight Sophie lay right next to Danni with her head between her paws.

"What's wrong, girl?" Danni brushed her hand across the dog's wide muzzle. "Were you worried about me tonight?"

The dog listened but didn't move.

"You're keeping an eye on me, aren't you?" Her instinct had to be telling her Danni had been in serious danger. "I appreciate your keeping watch for me."

With that, Danni turned over on her side. Despite two cups of coffee, she had a good idea she wouldn't have any problem sleeping.

CHAPTER 31

Sharing a night with a complete stranger made everything more exciting. No commitments. No rules. No holds barred. He did enjoy a challenge.

"Rob." The beautiful magazine reporter brought him back to the present. "Can we continue the interview now?"

Robert Evans smiled, dismissing his fantasy. "Of course. I'm sorry."

She flipped on her tape recorder. "We talked about Nashville yesterday. Now I want to ask you about life on the road."

"I find it to be accommodating." He winked and settled into the leather sofa in the front half of his bus.

"Once again, thank you for giving me so much of your time for this interview." She made a point of taking in the luxurious surroundings. "And for the opportunity to see the inside of your home away from home. Thank you for the tour. How many days a year do you travel in it?"

"Last year, I was out for more than two-hundred days."

"Really? Is that typical for an entertainment manager?" She opened her pad to take written notes, along with the recorder.

He smiled. "It's not even close to being typical. I do it because I love it, and because it gives me empathy for my artists." Gesturing to the driver's compartment and kitchen galley, he added.

"How can I ask them to live in such a confined, although accommodating space, when I'm not willing to do it?"

"I admire you for that, of course." Her eyes twinkled. "But I suspect there is more."

"You're very insightful." He cleared his throat. "It also gives me a better perspective about the audiences who pay to see my acts. I'm out here with them. I see what age groups are coming to the shows, what songs they react to the most, and I calculate that information into my managerial plan."

"*Calculate.* An interesting word choice . . ."

"As you know, I have a degree in business. I love numbers. Especially big ones." He smiled.

She jotted down his words.

"It's not only rewarding to see the satisfaction my acts give to their fans. It's financially rewarding to know what works and what doesn't." He paused and studied her for a reaction.

"So money is the bottom line for you?" She poised pen over paper.

"In the end it is, because—and follow me here, as I was trying to say earlier—if the audience is happy when they leave, they'll come back again. They'll buy a T-shirt and the album. They'll request your songs on the radio. And in the end that's what provides a good living for my acts." He settled back into his seat. "And a very good living for me."

She scribbled and nodded before looking up. "And what about your family? Don't they miss you?"

"I'm single right now." He thought about dismissing the question. "It takes a special kind of person to be married to an entertainment professional. I wouldn't expect someone to go into it blindly, so I'm pretty much what you see is what you get."

She laughed. "Oh, so there are no secrets on the road?"

"Of course there are. But if I revealed them, they wouldn't be secrets, right?"

"You've got me there." The dimples on each side of her mouth deepened.

"No, seriously." Rob wasn't about to let her go on that one. "The road life is like anything else. We eat, work, and sleep, just like every other American worker. We just do it in a different place every night."

"Do you ever get bored?"

His phone rang. It was Ramirez. "Excuse me." He stood to walk to the back of the bus and closed the door behind him.

"Our guests are here."

Ridge summoned Caleb to the conference room early the next morning for an impromptu meeting with the Evans case team. When he arrived, Mack Brown and Danny Parker of the DEA and Sam Wiley of the FBI were seated around the table.

It appeared Wiley and Ridge had been verbally jousting. Both men guffawed. A sign they had news. Good news. Evidently the case was going well from the FBI's perspective.

"As I said before, our insider has paid off." Wiley handed Ridge a thumb drive.

His boss turned and passed it along to Caleb.

"Good to see you Agent Samuels," Wiley grinned.

Caleb was now certain that good news awaited. "Likewise," he acknowledged each of their guests. "Shall I play this?" He brandished the drive.

"Please. I think you're going to enjoy it."

Caleb inserted the drive into the conference room computer, followed the prompts, and turned up the volume.

"—what's going on?" It was Robert Evans's voice.

Silence.

"Phone call?" Caleb mouthed.

Wiley nodded, then mouthed "Ramirez."

"I told you, my girlfriend has nothing to do with this."

He had to be talking about Danielle.

"Explosion? What? Is she—?" Pause. "Yes, I—I understand . . . No!" A longer pause.

"Yes, sir." His final words were followed by what sounded to be a door closing.

"Who's your insider?" Caleb addressed Wiley.

"Actually, we should have two to tell you about soon." The FBI agent smiled. "I'm not ready to divulge the second, but the first is our agent, Cassia Kennedy. She's posing as a reporter by the name of Cassia Noelle, and she's been traveling with Evans for a few days."

"This is her work?" Ridge asked.

Wiley nodded.

"So we now know for sure Ramirez was behind the explosion." Ridge looked at Caleb. "We had already figured as much. Everything pointed to him."

"Where did you plant the device?" Caleb directed the question to Wiley.

"Near the back of Evans's bus."

"Great work. This case is moving quickly." Ridge continued. "We have extra security on the girlfriend. From the sound of that call, it appears she may be in imminent danger."

Wiley sobered. "I agree. I think she's going to be very useful." He addressed Caleb this time. "We need to keep her healthy."

Caleb's heart plunged to his stomach. "I'm . . . we're doing the best we can, sir."

The absolute best we can.

CHAPTER 32

Midmorning the same day – April 17

The headlines that morning didn't mention a car bomb explosion as Danni had expected. There was only a small report on the radio news about a vehicle fire in West Nashville. Perhaps, as Caleb said, it was because the investigation hadn't yet been completed.

Caleb called as Danni pulled her Escape into a spot behind Amoré. She'd said a prayer before starting her car this morning and had been grateful to see Agent Matheson standing in the shadows of the underground garage. She suspected he had watched the car all night. He'd tipped his cap to her as she unlocked her car door.

During their quick call, Caleb told her he had stepped up her security and to expect new faces watching her twenty-four hours a day—in the restaurant, on the street, and in and around her condo building. He said they would introduce themselves discreetly and to be aware if she saw someone suspicious. He also inferred Ramirez had been officially connected to the bomb, or at least that the TBI was leaning in that direction.

Before he hung up, he reminded her they would get through all of this one day at a time. Just hearing his voice gave her courage. But she braced herself for what could lie ahead.

Halfway been the back door of the restaurant and Danni's office, Jaycee ambushed her with a game of twenty questions. Thankfully, she had a lot she could share about the rehab center, keeping the topic of the explosion off limits.

"I had no idea something like the Hope and Grace Resource Center existed," said Danni as she dropped her bag onto her desk. "We need to look into hiring a few of their graduates. I met one woman who really touched my heart."

Jaycee listened intently while Danni told her about Rachel and her dream of being reunited with her daughter.

"I told her I would pray for her."

A slow smile spread across Jaycee's face. "I'm sure that meant a lot to her."

"I hope so. I know how much your prayers have meant to me."

Jaycee blinked away moisture in her eyes and swallowed. "You've got them, from now until forever, my friend. It's what friends do for each other."

The restaurant business was slow that day, likely because of the rain that continued to pour from bottomless dark clouds that had taken residence over the city. The forecast didn't offer much hope for relief during the next twenty-four hours. When a front stalled over the geographic bowl that encompassed Music City and its surrounding area, it could sometimes settle in for days. This particular storm was reminiscent of one that had brought flooding, devastating many parts of the city a few years after Danni moved to the area.

At Jaycee's insistence, Danni left for home earlier than usual that night. The clouds hung low, obscuring the half-moon that should have lighted her drive home, and by the time she took Sophie out for her walk, only the streetlights and the headlamps from passing cars provided illumination.

The unrelenting rain was coming down hard and, because the big dog loved water, Sophie managed to find every sinkhole and pothole on their usual circuit around the neighborhood. Her outer coat of fur was saturated by the time they returned to the front walkway of their building.

Water poured from Danni's umbrella as she folded it and stepped beneath the shelter of the narrow dark green awning. She tugged on the heavy brass door, opening it wide enough for both her and Sophie to enter the lobby. Without warning, the big dog started to shake—starting at the big Newfoundland's head and traveling to the tip of her tail.

"Sophie!" Danni jumped back, but it was too late. She was already drenched. Well, more drenched. And a small pool of water now covered three square feet of the Italian marble floor of the lobby.

A man in grey overalls, who worked silently a few feet away, scowled at them. He eyed the dog and then Danni, finally picking up his mop and bucket and heading their way. He shook his head as he stared at the mess on the floor.

"I'm so sorry." Danni held the Newfoundland on a short leash.

"*No te preocupes,*" the man said. "This is all I've done for two days. It's not your fault. I'm not sure if the rain will ever stop."

"I know. I can't remember when we've had so much at once." Danni thanked him for cleaning up her mess. "I hope your night gets better."

He nodded and went back to work.

Danni escorted the dog across the lobby and engaged the elevator button, hoping Sophie would hold off shaking again until she could towel her dry. When they exited on the seventh floor, she led the Newfie quickly to her condo and unlocked and opened the door.

She had just stepped inside when her phone rang. Grabbing a towel from the coat rack, Danni threw it over Sophie in an attempt to stave off immediate damage. She dug the phone out of her pocket and looked at it. Jaycee's number was in the caller ID.

"What's going on?" Danni blocked Sophie from the living room.

"We have a problem." Her friend's voice was thin, almost unrecognizable. "The restaurant is flooding."

"Flooding? How can that be?"

The big dog began to shake again. Danni launched herself across her, holding on with her free hand to keep the towel in place.

"We're already wading in three inches of water in the kitchen." Jaycee shrieked. "It's awful. It's coming in from the alley in the back."

"I'll be right there." Danni unsnapped Sophie's leash. "Let me change clothes. Do you need me to bring anything?"

"Just your office keys." Danni heard fear in Jaycee's voice. "We need to move everything out of there before the water gets to that point."

"Is there anyone helping you?"

"George and Trevor. Everyone else has gone home for the night."

"I'll see you in a few minutes!" Danni set the phone on her entry table, quickly towel-dried the dog, and then hurried to her closet to pick out a change of clothes.

After pulling on a pair of navy-blue sweatpants and an Iowa State sweatshirt, she swept her hair into a makeshift up-do and secured it with a hair tie.

"I'll be back in a while, Soph." Danni slammed the door behind her.

Punching the elevator button, she ticked through a mental checklist. She had her rain boots and her office keys. What was she forgetting?

Her umbrella. She fumbled with her keys and reentered the condo, grabbing the umbrella from the stand near the door and then relocking her door.

Should she drive? If the street was flooding, it might be hard to find parking. Besides, she could jog to the restaurant just as quickly as she could deal with the maze of one-way streets. Downtown Nashville's never-ending reconstruction and realignment often left even its residents confused as to which streets were open. Once they were finished with the cleanup at the restaurant, Jaycee could drop her back home.

Caleb slammed the door on his truck and started the engine. He loved to hear the purr of his 350. At this point in the day, it sounded much more relaxed than he did. Working twelve- and fourteen-hour shifts would eventually kill you, or at least wear you down. That was his theory, especially after a long day at the Bureau headquarters.

Walking the street all night was easier than staring at a computer screen, as he'd done today. But if researching the global narcotics ring that financed Valentino Ramirez's operation would put him, Evans, and their associates behind bars, it was worth the effort.

Caleb glanced at his watch. It was early enough to call Danni and check on her. He would think of some flimsy excuse to justify the call as business. But the truth was, he just wanted to hear her voice. To make sure she was okay.

He'd had a nagging feeling in his gut since the afternoon that something was wrong. Then again, maybe it was just his stomach complaining about the ten cups of coffee, two donuts, and half a tuna salad sandwich he'd called lunch—and dinner.

By his estimate, Danni should be at home or walking in the door by now. He speed-dialed her phone, mentally drafting an excuse for the conversation.

His call rolled into voicemail. *Interesting.*

She could be walking the dog. But why wouldn't she have her phone with her? He tried again, but it proved to be another futile attempt.

If she wasn't home or available by phone, she had to be preoccupied, in the shower, or still working. That wouldn't be unusual. But a quick call to Amoré would put his mind to rest.

After the restaurant phone rang three times, Caleb was about ready to hang up, when it was picked up.

"Yes?" It sounded like Jaycee Alexander, Danni's chef, was out of breath.

"This is Agent Samuels. Is Ms. Kemp still there?"

"She's on her way."

"From home?"

"Yes." A curt reply, which based on the tone of her voice, translated to, *Yes, now, go away.*

"Is everything all right, Ms. Alexander?"

"Well, actually, no, sir. Our restaurant is flooding, so if you'll excuse me, I have to—"

"Is that why Danielle is on her way back to the restaurant?"

A long sigh. "Yes."

"She's not answering her phone, and I'm concerned—"

"I just talked to her—" the chef paused, presumably to look at her watch—"not more than fifteen minutes ago."

"As soon as she walks in the door, would you have her call me?" Caleb was beginning to understand why his gut had been nagging him.

"Absolutely." Jaycee's voice quivered. "Now you have me worried."

"I'm sure everything's okay. Get back to your cleanup. I'll check on her."

"Thanks."

Caleb ended the call. Something was wrong.

He rerouted his truck, easily enough done on his way home. Danni's condo lay directly between TBI headquarters and his house on the West side of town. If she wasn't home, he would scour the five blocks between there and Amoré to find her.

And, in the meantime, he would pray.

With a wave to the night guard, Danni rushed out the front door of the Rutherford. A quick scan of the local landscape revealed a tired looking beat cop in deep discussion with a hobo standing beneath a Metro bus stop.

Perhaps another TBI agent she hadn't yet met. She smiled and took off jogging.

Under normal circumstances, it wouldn't have taken long to run five blocks, but the closer she got to the restaurant the more she realized how bad the weather had become. Large puddles, more like swirling ponds of water, had settled into low spots in the sidewalk, making her navigation precarious. She kept her eyes on the terrain in front of her, occasionally looking up to gauge her progress.

Lightning flashed, sending eerie shadows across the cityscape, its ricocheting booms of thunder startling her. But she was far more concerned about getting to the restaurant and forestalling additional damage. They couldn't afford to be down for long. Not when things were going so well.

She prepared to step off the curb and turn on to the brick-paved alleyway leading to the back entrance of the restaurant when a flash of lightning shot across her path. The bright light reflected off the dark and swirling water at her feet. She stopped short, her heart beating double time in her chest. More than a foot of water rushed into the nether lands of the narrow alley. If she had stepped into it, she might have been swept off her feet.

She would need to enter through the front door of the building, so she rerouted her steps toward the Second Avenue entrance. The rain was now coming down in pellets. Thankfully, the main street entrance was located on higher ground than the back. The kitchen might be taking in water, but so far the dining room should be dry.

Danni darted beneath the gold-and-white striped awning with the restaurant name screen printed on its front. Fumbling with her keys she could feel the wind picking up, blowing the rain sideways across her face. At least it wasn't pelting her now.

She fought to catch her breath as she struggled with the deadbolt securing the heavy stained glass and wood door that welcomed every guest to Amoré. Because one of the entrance lights was out, inserting the key became a chore. Why hadn't she brought a flashlight? She reached for her cell phone to engage the flashlight app, but a quick inspection of her pockets revealed nothing that felt like a phone. Had she left it at home?

The amber-colored streetlight and flickering neon from the storefront next door would have to be sufficient for her to insert the key into the lock. Finally, the key found the lock. But just as the latch turned, a shadow appeared in her peripheral vision.

Strong hands grabbed her by the shoulders and pulled her backwards into a rock-hard chest. As arms encircled her, she screamed.

One hand flew to her mouth, the other to her neck, making it difficult to breathe. She had to fight! If she passed out, this would end badly. Very badly.

CHAPTER 33

Caleb prayed God would help him get to Danni in time. Whatever this was all about, it wasn't good. He parked his truck on the street across from the Rutherford and approached the undercover agent posing as a homeless guy.

"Hey, buddy. Here's a dollar." He grabbed a single bill from his pocket and stepped close enough for a private exchange. "Have you seen our CI tonight?"

The man nodded. "Thank you, sir. You're very kind." He cleared his throat. "Not since she and the dog went inside, presumably for the night, less than an hour ago."

"You take care and keep your chin up." Caleb turned and rushed across the street toward the high rise. He entered the lobby through the double doors, stopping to place a phone call to Matheson before punching the elevator call button.

The agent in charge of watching the garage confirmed Danni's Escape was still parked where she had left it when she got home a couple hours ago. Caleb shoved his phone back into his pocket and waited for the elevator to descend. It was feasible Danni had been screening her calls—or was in the shower—earlier, and that she hadn't yet left for the restaurant. But he needed to be sure.

"Sir." The night watchman walked up to Caleb at the same time the elevator arrived. Caleb held the door open so as not to lose the lift.

"If you're looking for your pretty friend," the security guard said. "She's gone. She left a while ago."

"How long?" Caleb removed his hand from the elevator door, allowing it to close with a pop.

The uniformed guard looked at his watch. "I'd say about twenty minutes."

"Thank you!" Caleb slapped the man on the back and took off running.

What had Danni been thinking? Why hadn't she driven? That made no sense. And why wasn't she answering her phone?

As he turned the corner at the cross street on his way to Amoré, his head swirled with questions—the most important being, was she safe? He settled into an easy pace, slow enough not to miss something suspicious along the route to the restaurant, and fast enough to satisfy his worried mind. Urgency in his gut pushed him forward, but concern that she might be lying somewhere in a dark alley along the way tempered his speed.

He searched right and left for any sign of danger in the shadows, which had been deepened by the foggy rain. Pulling his jacket closer to his neck and the bill of his cap down over his eyes, he kept an even stride.

Danni kicked and clawed at her assailant. He would not win. Not as long as she had any fight left in her.

But she could feel herself losing ground, sliding toward the street. Her strength was no match for this guy. She calculated the location of his foot. What she wouldn't give to be wearing high heels right now. She landed a blow with the heel of her boot into the man's ankle.

"Ouch!" He cursed and loosened his grip.

Danni struggled to break free, but his upper body strength was too much for her. When he clamped down again, he tugged her toward the street with a renewed vengeance.

A block from the restaurant Caleb saw movement near the front door. The area was dimly lit, but he could see two people standing close together. Maybe embracing?

That couldn't be Danni. If she was anything, she was fiercely loyal. How else would she have put up with Robert Evans for more than two years?

The rain was now coming in torrents. Large drops of water pelted him mercilessly. He ducked his chin and averted his eyes toward the ground. At his feet was a massive stream of water. If he hadn't looked down, he would have stepped off the sidewalk into a maelstrom.

Where was it all coming from?

He looked to his left and then to his right. *Why hadn't he seen it before?* There was a breach in the fire hydrant across the street.

Turning his head in the opposite direction, and straining to focus, he could see another open hydrant not far from the back door of the restaurant. No wonder the place was flooding.

So it wasn't only rainwater filling Amoré? Most of this flood was manmade, leaving him with the obvious conclusion. *Luring Danni back to her work was a ruse.*

And that meant her life was in danger.

Caleb's presumption was punctuated with a scream. The two people, now less than thirty feet in front of him, weren't a happy couple after all. The man was dragging the woman toward a car.

It was Danielle!

With no time to calculate options, Caleb jumped across the tide of gushing water in front of him, clearing it without difficulty, and landing on solid pavement. If his old track coach could have seen the move, he would have been impressed.

Caleb sprinted toward Danni and her attacker, who by now had pushed her fully inside the sedan. He could see she was fighting with everything she had, but it wasn't enough.

Stepping up his pace, all Caleb could hear was his own breathing, ragged and rasping, and the memory of Danni's scream. He reached for the Glock inside his jacket, and taking one final, flying leap, closed the space between him and the car. Grabbing the man by the shoulders, Caleb threw him backwards and unto the ground. The thug bounced off the pavement, crying out in pain.

"Run . . . now!" Caleb grabbed Danni's hand and pulled her toward the curb. She scrambled into the shadows of the building several yards away.

Caleb turned to deal with her attacker, but in a split second, the man jumped to his feet and bolted to the other side of the vehicle.

"Stop. TBI." Caleb brandished his weapon. But the man dove into the backseat of the car, just as it sped away, tires squealing.

Caleb seared the number and letter sequence of the license plate into his memory, and then turned back to Danni. She was cowering in fear, staring at Chef Jaycee Alexander, who was holding a gun.

And it was pointed in his direction.

CHAPTER 34

The gun may have been pointed in his direction, but Caleb knew he wasn't the target. The woman holding the weapon was staring into the empty street behind him, reliving the past few, dramatic moments. He'd seen that kind of delayed reaction many times. Once the danger passed, it took a while for reality to take hold.

One wrong move on his part could be a fatal mistake.

"Jaycee!" Danni screamed.

Amoré's chef cocked her head but didn't change her focus.

"What are you doing?" Danni's voice was thin, and with good reason. She'd narrowly escaped death. Twice. Now her coworker had gone off the deep-end.

"Jaycee," Danni screamed. "Put the gun down!"

This time the chef looked fully at Danni. And a few seconds later, she lowered the weapon to her side.

"What just happened?" Jaycee switched her focus to Caleb.

He took a step toward her with his hand out. "Ms. Alexander, please give me the gun."

She handed the pistol to him, grip first, and as soon as he had wrapped his fingers around it, he let out a long breath.

Danni grabbed her friend and pulled her into a hug. "Where did you get that?" She pointed to the Smith and Wesson now in his possession. Caleb released the cylinder, emptied its contents into the palm of his hand, and pocketed the ammunition.

"I keep it in my car. I have a permit." Jaycee shook her head. "I just never thought I would have to use it." She lifted her chin and looked directly at him. "But I would have shot that man if you hadn't stopped him."

"Thank God you didn't have to." Caleb replayed the possibility in his head.

Danni patted her friend on the shoulder. "Let's go inside."

An hour later, after the fire department had shut off the water hydrants and Caleb had helped the crew mop up the remaining water, Jaycee offered coffee.

"That would be great." He gestured to a table in the front, the one where he and Danni had first sat and talked only weeks before. "I need to make a phone call. I'll join you in a few minutes."

While the women prepared the coffee, Caleb placed the call. A sleepy-sounding Martin Ridge answered. "This had better be good, Samuels."

Caleb chuckled to himself. "We've had a deal changer. Ms. Kemp was assaulted tonight in an attempted kidnapping."

"Is she okay?" Ridge's voice grew stronger with each word.

"Yes. Fortunately, I was here."

"Did you apprehend the guy?"

"No. He got away, and I didn't see his face. But I have a vehicle tag number. I've already called it into headquarters."

"I assume you're still with Ms. Kemp?"

"Yes, sir."

"Find out what she knows. I'll see you in the office first thing tomorrow morning."

Caleb started to hang up.

"Samuels?"

"Yes?"

"Good job. We need to keep Ms. Kemp safe. She's our best asset right now."

"I know, sir. See you in a few hours."

Caleb looked at his watch. Three a.m. Scratch the good night of sleep he'd hoped for.

Ten minutes later, Danni and Jaycee returned, both carrying large mugs of hot brew. Danni placed the delicious-smelling concoction in front of him.

He took a sip. *Perfection.* "This is a life saver."

She took the seat in front of him. "No. You're the lifesaver. Quite literally. That was another close call."

"*Another?* You mean this isn't the first?" Jaycee plopped down next to Danni. "I think it's time the two of you leveled with me. Does this have anything to do with Ramirez?"

Danni looked as if she was about to speak, but nothing came out of her mouth.

"I've got this." Caleb raised his hand, palm out. Then, taking a deep breath, he began. "Ms. Alexander, let me give you some background . . ."

Jaycee leaned back in her chair, her arms folded over her chest.

"First, please assure me this will be kept confidential."

She nodded. "You have my word."

"The TBI is investigating a case involving a global narcotics ring with ties to this area."

The chef's expression darkened, and she glanced toward Danni.

"That's unfortunately how Danielle became involved," he said.

"So it does have something to do with Michael's death," Jaycee half-whispered.

"Maybe not directly. We may never know for sure. But it does relate directly to the burglary that took place at Robert Evans's condo more than a month ago."

"I knew I didn't like that guy." Jaycee turned to Danni, who didn't look up.

"Although we're certain he's involved," Caleb said. "We can't, or more accurately, we don't want to prove anything yet. Not until we have enough to put him, as well as everyone else involved, behind bars for a long time."

Danni's hands were trembling as she fiddled with her coffee cup, still not looking up.

Jaycee leaned toward Caleb. "So what was the other close call?"

"Two nights ago, there was an explosion at the rehabilitation center where Danni visited." Caleb took a breath. "The vehicle she was about to get into went up in flames."

Jaycee paled, gathered her thoughts, and finally said, "Please take good care of my friend."

"We're doing the best we can," he said.

"I'll be praying." She looked from Danni to Caleb. "And for you too. I have a feeling there's more going on than I know, than I *want* to know. But you'll both be in my prayers, and if there's anything I can do . . ."

Caleb took a long draw from his coffee, saying a silent prayer of thanks for Jaycee Alexander. He liked her a lot. It was obvious God had put her in Danni's life.

Just as he was beginning to believe He had also put Danni into his.

"Go home and get some sleep," Jaycee said as she pushed Danni toward the back entrance of the restaurant. "We'll be fine this morning."

"But—"

"Don't argue. You may need to close for me tonight."

Likely story. Jaycee never left early. But you couldn't win an argument with her either. She had always been a good negotiator. Danni remembered watching her verbally spar with a street vendor in Mexico on the trip they had taken last year. Jaycee had walked away with a necklace at half price. Afterward, she had returned to slip the young girl an extra coin or two as a tip. Her friend might be feisty, but she had a soft heart.

"Please take care of her, Agent Samuels."

"Yes, ma'am." Caleb cupped his arm lightly around Danni's waist and escorted her out the building.

"I'll be back soon." Danni shouted over her shoulder before Jaycee closed the door behind them.

"Notice anything different?" Caleb asked.

"The rain has stopped!" The moon was peeking through the clouds. "What a difference a few hours can make."

Not just with the weather. If Caleb hadn't come along when he did, she might not be alive right now. "How are you holding up with no sleep?" she asked as they walked.

"It's overrated, don't you think?" The light from storefronts along Second Avenue twinkled in his eyes. Was it just her, or was he a devastatingly handsome man? Especially in the moonlight.

"If not, we're both in trouble," she laughed. "I haven't slept well in weeks."

He stopped walking. "I hope to fix that for you soon."

She turned to look at him. "I know. But I have to do my part too. I can't expect everyone else to fix the mess I've gotten myself into."

He studied her, nodded, and started walking again. He was not only handsome, he was a generous man. He hadn't hesitated to help with the cleanup they had done tonight after the rescue.

Rob wasn't exactly a roll-up-your-sleeves kind of a guy. He would never have helped the way Caleb had. Caleb had done whatever was needed, including carting out the trash. None of that fell under his job description. The only thing he was supposed to do was keep her safe. And he had done that too. Several times.

Maybe someday she would find a man like that to love her.

"Thank you for helping me," she said, catching her breath.

"With what?"

"With everything. Cleaning up tonight. Keeping me safe. And mostly for helping me see the truth."

"About Rob?"

"About life in general."

His glance lingered, but he kept walking. "How's that?"

"By setting a good example."

"Wow . . . you're too kind—"

"No. Just smart enough to know a good man when I see one."

He stopped walking again and looked around the landscape. *Was he embarrassed?*

He suddenly grabbed her arm and tugged. "You have no idea."

Danni bit her lip. "About how good you are?"

"No. About the things I've done in my life." He shook his head. "I'm not proud of my past." He kept a good pace as he looked behind every tree and signpost, and up every alley, for trouble.

"Hope and grace," she said.

He glanced toward her. "What do you mean?"

"I know what it means now. The name of the rehabilitation center."

"Okay." He didn't seem to know where she was going with this.

"Those girls are being given the hope that they will have a better future. And the grace to put their past behind them. How beautiful is that?"

"HGRC is a great place."

"I agree," she said. "It's a reminder to all of us—not just to those girls but to every one of us—that we can move beyond our past mistakes. Right?"

He shook his head, finally understanding her point. "Yes, but some things can't be so easily forgotten. Or forgiven."

"Caleb! There is no qualifier in God's grace. I know you can't forget about what happened with your brother. I understand that. But," she said softly, "it's as far behind you now as the things those girls may have done before they entered rehab. Aren't you willing to forgive them, to try to help them?"

"Of course."

"God has given you that same grace."

His jaw tensed, but he continued to look ahead.

They remained silent until they had reached the Rutherford. Caleb opened the massive entry door, nodded to the night guard, and escorted her to the elevators.

The lift arrived on the seventh floor, and the doors opened with a bang. Caleb scanned the hallway before walking her toward her unit. As soon as they reached her door, he turned to her. "My parents almost never got over it, Danni. I vowed to turn my life around then and there, but nothing . . . nothing can ever make up for that loss."

Danni reached out to him, then thinking better of it, handed him her key. "I know." There was so much more she wanted to say. But it would wait until another time.

He inserted the key into the deadbolt, the lock clicked, and the door drifted open.

Danni called for Sophie, but she didn't appear. "That's not like her. She's usually here the minute I walk inside."

Caleb stepped in front of her, secured the door behind them, and told her to wait in the entry. "Let me look for her. Where would she likely be?"

"Probably the closet, or in the master bathroom. End of the hall to the right."

Spotting her phone on the entry table, he handed it to her. "Dial 911 if anything goes wrong." He looked to his left and right, made a detour through her dining room and kitchen, and then headed down the hall.

She was pacing the foyer, weighing her options when Caleb emerged with Sophie by his side.

Danni exhaled a deep, shaky breath. "Where did you find her?"

"She had burrowed between two suitcases in the back of your closet. "Is that normal?"

"No." Danni wrapped her arms around the dog's neck. "Are you okay, girl?"

The dog leaned into her.

"She seems okay now." Danni shrugged. "Maybe she was worried because I was gone so long."

"Could be." Caleb seemed to be convinced that everything in the condo was okay. "I've checked everywhere. Lock your door when I leave." He stepped around her. "And don't open it for anyone you don't know."

"I guess you know you're scaring me." She did her best to smile.

"Don't be scared. Just be cautious." He opened the door and started to leave.

"Caleb."

"Yes?" He hesitated.

"Be careful. I don't want anything to happen to you either."

The muscles in his jaw tightened, and he took a step closer. Drawing her to him, he placed his lips on hers, then pulled away.

"Another stalker?" she asked.

"No." He whispered in her ear. "I'm just not sure I should be doing—"

"This?" She finished his sentence and moved her lips toward his.

Dear God, please protect this man. I'm falling in love.

CHAPTER 35

Caleb watched the lighted numbers descend. What had he just done? This was not business as usual. By the time the elevator doors had opened and he stepped into the well-lit lobby of the Rutherford, he had replayed the last few minutes in his mind over and over again.

There was no doubt. He had crossed the line. He had made this case personal. And it could cost him everything. Even the case.

He cradled the back of his neck with his hand. Things had just changed between him and Danni. Between him and his confidential informant.

What would he tell Ridge if he found out? Hadn't his supervisor already known that things were going in the wrong direction? He had seen it coming when he had thought about taking Caleb off the job a few weeks ago.

Am I really that transparent? And out of control? An agent has to be in control at all times or someone gets hurt. The case could suffer, would suffer, if he didn't get ahold of himself.

This wasn't about him. It was about serving justice to the jerks who had killed Jonathan. Or, if not Jonathan, hundreds of innocent kids just like him. The thought of losing that opportunity was unacceptable. Evans, Ramirez, Roman, and the man who attacked Danni tonight. All of them. They had to be locked away for a long time. If not forever. They had already caused too much heartache.

Caleb had collected files on local teens for years. Good kids who had stumbled into the drug scene and never returned. Some had been hooked, hopelessly, on meth or heroin and sold everything but their souls—sometimes even that—to get their daily fix. Others' lives had ended far too soon, if not by an overdose then by a related car accident, a shooting, or a steady decline in health.

No one was immune from falling victim to a drug dealer's wares. The streets were unsafe because of those thugs, and he had to do everything he could to stop them. But he couldn't do his best if he let his heart go off leash the way it had tonight.

Off-leash? He groaned. Where had that come from? Danni Kemp, and her big, goofy dog had gotten to him. Big time.

He relived the kiss again. Why had he let that happen? Because she had been willing? There was no doubt she had responded to his overture, and because of it, their relationship had taken a mutually acceptable turn. But despite the guilt and pain that hitched a ride, he wasn't about to stop the speeding train. He just had to slow it down for the sake of the investigation. It was his job to keep everyone safe. He had to put the bad guys behind bars first.

And then he could move on with his life.

He glanced at his watch, weighing his options. He could go home and change clothes, or he could go on into the office wearing water-soaked pants and shoes. He had made the decision to drive home when his phone rang.

"Where are you?" Ridge asked.

"Downtown."

"Get to the office as soon as you can. We have breaking news coming in."

"What is it?" Caleb hoisted his tired body into his Chevy.

"I'll know more by the time you get here, but it sounds like something explosive is about to go down."

Caleb closed his eyes and prayed to God there wouldn't be a literal fulfillment of Martin Ridge's prophecy.

"Let's start shooting over here, Tom." Cassia Noelle directed her photographer to a large stack of rocks. Then she turned to Rob. "If you would, please stand here."

Rob tugged at microscopic wrinkles in his shirt and walked to the X Cassia had drawn in the dirt, pivoting toward her and her photographer.

A satisfied sigh fell from her lips. "Perfect. This is going to look fantastic!"

Rob relaxed. In the last few days, it had become apparent that Cassia Noelle's work was stellar. She had shown him several of her finished projects, including photos she had art directed and stories she had written. Every one of them was top notch. His cover story was going to blow the roof off his profile in Nashville. It was about time he got some respect in Music City.

He grinned.

"Great! Show those dimples." Cassia cooed. "Keep snapping away, Tom."

Rob switched positions and tilted his chin down. He'd watched dozens of celebrity photo shoots, many for his own artists. He had the poses down. This was going to be fun.

"Work it, baby." Cassia knew how to get the best out of him.

He laughed and blew her a seductive kiss.

"Now do that, but for the camera." She winked and took a step behind the photographer so Rob could react to her, but it would appear he was looking into the camera's lens.

He threw out another kiss. This one even more impassioned. He trusted Cassia to cull out the bad shots and make him look great. Not just great but amazing. Just like she had done with her other features.

He took a break while the beautiful journalist and her photographer brainstormed more ideas for photos. This cover story would be one of the best hits he'd had in a long time. His peers in Nashville would be so—

His phone vibrated from inside his boot where he'd hidden it for the shoot. He bent to retrieve it and saw Ramirez's number flashing on the screen. Not a convenient time.

"Hello."

"You sound irritated, Robert."

"It's just not a good time—"

"If it makes you feel any better, I'm not having a good day either."

Rob sighed. *Now what?*

"I'm losing my patience with that pretty little brunette of yours in Nashville. When are you going to take care of her?"

"It has only been twenty-four hours since I talked to you last—"

"The woman seems to have nine lives."

"What do you mean by that?"

"Let's just say one of my men found her especially attractive and became impatient." Ramirez laughed.

"Who? What did he do?" Rob stepped farther away from Cassia and her photographer.

"Am I detecting a bit of jealousy? *El comal le dijo a la olla, que tiznada estás.* Perhaps you need to look in the mirror, my friend."

Ramirez clicked his tongue. "You should be more concerned about that cop she's cozying up to. He's digging for information."

"It's nothing I can't fix when I get home."

"Then it's time you go home."

"My business is on the road, you know that."

Rob heard breathing on the other end of the phone. "Robert. Robert. Robert." Ramirez sighed. "You need to slow down and remember who's in charge here."

Rob bit his tongue, pushed his pent-up frustration aside, and waited.

"Perhaps you don't understand me. This is a matter of life and death." He paused. "Hers and yours."

"Is that a threat?"

"Take it any way you want to take it but get your girlfriend under control, or I'll do it for you. And you may not approve of my method."

Rob's heart climbed to his throat.

"Do you understand?" Ramirez prodded for a response.

"Yes."

"Good. And if you want my advice, it's time to marry her." He cleared his throat. And the air. "Now, let's talk business."

Rob glanced impatiently toward Cassia. Thankfully, she was preoccupied.

Ramirez continued. "Are you serious about retiring?"

"Yes." Now Ramirez had his full attention.

"I've been thinking about it, and I hate to lose you. But . . ." He paused for dramatic effect. "You've been such a good employee. I wouldn't feel right standing in your way."

Could it be this easy?

Rob envisioned warm sun, sandy beaches, and palm trees swaying in the breeze. No more cramped tour busses or small towns. No more surreptitious business transactions. For that matter, no more Music Row competition. He would miss the women on the road, but . . .

"But," Ramirez broke into Rob's thoughts, "I need you to do one more job. A big one."

"The bigger the better." Rob said enthusiastically. A little extra cash before retirement would be handy.

"Good," Ramirez said. "I'll be back in touch soon."

The call ended, and Rob put his phone back in his boot.

"Is everything okay?" Cassia slipped up beside him.

He smiled. "Yes. I'm ready to get back to work."

"Great. We have one more shot over here." Her voice drifted off as she walked away from him, hips sashaying.

Rob shifted his eyes to the ground and thought about Ramirez's advice. Why did he need to marry Danni right away?

Cassia looked back to see if he was following her.

Of course! If he married Danni, she couldn't testify against him. Danni didn't know much, but she knew about the money stash. And Ramirez had said something about a cop. Danni wouldn't do anything stupid like talk to a cop. She had proven her loyalty over and over. Still, it appeared that he needed to get back to Nashville.

He hurried to catch up with the beautiful blond reporter, to finish the work at hand and get it out of the way. Then he would schedule an unexpected visit to Music City. He would get everything worked out. His dream of retirement would soon be a reality.

Cassia directed him to stand in front of the bus, which Hank had parked in the middle of a long stretch of road.

"The Endless Road," Cassia said, gesturing wide with her hands. "That's what we're calling this shot and your feature." She smiled. "Don't you love it?"

"Very creative." Rob nodded and assumed a pose. *But it might not be completely accurate.*

CHAPTER 36

The next day – April 18

Just as Danni had expected, Jaycee refused to leave work early. The two walked out of the restaurant together, locking the back door behind them.

Jaycee gave her a quick hug. "Be careful, Danni. Your hero isn't here tonight." She nodded toward Matheson and another agent who watched from the shadows.

"You be careful too." Danni waved to her friend as they got into their respective vehicles to leave.

The idea that Jaycee's life could be in danger, *was* in danger, because of Rob infuriated Danni. But there was nothing she could do about it except pray—and hope that Caleb was right. That it would all be over soon.

He had ordered twenty-four-hour security for Jaycee after last night's kidnapping attempt. The new agent, dressed in motorcycle gear, hopped on his Harley to follow Jaycee home.

Matheson drove Danni home in her car. And, because security had been further tightened, he also escorted her to her condo, following her inside to be certain everything was okay.

When Sophie didn't meet them at the entry, Danni had to search for her, finally finding her hiding in the closet, just as she had been when she and Caleb entered earlier that morning.

Did the dog know something Danni didn't know?

After the agent left to spend the remainder of the night outside, Danni shared a late-night supper of peanut butter and crackers with the big Newfoundland. Then she changed into her pajamas, and as soon as she climbed into bed, Sophie jumped in beside her.

"What's up with you, Soph?" It was completely unlike the big dog to hover. Danni threw her arms around her. "You need to relax, girl."

Sophie pulled away and jumped off the bed.

"Where are you going?"

Sophie shook her entire body, as if shaking off water again, and then began pacing around the room. She walked out of the bedroom, down the hall, and into the foyer. Danni could hear the tap, tap, tap of her toenails on the foyer floor. A few minutes later, she paced back into the bedroom, made a U-turn beside the bed, and went into the bathroom. A few seconds later, Danni heard a bump, followed by the clatter of bottles, which had to be knick-knacks hitting the tile floor. Then Sophie came pacing back into the bedroom.

"Hey, you . . ." Danni reached her hand out to the dog.

Sophie stopped, gave Danni a worried look, and walked back into the hall, reappearing again at the bedroom door in less than a minute. Danni called to her again, but this time Sophie ignored her and kept walking.

"Sophie? What's the matter?" Danni patted the top of the mattress with her hand. "We need to get some sleep."

The dog stopped, eyed Danni suspiciously, and then jumped up on the bed. She turned a counter-clockwise circle and plopped down with a grunt.

"Thank you!" Danni voiced to no one. Now maybe they could get some sleep.

Danni set the alarm, switched off the lamp, and settled in, hoping Sophie's disturbing behavior had stopped for the night. But the dog remained restless. It was time for a visit to the vet.

The next morning, Danni made a work-in veterinarian appointment. She called Jaycee to let her know she would be late getting to work.

Sophie seemed to relax once they left the condo. She stuck her big head out the window of the Escape for the entire three-mile ride to Dr. Bradley's office. And once there they didn't have to wait long.

"It's always good to see you and Sophie," the veterinarian said, closing the exam room door behind him. "What's going on?"

Danni took a seat in the chair in the corner of the room. "This may sound strange, but she's just not been herself. Several times when I've come home, she's been hiding in the closet. Then, last night, she started pacing around the house and was unsettled all night. It's almost like she's worried about something."

"Does she seem to be in any pain?"

"Not that I'm aware. And she's eating okay."

The veterinarian gave Danni a curious look.

"Anything changed in your routine?"

"Not really."

The doctor reached for Sophie's leash and pulled the big Newfoundland close to him.

About ten minutes later, after doing a quick, hands-on exam, listening to her heart and lungs, and drawing blood, he took a seat on a nearby stool.

"I don't mean to get personal, but how about you? Are you anxious about something?"

How could she answer that? She finally shared. "There are some changes going on in my life right now."

"Okay. Well, I'm not seeing any sign of physical illness in Sophie, so I'm guessing her anxiety may have been triggered by something in her environment. She could even be picking up on your anxiety." He searched her face.

"How did you know that?" Danni asked.

"It's more than a hunch." Dr. Bradley raked a hand through his graying hair. "You seem to be stressed."

Danni attempted a smile. "I am. And I hate that it's affecting Sophie." She focused on the dog. "I'm going through some hard things right now. At work and personally. Hopefully it will be over soon. I'm working on it, Dr. Bradley." She stopped, not willing to share more.

He nodded. "Sophie loves you. And I'd say she's reacting to your stress." He rubbed the Newfoundland behind her ears. "So let me ask you this, has anything unusual happened inside your home lately?"

"We had a break-in next door. The police were all over my place that night."

"She's probably reacting to that. And . . ."

The veterinarian waited for her to continue.

"Because of the break in, there has been extra security around the building.

The veterinarian finished her conjecture. "I think you've figured it out. Sophie's home—her secure place—and her routine have been upended recently. I'm guessing she's uncertain how to respond to it."

"So . . ." Danni studied the dog. She was now lying with her eyes closed between the two of them. "What should I do?"

"What would you want someone to do for you if something like that happened?"

"I'd want to be reminded that it's going to be okay." Danni thought about how Caleb had reassured her over and over. "I guess I need to make sure Sophie knows she can trust me to take care of her through this. Right?"

The veterinarian smiled and nodded. "Yes."

"Do I need to pay you a personal counselor's fee, as well as a veterinarian fee?"

He laughed. "No, it's just part of my service to longtime clients."

"I appreciate it, Dr. Bradley."

"If you'd like, while you're in the process of making a few changes, I can give you a homeopathic supplement for Sophie that will help her relax." He looked at Danni over the top of his glasses. "If that doesn't work or she gets worse, let me know."

"That sounds perfect." Danni's phone vibrated in her pocket as she stood and reached to shake this doctor's hand. "Thank you again."

"I know you'll work everything out. You're a smart young woman. Take care of yourself."

He offered her a reassuring smile and opened the exam room door.

"I'll take care of myself and Sophie. I promise." She led the dog out of the exam room. "We'll get through this."

After paying the bill and purchasing the small bottle of tincture the veterinarian had prescribed, Danni loaded Sophie in the car. It had turned out to be a beautiful day. She rolled down all the windows and opened the sunroof, after starting the car and buckling her seatbelt. Then she pulled her phone from her pocket to see who had called.

Rob Evans.

She hit redial, and Rob answered on the second ring. "Hey, babe. Thanks for calling me back."

"I'm better at it than you are."

"Nice to talk to you too." He sounded genuinely hurt.

"Sorry." But she wasn't.

"I couldn't wait to tell you my news!"

"What?"

"I'll be home tomorrow."

"Oh." Danni flinched, and then reminded herself to be happy. "That's great!"

"Can you take Sunday afternoon off for lunch and to look for rings?"

"I—I guess so. Jaycee shouldn't mind, but let me talk to her."

He laughed nervously. "She probably would, if you tell her why. She's never liked me, you know."

"Her bark is just worse than her bite."

"Well just in case. Let's keep your ring as our little surprise until you show it to her. Okay?"

"Okay."

"Hey, I need a little more enthusiasm than that. I'm asking you to marry me, you know."

"I'm sorry, Rob. I've just got a lot of things on my mind. I had to take Sophie to the vet this morning—"

"I can't wait to see you. I've got more good news I'll share with you tomorrow."

"Sounds great."

"I love you, Danni."

Danni's phone beeped with another call, and Caleb Samuels's name appeared in the window.

"Rob, I need to go. It's my other line."

"Okay, but I want you to think about something. I want you to reconsider my suggestion to elope. Maybe to the Caribbean? Maybe next month."

What? "I thought we'd agreed to have a big wedding . . . in January. I've already started to make plans, and—"

"I guess I'm just ready." His voice wavered. "You know me, I may take a while with something, but when I'm finally ready—"

Call waiting beeped again.

"I'll think about it." She bit her lip. "We'll talk about it this weekend. Okay?"

"Okay. See you then! Bye."

Danni's hands were trembling. How many times had she hoped that Rob would ask her to marry him? And now that he had . . . it didn't matter. She connected the second line.

"Hi."

"Are you okay?" Caleb asked.

"Not really. I was just on the phone with Rob. It's been a busy morning . . . And I'm just now leaving the vet with Sophie. She's still acting funny." She told him about her unsettling night, and what the vet had told her, rattling on and on.

Caleb listened patiently until she was finished, and then asked, "Is she going to be okay?"

Danni thought about her answer. "Yes. As soon as I am."

"That's why I called." He hesitated. "I just walked out of a meeting with my team, and we think something big is about to go down."

Danni took a long breath and steadied herself. "I'm ready," she said. "For whatever it is."

CHAPTER 37

Midmorning – April 19

aleb knew he couldn't talk candidly on an unsecured line. "Do you have time to meet me at your place before you go to the restaurant?"

"Sure. I'll be there in twenty minutes."

"See you then." He turned his truck toward downtown Nashville. Sleep could wait. He owed Danni the truth. And a choice.

Glancing into his rearview mirror, he ran his hand across his beard. It had been two days since he had shaved. But it would have to do. She might as well know now that being involved with a law enforcement agent had consequences.

Twenty minutes later he waved to the agent on duty and walked to Danni's condominium door. He tapped lightly. She answered almost immediately.

"I knew you'd be here on time." She smiled, nodding to the other agent in the hallway.

Caleb stepped inside the apartment, and Sophie greeted him with a wag of her tail.

"Hey, girl. I hear you've been to the doctor this morning."

"She's just about ready to take her first dose of medicine. Come on into the kitchen." Danni turned toward the dining room, and Caleb followed. "Can I get you something to eat?"

"No. But would I be imposing to ask for a cup of coffee?" He stopped at the dining room table and pulled out a chair with a view into the kitchen.

"No sleep, huh?" She engaged her coffee pot. "How do you do it?"

"What?"

"Work with no sleep."

He scrolled through his emails and muted his phone before setting it on the table. "About the same as you."

"But God will get us through this."

He prayed she was right.

A few minutes later, Danni and Sophie walked into the dining room. Danni was holding something that had the dog mesmerized.

"Sit, Soph." The Newfoundland immediately landed on her furry bottom, wiggling with excitement.

"What has her so stirred up?" Caleb leaned back in his chair, tired but revitalized in Danni's presence. He could get used to coming home to a beautiful woman and her dog.

"Liverwurst." Danni winked. "It's my go-to cover-up for doggie medicine."

"Lucky dog." Caleb chuckled and watched as Danni added a few drops of something to the meat. "What is that?"

She capped the vial in her hand and gave it to him. "Homeopathic. My vet says it will calm her nerves." She held out a golf ball size of the processed meat. Sophie took it from her hand, devouring the meat quickly.

"Here, one more piece for being such a good girl." Danni gave the dog an untainted piece and patted her on the head.

Sophie grabbed the second bite and took off for another part of the house, and Danni took a seat next to Caleb.

"What do you have to calm my nerves?" she asked. "Or is your news going to upset me more?"

He rubbed the back of his neck with his hand. "May I have my coffee first? Then I'll give you the full rundown."

"Sorry, I forgot."

He handed her back the vial. "And no medicine for me thanks."

A few minutes later, Danni returned with two coffee cups, his light and hers dark.

"I'm ready," she said, taking her seat.

He took a sip. "What I'm about to tell you is, of course, confidential. But the feds now have someone on the inside with enough information to put Ramirez behind bars for a long, long time."

Danni's mouth dropped open.

He continued. "Before you ask, it has nothing to do with Rob. This informant is involved in a different aspect of Ramirez's operation."

"Okay . . ." She paused to think about what he had said. "So what does this have to do with me?"

"A lot actually." He studied her. "Your assistance is no longer needed."

"Wow." Danni's hand flew to her mouth, and she sat back in her chair, not speaking.

He sat quietly, waiting for her to process the information. If he knew her like he thought he did, she would realize what was missing. In a few seconds, the light came on in her eyes.

"Let me see if I understand." She drew an imaginary line on the surface of the mahogany table. If Ramirez is put away for a connection over here." She tapped one side of the line. "What happens to this side of his operation?" She pointed to the other side of the line.

"It will likely go away because the source, the mastermind of the operation, will be in prison."

She nodded. "Then most likely the other people, those involved over here . . ." She pointed to the other side of the line again. "They won't be prosecuted?"

"You're correct."

"Which means that Rob—and anyone involved in the distribution of the drugs—will not be charged?"

"Could happen."

She thought for a minute. "That's not right."

Caleb smiled to himself. He'd bet she would come to that conclusion. He shook his head. "I know."

"Are you giving me a choice?"

"Yes." She was not only beautiful; she was smart.

Her hand flew to her mouth again, and her eyes grew moist. Caleb watched as the decision battled within her, but he knew what she would do. At least he hoped he did.

"I can't stop now. Not when we're this close. We are close, right?"

"Yes, but you do have a choice."

She shook her head. "No. Not really." She stared into his eyes, her expression set. "For the sake of Michael, Rachel, and everyone who has been hurt by these people, I want to help."

Caleb nodded, hesitating before he spoke. "You realize that means Rob will likely go to prison."

She held his gaze.

"For a long time."

She nodded and clutched her trembling hands. "I know. But he's no better than anyone else. If it's proven he's involved, he should be punished."

Before Caleb left, Danni told him that Rob would be back in town for the weekend.

"He asked me to go with him on Sunday to pick out rings." She searched for the right words, but there were none. "Caleb, I'm not . . . I don't—"

He held up his hand to stop her. "I know. But don't let him know that. Not yet."

She willed herself to relax.

"Don't break your cover. It's important you respond normally to him. But there's no need for you to lie or do anything misleading."

"Okay."

"As cliché as it may sound, your heart will lead you. Don't overthink it." He searched her face and covered her hands in his. "The important thing is not to commit to the wrong thing."

"If you mean don't commit to marrying him, there's not a chance."

Not a chance whatsoever.

She was hurt. And disappointed. Rob had stolen her future— the future she once thought they would have together. This should have been one of the happiest days in her life, but now that it was here, she wanted to run from it.

Of course she was capable of playing along. Looking at rings wasn't a commitment. And if she could get important information from Rob, information that would be instrumental in saving lives and families, she could be completely committed to that.

Caleb cut into her thoughts. "Depending on how much he shares with you in the afternoon, we may fit you with a wire before dinner that evening, assuming you go out to dinner with him."

She nodded. "I'll make sure we do."

"It's your job to try to get details that could help secure a conviction against him, and the many others involved in the cross-country drug distribution ring Ramirez has set up." He hesitated. "I know that's difficult for you to think about."

"It's easier than it was." Her thoughts drifted again to the people who had been hurt by the Nashville operation. And that included Agent Jamie Wade, who was now recovering at home. Each of them—all of them—deserved to be vindicated. And potential victims deserved the chance to be spared the agony. "I'm ready to do my part."

"You're making a difference." Caleb stood to leave. "I'll check in with you soon."

"Good. I need your encouragement."

He stopped just short of the door. "What are you going to tell Jaycee?"

"How much can I tell her?"

"Want me to meet you and her for coffee after the restaurant closes tomorrow night? We can talk about it together."

"Great." Danni planted a quick kiss on his cheek. "Thank you for walking me through this. For making it as easy as it can be, considering the circumstances." She stepped back from him and felt her face flush. "You're a special guy."

"And you're an important part of this case." He hesitated. "But you've become an important part of my life too." He grimaced. "I need to take Zach to the park Sunday afternoon. That's where we'll be when you and Rob are together, and we'll be praying for you."

"I wish Sophie and I could go with you. It would probably do her a lot of good."

"There will be time for that soon." He reached to take her hand, hesitated, and then left.

Rob took Cassia's hand and kissed it. "I've enjoyed the last few days. I hope you won't be a stranger."

She smiled in her shy but provocative way. "And I hope we will have that opportunity soon. It's been a pleasure to get to know you." She glanced toward the bus, where Hank was seated in the driver's compartment in preparation for their drive to another city. "You and your staff have been very accommodating."

Something about that thought irritated Rob. She and Hank had become cozy. Of course, there was no way that brute of a man could win the affection of a beautiful woman like Cassia.

A pang of insecurity struck. Hopefully he wasn't losing his charm. It would be good for him to return home tomorrow. To see Danni and to start making plans for his future as a man of leisure. Retired at thirty-five. But married?

He had some adjusting to do.

CHAPTER 38

The Next Day – April 20

Ramirez called as Rob was packing for his trip back home.
Tonight's show would be his last before the bus deadheaded
to Atlanta and Rob would fly back to Nashville.

"Yes, sir."

"I have your arrangements made."

"My arrangements?"

"For your last job."

"Oh, yes, sir. That didn't take long."

"We've been in the planning stages for a while. I have an
unusual pickup for you. This one is just outside Nashville."

"Really?" Rob had never made a connection in or around Middle Tennessee. It had helped him avoid suspicion from authorities
in Nashville and kept him more than an arm's length from local
narcotics thugs.

He had hoped to keep it that way. Although, with this being
his last job, there should be no reason for concern.

"Where?"

"That's still to be determined, but I want you to be prepared
to stay in Nashville until I call you again."

Rob didn't understand, but it shouldn't be a problem. Except
for the honeymoon trip he was planning in May.

"We'll need your coach too."

"It will be back in town by Sunday. After the drop-off in Atlanta."

"We'll also need Danielle."

"Excuse me, sir?"

"I want her to make the pickup with you."

"But I don't see the point in that. She has nothing to do with my—"

"Robert, please." Ramirez interrupted. "Danielle has *everything* to do with this. Not to mention I'm fully aware that you've had her hiding money for you."

"But she doesn't know . . ."

"Then what she doesn't know won't hurt her. At least we hope it doesn't." Ramirez chuckled. "Because if you don't deliver her at the same time you pick up the goods, I must unfortunately eliminate her from the happy little picture."

Rob remained silent.

"You don't want that, do you, Robert?"

"Of course not." Fear rose in his gut. If they would kill Danni, they would come after him too.

"Of course, you don't. Because if she dies, you're going with her." The man on the other end of the phone talked as matter-of-factly about his potential demise as most people talked about the weather.

"I don't understand why there's a need to bring her with me."

"First of all, because I said so, Robert. And, secondly, I want to meet the woman who has obviously taken your heart, if not changed your ways." Ramirez laughed. "You're a bit of a playboy for someone who's almost married."

"If I may say so, sir, it's none of your business how I handle my personal life."

"Oh, but it is. You see, I'm smart enough to know that if you cheat on her, you'll cheat on me."

"I would never—"

"Spare me the drama, Evans. I know you have designs on the reporter I sent this week."

Ramirez had sent Cassia? Rob cursed his boss underneath his breath.

"Yes, it was me who sent Ms. Noelle to interview you. Are you surprised?"

Rob could hear the smile in Ramirez's voice.

"Why would you do that?"

"I wanted to know more about you, Robert. Is that a problem?" He chuckled to himself. "She's sending the transcript to me straight away."

Rob swiped his hand across his forehead. "Sir, you know I would never divulge anything that would put our work in jeopardy. I did the interview to talk about my music career."

"The size of your ego amazes me sometimes, Evans. If nothing else, I'm sure that hearing you boast about yourself will provide a few minutes of entertainment for me and my associates."

"Sir, with all due respect, I don't think that's appropriate."

"You don't think that's appropriate?" Ramirez roared with laughter. "You really need a sense of humor. Enjoy your trip back to Tennessee. I'll look forward to seeing you and meeting your beautiful, naive, and might I add, *very compliant*, bride-to-be. She's the perfect woman, you know, Robert. Marry her as soon as you can so she can't testify against you."

He hung up the phone.

Rob stared into the bathroom mirror. His cover story may have been a sham. His retirement plans seemed to be going awry.

But he was smarter than the rest of them, and that included Ramirez. He just needed time to think.

A loud knock on his bedroom door jarred him from his dilemma.

"What is it?"

"Boss, one of the band guys has a question. I told him he needed to wait, but he said it was important."

"I'll be there in a minute." Danni yelled across the room as Caleb settled into a booth near the front of the restaurant. It was his favorite place to sit. He could keep an eye on the front entrance and still watch Danni work.

She ran a tight ship. It was no accident her restaurant had become one of the best known and loved in Nashville. While he was watching her and her crew cleaning and checking every table, one of the kitchen workers came to her about a sack of flour that had been found on the storeroom floor.

"Throw it out," Danni told the girl. "It's better to lose a bag of flour than to take a chance on harming one of our customers."

Even after one of the sous chefs tried to convince her the flour was okay, despite potential exposure to the flood water a couple of days ago, Danni stuck to her guns, suggesting the outside appearance of the sack didn't tell the full story.

The irony was not lost on Caleb. Why would a woman who sought out perfection in her work settle for someone as lacking as Robert Evans? Then again, why would she be interested in someone like him? His past wasn't much better than Evans's. It was only by God's grace that he had moved beyond it.

Evans's surface appearance might be untarnished, but Caleb knew you didn't have to dig deep to find the real man, tainted by the greed of drug money. And he didn't seem to be the least bit concerned about his customers, young men and women, some only twelve or thirteen, who would be lured into drugs because of the convenience of buying them.

Even some kids who initially resisted would eventually buy into them because of peer pressure and the illusion that drugs wouldn't harm them. Like most people in today's culture, they had been conditioned to think it was only the unlucky few who drew the bullet. And they all trusted their own luck.

He had thought the same thing when he was younger. Unfortunately, it was Jonathan who had taken the bullet. Part of Caleb had also died that day. The other part had to live with the regret, guilt, and the dread that his mistake had cost his brother's life— and that someone else he loved could be taken from him. Which had left him with only one choice. If he spent all of his time trying to rid the world of the bad guys and educating kids, it would leave no time to lose his heart—

"You look like a man who could use a good cup of coffee and a bowl of apple crisp." Jaycee broke into Caleb's self-absorbed, internal monologue, setting a cup of steaming coffee and a dish of sweet-smelling dessert in front of him.

"How did you know?"

The chef smiled. "That you wanted coffee?"

"No," he said. "That apple crisp is my favorite dessert?" The smell of cinnamon-covered apples took Caleb back to his childhood.

She lowered herself into a seat across the table from him. "Well, my first clue was that you're from the South." She raised an eyebrow. "But who doesn't love cinnamon, brown sugar, and apples all rolled into one?"

"Especially with fresh cream on top." Caleb ceremonially toasted her in mid-air before pouring a half-cup of cream from the pitcher she had placed on the table.

Jaycee laughed.

Before setting the pitcher back on the table, he splashed a small amount of cream into his coffee. "This is good for my heart, isn't it?"

"Well . . . maybe not long-term." She grinned. "But it's good comfort food."

"I needed that tonight."

She sobered. "You appeared to be a bit introspective."

He took a bite, and the flavor took him back to his childhood. "This tastes just like my mother used to make."

"She probably used the same recipe. It's straight from the Betty Crocker cookbook that most of our moms used when we were growing up."

Caleb laughed and shook his head, "I thought you were some fancy kind of chef."

She laughed. "Most people think the same thing, that chefs are supposed to always be creating innovative new recipes with *contemporary cultural significance*." She pronounced the final words with a fake, intellectual flare. "But it's often the time-tested ideas that work best."

"You're a wise woman." He took another bite. "Whatever you do, don't mess with this recipe."

Jaycee sobered again. "So . . . what has you so worried tonight? I could tell from the back of the room that you have a lot on your mind."

"Honestly?"

"Absolutely."

He hesitated. "Maybe a little bit of everything."

She nodded.

He took his watch off and laid it on the table in front of her. "This belonged to my brother Jonathan, who was killed when he was a young man."

Jaycee studied the watch but said nothing.

"I was only a few years older, so needless to say, it was a life-changing event for me." He cleared his throat, not sure whether to go on.

When she didn't speak, he continued. "I decided then and there not to risk my heart again. You know, not to get close to people, because I might lose someone else."

"How's that working out for you?" She had both compassion and mischief in her eyes.

He laughed. "Not too well."

"I didn't think so." She tapped the table with her fingertips. "If you figure it out, you could get rich selling it to the rest of us. None of us want to be hurt any more than we have to—"

She hesitated, seeing Danni approaching from the far side of the restaurant.

"Just remember one thing."

Caleb set his napkin on the table and leaned back in his chair.

"Perfect love drives out all fear."

"Hey, there. The two of you look serious." Danni stepped up to the table. "What's going on?"

"We were just debating about another piece of apple crisp." Jaycee stood and reached for Caleb's bowl.

Danni settled into the seat next to her. "None for me, thanks. But I will have a cup of coffee, if you're heading back to the kitchen."

"Absolutely," Jaycee said. "Caleb?"

"No, thanks. I'm good right now." He patted his stomach. "But after you return, let's make sure we all know what we're doing tomorrow."

CHAPTER 39

Sunday – April 21

When Rob walked in the front door of Amoré at one o'clock on Sunday afternoon, Danni was ready to leave. The less time he spent at the restaurant the better.

"Are you okay if we look at rings before we eat?" Rob planted a kiss on Danni's cheek.

"Works for me." She said, throwing her handbag over her arm.

They had almost made it out the front door when one of Amoré's servers stopped them. "Ms. Kemp, do you know if that police officer will be back today?" A watch dangled from the girl's fingers. "He left this at his table last night."

"Oh . . . I don't know." Danni gave a sideways glance to Rob. "I don't expect him, Meg. Just give it to Jaycee to keep."

"She's not working today, ma'am. It's Sunday."

"Of course. Tell you what. Give it to me. I'll put it in the safe when I return."

"Yes, ma'am." The server handed Danni the watch, smiled flirtatiously at Rob, and then took off for the kitchen.

"Why have the police been hanging around here?" Rob scowled as he opened the door.

Danni slipped Caleb's watch into the zippered pocket of her handbag. "Maybe because one of our servers died of a drug overdose." She kept walking. "Which way to your car?"

Rob nodded to the left and latched onto her elbow. "Those idiots who take drugs never cease to amaze me. What do they expect if they're going to play with fire?"

Danni resisted the urge to slap him. Instead, she reached back into her handbag for her sunglasses. She had never been good at lying. It was probably a good idea to hide her eyes and keep her mouth shut.

"It's bright out today, isn't it?" Rob opened the passenger side door of his car for her and then walked to the driver's side.

They remained silent while Rob fought his way through the maze of downtown construction and lunch-hour traffic. Busier still was Hillsboro Road, the main access road to Green Hills, Nashville's premier shopping area for urban dwellers. Traffic to and from the mall could be even worse than downtown.

"So tell me about your trip." She broached a noncontroversial topic as they neared the Green Hills Mall.

"It was okay." He glanced her way. "But I'm getting ready to make some big changes." Pulling to a stop at the next red light, he reached to take her hand, massaging her ring finger.

"I was going to wait and tell you later, but since we're talking about it now, I have a wedding gift for you."

What now? She didn't want or need another gift from him.

He patted her hand, returning his attention to the road. "I'm making plans to retire this year."

Danni's hand flew to her heart. "Seriously?"

He laughed. "I knew you would be surprised. Can you believe it?"

"No! Rob . . . I can't even . . . why? You love your work."

"I know." He eased into the right lane, and then turned right into the mall parking lot. "I've been putting money away for a while so I can slow down and enjoy life." He glanced to her again. "I'd like for us to travel. Maybe buy a place in the islands."

Danni forced air from her lungs. "I-I'm shocked. I don't know what to say. I mean, I still have my career, and it's a time-consuming job, and . . ."

He found a parking place near the front of the mall and pulled to a stop.

"No worries, babe. You can travel with me as you can. I'll be home most of the time, and that's another surprise I want to talk to you about. But let's relax right now and enjoy the day. We can talk about everything after lunch."

A few minutes later they walked hand in hand into Swartz Jewelry, a well-established family-owned store known for its prestigious brands and celebrity customers.

Danni's eyes widened as they walked toward the back of the store, passing displays of everything from tiny charms to expensive watches encrusted with diamonds.

"I have an appointment," Rob caught the attention of the first available clerk. "It's Robert Evans."

"Yes, Mr. Evans." The clerk demurred. "Our manager will be right with you."

The woman left to retrieve the manager, and within a few minutes, a smiling, middle-aged man wearing wire-rimmed glasses appeared from the back. "Robert! How nice to see you again."

He shook Rob's hand and turned to Danni. "And this must be—?"

"Danielle." Rob grinned from ear to ear.

The manager, who was introduced as Henry, grabbed her hand and held it. "You are a lucky man," he gushed in Rob's direction, and then looking back to Danni said, "Congratulations on your impending marriage."

"Thank you." Danni shifted her gaze to the rows of wedding bands and solitaires. This was more awkward than she had imagined.

"Danielle and Robert, please have a seat. Would you like coffee or tea?" Henry asked.

"Not for me." Danni said.

"We have lunch plans later," Rob said, ushering Danni to a chair near a large display case.

"Then let's get started! We'll find the perfect ring for this perfect bride."

"Show us only the best," Rob said.

"Of course, sir." Henry smiled, pushed his glasses higher up on his nose and rolled up his sleeves, while no doubt counting dollar signs. He selected several samples for their perusal.

It's you I should love. Not the ring. The phrase kept playing over and over in Danni's mind as she and Rob exhausted their search for what Henry had called the "perfect" ring.

Finally, after everyone's enthusiasm had almost run its course, the store manager took a seat. "If nothing I've shown you catches your eye, we can design something for you. But you won't, of course, be able to walk out of here with it today."

"I'm just not seeing it," Danni said. "I want something simple. Almost plain, but unique."

"Wait!" The smile returned to the manager's face. "I have something in the back."

When he returned with the ring, he held it out for both of them to see. Rays of light scattered from every angle. Danni's heart took a plunge. She had to admit it was the perfect ring. Simple but elegant.

Rob grabbed her hand. "Try it on."

She put it on her finger and slid it in place. It fit perfectly.

Henry raised an eyebrow and grinned. "Oh, yes . . ."

Rob nodded his approval as Danni admired the sparkling bauble. It looked great on her hand.

"It fits you beautifully." Henry gushed. "You have exquisite taste."

"I—I don't know." Danni now regretted even trying it on. How could she say no? She loved it.

"What do you think?" Rob was hovering, hanging on her decision. And appeared to be almost nervous.

Why was he so eager now to have her in his life, to marry her? He hadn't been around when she needed him. For the break-in. Or the flood. Or even when her father had nearly died.

She shook her head. "No . . . this isn't it. There's something about it that's not quite right."

Henry and Rob deflated simultaneously.

"I don't think I can make a decision today." She took off the ring, handed it to the store manager, and leaned back in her chair.

Rob squirmed in his seat.

"Are you sure?"

"Yes. I'll know it when I see it." She assured him. "Can we eat lunch now? I'm starving."

After lunch at a restaurant in the mall, Rob escorted Danni to the car. "I think we should elope, with or without a ring." He took her hand. "I want my new life to start with you in it."

"Rob, I'm already planning the wedding."

"Can't you cancel what you've started? It's not like the invitations are ordered. You told me the other day that it was a lot of work."

"I know, but—" *Was that desperation in his eyes?*

"Danielle, please. Think about it." He opened the car door for her.

"Okay. I promise. I will."

"Good." His smile returned. He expected her to give in, as she always had.

"Now, I want to show you something." He said, taking the driver's seat. "I have another appointment for us." He looked at his watch. "In ten minutes."

"Where?"

"You'll see." He grinned and started the car.

Two blocks up the street, on their way toward downtown, he eased his Mercedes into the left lane.

"Why are we turning here?"

"Just wait." He patted her hand and smiled. "It's a surprise."

Danni sat back into her seat and enjoyed the scenery. Woodmont Avenue was lined with beautiful older homes in a fairytale setting. Each home had a manicured lawn, and most were set back from the street in a small grove of trees and featured exquisitely designed landscaping. A number of the larger homes had circular drives.

For years, it had been one of the most exclusive addresses in Nashville. At least by Danni's estimation. She had driven down Woodmont countless times to and from meetings or to shop at the mall. Convenient to downtown, most of Woodmont Boulevard's stately homes and mansions were off-limits to even upper-middle class families.

"Why are we stopping?" She asked, as Rob pulled into the circular drive of a beautiful two-story brick.

"I told you, we have an appointment." He checked his watch again.

"Here?"

"There she is." A silver Lexus pulled into the driveway in front of them. Then Danni noticed the realtor sign in the front yard. *Offered exclusively by Mansion & Manor Realty. Shown by appointment only.* Even the real estate signs in this neighborhood touted its exclusivity.

"Why?"

She had been reduced to monosyllables. And Rob couldn't wipe the smile from his face.

"Because you've always wanted to live on this street. And I want a nice place to raise a family. And to live with my wife." He emphasized the last word.

Was this a test of her strength? To her commitment to stay true to the right thing? The house in front of her was the home of her dreams with its Old South architecture and its manicured lawn.

Within minutes, the tall, blond realtor had unlocked the front door. The entry inside featured a winding staircase. The completely remodeled kitchen would be a chef's delight. Danni could imagine inviting Jaycee over to spend the evening inventing new entrees. And the fenced-in backyard was perfect for Sophie. Or a pool party. Or a garden.

But while Sophie would tolerate Rob, Jaycee couldn't. The truth was, she would be spending evenings in this big place with Rob. Alone.

And that thought was not inviting.

The biggest surprise of the day, despite what Rob might have planned, was how easily she could envision her life without him. And this house, which from outside appearances was everything she had ever wanted, could never be her home.

CHAPTER 40

After saying their goodbyes to the realtor, Rob turned his white Mercedes toward the Rutherford. He was still babbling on and on about the house. He loved the den. He loved the wine cellar. He loved the pool.

Never once today did he tell Danni how much he loved her. But he did ask her for a favor. He wanted her to help him with a business deal he had to close before he retired. He asked if she would go with him.

"When is it?" she asked.

"I'm not sure yet," he said, looking somewhat confused about the whole issue.

"Then I can't tell you for sure. I'll do my best" was all she could say as he pulled in front of the restaurant to drop her off.

"Where are you going from here?" she asked.

"I'll stop by my office and then head on home to make phone calls. I need to organize a few things, since I'll be working from home for a while."

"Why is that?"

He frowned. "I told you I'm retiring from the road. What about that do you not understand?"

Danni recoiled. "Sorry. I guess I'm just stupid." She opened the car door to get out, and he grabbed her elbow.

"I'm sorry. Please stay." He took a moment to compose himself. "Danni, I'm sorry. These changes are hard for me. As I'm sure they will be for you. But please have patience with me while I adjust."

She nodded and gripped the handle on the door. He was beginning to scare her. The Rob Evans she knew had never begged. Or shown fear. But within the passing of a minute she had seen both.

Something big had to be getting ready to happen, just like Caleb had warned. And it must be bad. Rob was out of control.

"Rob." She chose her words deliberately. "I'm here, just like I always have been."

He smiled and leaned forward to kiss her on the cheek.

As she waved goodbye from the sidewalk in front of Amoré, one question haunted her. Although the answer didn't really matter. *Why now?* Why did he need her so much now when he hadn't seemed to need her before? The possible answers to that question sent a shiver up her spine.

As she opened the front door of the restaurant movement in her peripheral vision caught her attention. It was Agent Matheson. He winked and held the door for her, following her inside.

She had wondered how close the TBI had been watching today. Although she hadn't noticed anyone, Caleb had promised she would be under intense surveillance while she was with Rob. Not because they didn't trust her, but to keep her safe.

And even though Caleb had spent the afternoon with Zach, he had assured her they would be praying for her. That thought made her smile. So did knowing she would be hearing from him before the end of the day, to check in with her and to let her know if she would need to wear a wire at dinner.

Dinner? Rob hadn't mentioned going to dinner. Maybe she should call him and ask if he wanted her to bring something home. But before she could pick up her phone, a flurry of work-related calls kept her busy for an hour. Then Amoré's pre-dinner traffic started to arrive.

"Are you in Nashville, Robert?"

It was Ramirez. Perhaps his wait would be over, and he could get this last job behind him.

"Yes, sir. I flew into town yesterday."

"And the shipment?"

"Should have already been delivered, sir. The bus will be back in Nashville tonight."

"Good. That means we can move forward with the completion of our final business."

Rob breathed easier. "I'm ready, sir. What do you need from me?"

"I need you to stay vigilant," Ramirez said. "Did you learn anything about that cop your girlfriend has been spending time with?"

"I can tell you it's nothing to worry about. He's investigating the death of one of Danni's coworkers, there's nothing personal—"

A message alert pinged on Rob's phone.

"Go ahead. Check your text." Ramirez chuckled.

Rob clicked on the message icon. At the top of the list was a message from an unknown sender. It was a photo.

Of Danni? He clicked to enlarge the picture, and his heart dropped. It *was* a photo of Danni. The Parthenon at Centennial Park was in the background, and she was kissing another man.

"Are you convinced now, Robert?"

Rob's response caught in his throat. He'd been a fool.

"Who is he?" he asked, his voice measured.

"He's your girlfriend's new best friend, Mr. Evans. He works for the Tennessee Bureau of Investigation. Do you see now why I've been so concerned?"

Rob slumped into the bucket seat of his Mercedes. Everything. *Everything.* Was falling apart.

And suddenly Ramirez became his only hope.

"What do I need to do, sir?"

"Stay vigilant, Robert, just like I said. We will get through this. I have a plan." Ramirez sounded both comforting and cocky. "But you must follow it to the letter."

"Yes, sir. Anything, sir."

"The stakes have been raised this afternoon. In fact I have a few surprises for you. But you'll find out about those soon enough."

Rob remained quiet.

"Keep your schedule clear for the next few days. I may call you on a moment's notice. When I come to town, we will take care of all of this."

"You're coming to town, sir?" But Ramirez had hung up.

Rob dropped the phone to his lap and collapsed onto the steering wheel of his car.

What had Danni done? And what would it take to get him out of this mess?

A few minutes past five o'clock, Caleb's number lit up Danni's cell phone. She rushed into her office and closed the door. Finally she would have a chance to tell him about her day.

After hearing about Rob's unexpected plans to retire, and seeing the desperation in his eyes, she needed the reassurance that Caleb had never failed to deliver.

"How are you?" she asked.

"Not well."

"Caleb?"

"I'm here." His voice cracked. "But Zach has disappeared."

Danni fell into her office chair.

"After I dropped him off for the day, his mom let him go outside to play, and he never came home."

"There has to be an explanation. He's at a friend's house or—"

"No." Caleb interrupted her. "Ginny, his mother, has already received a call. Zach has been kidnapped, and he's being held for ransom."

CHAPTER 41

D anni paced around her office, one hand holding her phone, the other cradling her forehead as the possibilities raced through her mind. But everything led back to her first, horrible thought.

"Is his disappearance related to the narcotics ring?"

"We don't know. We suspect it is."

"But the only connection is . . ." She stopped when she realized what she was about to say.

"Me. The only connection is *me*." Caleb completed her sentence. "Nice, huh? I've managed to draw an innocent boy into this."

This was no time for blame. She could wallow in it too. Right now, they had to be proactive. "How can I help?"

"Are you going to dinner with Evans tonight?"

"He hasn't asked yet."

"If you think you can make it happen, I want you wired."

"Anything." Danni leaned against her office door, wondering what madness might walk into her life next.

"I'll send Agent Wade to the restaurant. She's back at work, and she'll get you set up."

"Okay."

"I'll have her call you. I need to run."

"I'll try to reach Rob and arrange for us to get together."

He mumbled something away from the phone. Then, "Thank you." He hesitated. "I'll be back in touch as soon as I can."

"Be careful."

"I was about to tell you the same thing." Unspoken words hung in the air between them. "Jamie will be in touch."

With that he disconnected the call.

Danni lowered her phone to her desk. What a mess she had made of her life. And the lives of others. All because she had been infatuated with Rob Evans.

How could she have been so blind? Because she had believed that money meant security. She had bought into his decadent life-style—her decadent lifestyle, she might as well admit it—at the expense of others.

Tears rimmed her eyes, but she refused to oblige them. She had too much to do to waste time feeling sorry for herself. She collected her thoughts, picked up the phone, and dialed Rob. If he knew anything—anything—she would get it out of him tonight. Within thirty minutes she had dinner plans with Rob at her place, and Agent Wade was on her way to Amoré to install the wire.

One more thing had to be handled. Danni stood, crossed the room, and opened her office door. Jaycee was standing there, her hand in midair about to knock.

"What are you doing here? You're supposed to be off today."

"I was worried. You've been on my mind all day." The normally upbeat chef wore a concerned look on her face. "I had to come."

"Step inside." Danni opened the door wider. "I need your help."

Jaycee slipped through the door and closed it behind her.

"Have a seat." Danni nodded to a chair.

Jaycee set her handbag on the floor and took a seat. Danni leaned against her desk. "I'll give you the five-minute recap, and then I have a request."

The chef listened without interrupting. When Danni stopped talking, she asked, "What can I do besides pray? I've already got that part covered."

"I need you to prepare two dinners for me to take home in—" she glanced at the clock on the wall—"an hour. I'm going to do my best to pry the truth out of Rob tonight. If he knows anything about Zach's disappearance, I'll find out."

Jaycee stood. "Veal Piccata okay?"

"Yes, he'll love that."

"With risotto and asparagus." She paused to think. "And *zuppa inglese* with fresh fruit for dessert."

"That's perfect, Jay."

"I'm on it." The chef took off for the door, then turned back and enveloped Danni in a hug.

"It will work out," she said. "In fact, God already has it handled. Do the best you can, and let Him take care of the rest."

Danni nodded, forcing a weak smile. Trusting God was the only thing left.

Although she did have an idea that might help move things along.

Caleb walked the circumference of his office and back again, trying to put the pieces together. His heart told him to pound doors and turn over every rock to find Zach. But his training reminded him it was best to stay here.

They knew with little doubt who had taken the boy, which meant an ordinary street search wasn't going to help. Zach was most likely already out of town, whisked away before anyone even knew he was missing. Ramirez's crew wouldn't risk showing their hand unless they knew they were holding aces.

The logical next step was to prepare for a phone call. Or hope Robert Evans had information that would give them a lead.

Caleb slammed his fist against the wall.

The boy would have been better off without him in his life. How could he have let him down like this? He should have known Ramirez was capable of anything. But a ten-year-old child?

I should have watched Zach closer and instructed Ginny Franklin to take extra precautions. There were so many things he would have done differently, if only he had a do-over. A second chance.

And then he remembered Zach had been his second chance. Had he learned nothing from his brother Jonathan's death? You play with fire, and you get burned.

Almost on cue, Caleb's phone pinged. It was a message from Ginny Franklin.

Caleb, I just received this. PLEASE tell me what to do.

Attached to the message was a video. It was Zach. His feet and hands were bound, and he was leaning against a wall next to a blond woman whose face had been obscured.

Caleb pushed play on his screen, and Zach came to life. The boy's voice was strong.

"Caleb, please help me. And tell my mom I love her."

The video went dark. And Caleb struggled to maintain his composure. The boy was stronger than he. Zachary hadn't given up. He trusted Caleb to get him through this.

And he would.

Caleb started out the door. He had to get the tape to forensics. Maybe they could trace—

And then he remembered. He stopped walking and bowed his head. *Father, please don't let me take this into my own hands. I know how that story ends.*

He had been running away from God when Jonathan was killed. This time he wanted God on his side. The image of Zach in the video played over in his head, and Caleb's own prayer echoed the boy's words.

Please help me, he prayed as he rushed out the door.

By seven o'clock, Danni had everything ready. Jamie and another female agent had installed the wire, which wasn't really a wire at all. It was a digital device small enough to fit on Danni's fitness bracelet, something Rob was used to seeing her wear.

Now . . . she had to relax and forget it was there.

The candles were lit and the dinner was warming on chafing candles. She checked her hair in the hall mirror. As soon as she'd gotten home, she had changed clothes and touched up her makeup.

She had also fed Sophie, which included giving the dog her nightly dose of calming tincture. The stuff had worked miracles for the Newfoundland. Danni hoped it would work as well on Rob.

She read the instructions on the bottle. It was purely homeopathic, odorless, and colorless. And if it was safe for canines, it must be safe for humans. She had made up her mind. If Rob hadn't told her what she needed to know by the end of dinner, she would be serving *zuppa inglese ala relaxation* for dessert.

When he arrived a few minutes later, he looked beaten down. Either planning for retirement was harder than working, or something bad had happened since she had seen him. She guessed it was the latter.

Now to get him to talk about it.

She kissed him lightly on the lips and led him to the dining room. After he had taken his usual seat at the head of the table, she poured their drinks and chatted about her afternoon.

"We were crazy busy today; how were things at your office?"

"Oh . . . I wasn't there for long. I came home early and tried to take a nap."

Danni took a step back for dramatic effect. "And you still look tired. But you've been on the road for almost a month."

He nodded. "That's probably why I'm tired." He averted his gaze, changing the subject. "Where's Sophia?"

"Sophie? She's already in bed asleep. She's been anxious about something lately, and it's wearing her out." Danni scooped veal onto Rob's plate. "Maybe that's why you're so tired. Have you been under a lot of pressure?"

"Yes, some. You know how work is."

"You seem extra tired tonight, Rob." With silver tongs, she arranged stalks of asparagus artfully beside his entrée. "Maybe you should see your doctor?"

"I'll be okay. I just need to rest." He flickered a smile as he unfolded his napkin.

"Jaycee made your favorite risotto." She handed the plate to him and then prepared hers before taking a seat beside him.

"Here's to us." She said picking up her water glass.

"Yes, to us," he said, raising his glass.

"So—" she took a bite—"tell me about your schedule for the next week."

Rob put down his fork. "What is it with your game of twenty questions tonight?"

Danni swallowed. Fanning her throat, she took a sip of water. "Oh, sorry. That bite went down wrong." She dotted her napkin to her mouth. "I guess I'm just giddy." She smiled. "With looking at rings and houses today."

He nodded, seeming to relax. "I understand, babe. It's a big life change." He picked up his fork and took a bite of the risotto. "This is delicious. Tell Jaycee I appreciate her making it for me."

While they finished eating dinner, Danni told Rob about her trip to Iowa, shared her challenges at work, and joked about how Jaycee wanted to join her choir at church.

Rob seemed to enjoy the meal and letting her carry the weight of the conversation. For once he stayed off the phone and never broached the subject of his work. As she cleared the plates, she knew it was time to implement her plan.

"Would you like coffee with dessert?"

"That sounds great. Can we eat in the living room?" He stood.

"Of course. I'll make the coffee and bring it right in. Why don't you turn on the TV?" There was no way he would see her spike his dessert if he was watching television in the next room.

Danni retreated to the kitchen, pulled two parfait glasses from the cabinet, and filled them with Jaycee's decadent concoction of pudding, sponge cake, and fruit. The fragrance of the rum flavoring the chef had sprinkled on the fruit was enticing. Even if the tincture hadn't been odorless, the exotic scent would have masked it perfectly.

Danni decided she'd better check on Rob and serve the coffee before she made her final move. She filled a mug to the brim and took it into him.

"That looks great. Thanks, babe." He smiled and resumed his channel surfing.

She returned to the kitchen, wiped her brow with a napkin, and tossed it into the trashcan. Finally, she took a deep breath. She could do this. Slipping the vial from the spice drawer, she unscrewed the lid, which was attached to an eyedropper. If five drops worked for Sophie, they should work for Rob.

She squeezed the bulb once and a drop of tincture fell into the pudding. Four more squeezes and . . . oops. Two drops fell into the pudding for a total of six. Should she try to spoon the extra out? No, that would risk not giving him enough.

She would go with it. Hopefully he wouldn't fall asleep before she had gotten what she needed. She returned the vial to the drawer and picked up both parfait glasses, carrying hers in her left hand and his with her right hand. When she walked into the living room, Rob didn't even look up. She set her dessert on the side table next to her chair and took a step toward him.

As he reached for it, the doorbell rang.

CHAPTER 42

W hen Danni opened the door, her heart took a plunge. Four men stood in the hall holding guns. And badges.

"Tennessee Bureau of Investigation, ma'am," one man said before charging past her. Two more followed him, leaving Caleb standing in the hallway. He nodded at her and then rushed in behind the other men.

She spun around in time to see Rob drop the remote.

"Are you Robert Evans?" One of the men now stood over him. Rob nodded.

"Mr. Evans, you're under arrest for transporting narcotics across the state line with the intent to sell."

"What?" Rob looked to Danni. "Do you know anything about this?"

She stood there, holding his parfait in midair, unable to respond.

"Please stand up, sir."

He obliged, shaking his head.

"Cross your wrists behind your back and turn around."

"Get your hands off me," Rob protested. "I have a right to an attorney."

"Yes, sir, you do. And we'll be happy to provide a phone. But first I need to read you your rights."

"Danni!" Rob screeched, his back to her. "You had something to do with this, didn't you?"

305

She walked to the nearest chair and braced herself against it.

"No." The word came out as a whimper.

Caleb stepped to her side. He was with her. She could do this.

She straightened her shoulders. "This is your mess, Rob, not mine."

"But I'm innocent, babe, don't you see? I'm being framed." He turned in her direction, his face contorted and red.

"If you're not guilty, I'll fight right along beside you."

The muscles in Caleb's jaw tensed.

Danni directed one final vow to Rob. "But if you're guilty, I'll help them put you away."

Before he could respond, the arresting officer grabbed him by the shoulder and propelled him forward, and for the second time today Danni witnessed a broken and bitter Rob Evans. The charm was gone. The expensive clothes didn't matter. And fear clouded his striking blue eyes.

As the officer led him past her, Rob shook his head, and then looked away. "You will regret this."

Danni slumped, but Caleb caught her. He took the parfait glass in one hand, holding her upright with the other, and walked her around the chair. Setting the dish on the side table, he eased her into the chair.

"Wait here. I'll be right back."

She nodded, praying she wouldn't faint. Hoping if she did that she would wake up to find this was a nightmare. But remembering Zach, she knew it wasn't. For his sake, she fought to maintain her consciousness. She couldn't put any of this behind her until the boy was home safe.

Caleb escorted his fellow agents to the elevator.

"We've got this," Langley told him. "Take care of the girl."

"I appreciate it." Caleb slapped him on the shoulder in celebration of their victory. A bittersweet one in light of the circumstances. Zach was still being held, probably hundreds of miles away, and his safety depended on how they handled the next twenty-four hours.

If they didn't keep Evans's arrest a secret, Ramirez might react. And a sudden defensive move could be deadly for Zach. They were better off to let Ramirez's plans play out, to let him show his hand. Then, with the combined resources of the Feds and the TBI, they could stack the deck in their favor.

At least that was what he hoped.

When he returned to Danni's condo, she was still sitting where he had left her. He settled into the chair beside her.

"Are you okay?"

She tipped her chin toward him. "I'm not sure what just happened."

"We received new information." Before he could explain, movement in his peripheral vision caught his attention. He turned to see Sophie amble into the room. The dog stopped and stared at him. "She looks relaxed."

"Tincture," Danni said. "I was about to give some to Rob."

"Huh?"

"Never mind." She waved away the question. "Tell me why you're here. I thought I was—"

"The Feds got to his bus driver. They intercepted him en route to deliver a load of narcotics in Atlanta." A cell phone caught Caleb's attention. "Is this Rob's?"

She nodded.

He slipped it into his pocket and resumed his explanation. The driver confessed everything, explained how the operation worked, gave them times and dates, and showed them the goods. He basically sold Evans out in exchange for a lighter sentence."

She clasped her shaking hands. "So Rob's going to prison?"

"Yes, for a long time. I'm sorry." This couldn't be easy for her. Whether she liked Evans now or not, she had loved him at one time.

"Don't be." She stiffened. "It's his doing. Zach is my concern."

"That's why I'm here. I think I can get more out of Evans than you were."

The corners of her mouth formed a faint smile. "My interrogation skills are lacking, aren't they?"

"It's not that. We have leverage now. Securing the bus driver's statement and a hundred pounds of cocaine can make all the difference."

"That much?"

"Yes, over a half billion dollar's worth."

"No wonder Rob was planning to buy a house on Woodmont Boulevard."

Caleb startled. "When did you find that out?"

"Today on our outing. He took me to see it. It was supposed to be my wedding present."

His expression darkened. "I'm afraid most guys couldn't offer you something like that."

Danni held her left arm out to him. "Take it off."

When he didn't move, she persisted. "Take the recording device off my wristband. She pointed to it with her free hand. "I don't need it anymore, do I?"

"No, you don't. I'll disable it for you." He detached the device from the plastic band, neutralized it, and slipped it into his pocket.

"Were you about to say something you didn't want recorded?"

"Just that I can't be bought. Not with drug money. Not when I know about it anyway." Her green eyes searched his face. "I just want you to know that a big house isn't important to me. I figured that out this afternoon."

"I knew that," he said. "Probably even before you did."

CHAPTER 43

The next morning – April 22

The following morning at eight o'clock sharp, Caleb called.

"Are you still at home?"

"Just about to leave."

"Stay there. I'll pick you up in twenty minutes. Evans heard from Ramirez this morning. I've arranged an impromptu meeting for everyone on our team."

So that was why Caleb had taken Rob's cell phone.

Timely as usual, Caleb knocked on her door in almost exactly twenty minutes. He looked tired, but he had to be with the weight of the world and a young boy's life resting on his shoulders. Interestingly, her personal insomnia had somewhat eased now that Caleb was firmly entrenched in her life.

"Where are we going?" She asked as she climbed into his truck.

"The Criminal Justice Center, also known as the county jail."

"Can't say I've ever been there before."

"Hang with me, baby. I'll show you the world." Even if he was tired, he still had his sense of humor.

She glanced his way. "I would love that."

Caleb reached across the console to take her hand in his. "I hope you mean it."

He pulled into a parking spot marked "official vehicles only" and walked around to open her door.

"Why are we meeting here?"

His expression sobered. "Because we may call Evans into the meeting. Can you handle that?"

"I guess I don't have a choice."

His smile reached his eyes, and he helped her out of the truck.

Danni tugged at her jacket as they walked inside the two-story red brick building. This was a different world from the one she had been living. And she had the feeling it had become as much a part of her future as it was her present. She glanced at the handsome man walking beside her.

Caleb opened the front door of the Davidson County sheriff's administrative offices, which was adjacent to the Hill Building Detention Center. He acknowledged the guard at the front desk and greeted Martin Ridge, who appeared to be waiting for their arrival. It was the first time Danni had seen him since the game of good cop, bad cop at police headquarters three months ago. Hopefully he had a better feeling about her now.

He greeted her. She nodded. And Caleb grabbed her elbow and escorted her down the hallway, through a security door, and into a second corridor. This place made the police headquarters look like a swanky resort. The gymnasium-like acoustics amplified every sound, from the *click, click, click* of her heels on the tile floor to the rustle of Ridge's suit.

Caleb, however, appeared to move effortlessly with a confident, deliberate gait. He fit in perfectly here but still rose above his environment. Danni had no doubt that, despite the terrible circumstances that had catapulted him into this life, he had been created for it.

They stopped just short of the end of the hall, and Ridge opened the door to a small conference room on the left.

"Everyone else is already here," he said, inviting Danni to walk ahead of him.

As she entered the rectangular room, more than a dozen men and women looked in her direction. Caleb steered her to the nearest chair and took the seat to her right. Ridge sat on her left. It was like having her own personal security team.

Jamie Wade, who was sitting directly across the table, greeted Danni with a smile, but there were no other familiar faces. The seat at the head of the table was empty. Was it for Rob?

Within a few seconds, the man sitting next to Jamie called the meeting to order. He introduced himself as Sam Wiley of the FBI. The men to the right of him were also FBI. Two other men worked with the DEA. Another was with ATF—the Bureau of Alcohol, Tobacco, Firearms and Explosives. Despite a knack for remembering names, Danni couldn't remember any of them, except Wiley, by the end of the introductions.

Caleb took the floor to introduce her. He praised her for her courage and explained that without her help they might not be this far along. At the end of his monologue, everyone applauded.

"I'm not sure how much I've done." She directed her words to Caleb.

Wiley stood and walked to a white board behind him.

"For those who don't already know, and I believe all of you do, with the possible exception of Ms. Kemp, Ramirez called Evans this morning, which is exactly what we had hoped would happen." He made an imaginary mark in the air. "Score one for the good guys."

Everyone laughed.

"Are we ready with the audio?" He directed the question to the man at the far end of the table. "Let's roll it. This is the recording of that call." He signaled the tech to begin.

Robert, I now have the final arrangements.

Okay.

Rob's voice wavered. Danni almost felt sorry for him. Almost.

In two days, I want you to meet me on a farm near the Tennessee-Kentucky state line. It's the vacation home of a country star who is on tour right now, so we'll have our privacy. Be there at three o'clock in the afternoon, and bring your bus. I will have the merchandise with me, along with two special guests.

Who are the guests? It was Rob speaking.

Do you remember the lovely Cassia Noelle?

Yes.

I've learned that she has been working for both sides. In fact, I've had more than one security breach in the past few days. Shortly after your driver delivered product in Atlanta, my facility there was raided. Did you know about that?"

No, sir! Not at all. Breaches aren't good.

Breaches aren't good, Evans. And, unfortunately, you're the common denominator in both.

I know nothing about them, sir.

I will need to talk with your driver.

Yes, sir.

Also on the plane will be a boy by the name of Zachary. He's a fine young man. His mother will be sending a stipend for his return.

You kidnapped a child?

Robert, I would never do something like that. You need to trust me.

An evil laugh from Ramirez made Danni's skin crawl. How could Rob have been working with such a wicked man?

I do trust you, sir.

Along with the bus and driver, I need you to bring your lovely bride-to-be.

Yes, sir.

Caleb grimaced and tucked his chin.

Is everything clear?

Yes.

Robert. I'm going to trust you not to share this with anyone.

Yes, sir.

Especially the authorities.

I would never do that, sir.

Once this delivery is done, you may retire with my blessing. It will be your independence day.

That sounds great, sir.

By now you should have received a text with directions to the property.

Got it now, sir.

I'll see you in two days, my friend.

The call disconnected, leaving silence in the conference room. Wiley stood and walked back to the white board.

"Here are the bullet points from the call." He picked up a maker from the tray and made notes as he spoke.

"Ramirez will be on site. He will have two hostages with him. One is an FBI undercover agent. The other, we believe, is our missing boy, Zachary."

Wiley moved his marker down the board and wrote, *a possible exchange of merchandise.* He scanned the faces in the room. "This is never going to happen, folks. That's not what this is about."

He put down the marker. "Ramirez may have summoned three people and asked that authorities not be notified, but we believe this is about killing as many people as possible. Not just those he's summoned, and the hostages, but as many law enforcement officers as he can draw into the fight."

A deathly hush filled the room.

Wiley walked back to the table and took a seat. "I'd say he knows we're on to him and that we're taking him down one operation at a time. Or at least he fears that. And he wants retribution."

When Wiley opened the planning discussion, Caleb took the lead.

"Before we talk details about the best way to fortify the farm and to preempt, or at least limit, a deadly strike from Ramirez, I'd like to suggest a female agent fill in for Danielle on site."

Jamie Wade raised her hand. "I'd like to do it."

"You have a baby!" Danni protested. "I can't let you put your life at risk, again, for me. Besides, you have blond hair."

Jamie chuckled. "Hair color is subject to change without notice. Have you forgotten that I'm a hairdresser?" She grew serious. "And this is my job. I'm trained to stay safe. You don't have that kind of training."

"But I got myself into this. I should be the who takes the risk." Danni looked to Caleb. "I don't want anyone taking my place."

Caleb's stomach churned. He couldn't let her do this. "Ramirez is leading you into a trap. You don't understand."

"I do understand. And I want to finish this myself."

CHAPTER 44

Two days later – April 24

aleb watched as Danni stepped confidently aboard the traveling coach. He had to hand it to her, she didn't seem to be bothered by the task at hand. The woman was determined, even downright stubborn, when she set her mind to something.

On the other hand, Robert Evans, who, along with his guard, waited to board behind her, stood on one foot and then the other. He looked a wreck. Incarceration hadn't served him well. To keep news of his arrest off the street, he had been held in solitary confinement for the past few days. He would soon find that was easy compared to life in the general population.

Sam Wiley boarded next. He had Evans's cell phone with him in case the drug boss called with a location adjustment, which would be a smart move for the bad guys and a potentially deadly one for Caleb's team.

Ridge followed Wiley, then Jamie Wade, and Caleb boarded last, pulling the door closed behind him and acknowledging Hank Porter, who was already belted into the driver's seat. Because of his classification as a flight risk, he'd been fitted with a GPS bracelet around his ankle.

Evans, on the other hand, was wearing leg irons.

"What have you done to my bus?" He bellowed as he hobbled to his seat.

"Sit down and shut up." Wiley said. "We had to go through it. Sorry if we didn't put everything back the way you like."

"My attorney will hear about this. I thought if I cooperated, you'd treat me better." His guard directed him to the sofa, then took a seat beside him.

Wiley settled into one of the side chairs. Ridge took the other, leaving Caleb with three choices, sitting next to Evans—a completely undesirable option—riding in the jump seat, or joining Danni and Jamie Wade in the back lounge.

Despite Danni's protests, Agent Wade had been assigned to provide support and backup. Ridge had made the decision yesterday to keep every option in place, so there was still the chance he would substitute the TBI agent for Danni at the last minute. From a distance, the two women looked remarkably alike now that Jamie had changed her hair color.

Caleb chose to lean against the kitchen sink for a while. He wanted to stay in the loop. They still had information coming in. An hour before, they had received confirmation that every member of Ramirez's ground crew was under surveillance and would be neutralized as soon as the plane landed. The FBI, DEA, and highway patrol, as well as the Macon County Sheriff's Department, had joined their offensive operation on the farm near Lafayette, Tennessee, where Ramirez had chosen to rendezvous. It was the Macon County boys who had been the most help. Those guys knew every hill, holler, and back road in the area. They had also pointed out a little-known way into the farm, which could be used for an exit if necessary.

Caleb knew there would be no time for that, however. Today was going to come down to a gun battle. Hopefully, if all of their plans had been executed properly, it would be a short one. And the good guys would win.

An ATF sniper team had been inserted around the landing strip on the property without Ramirez's people's knowledge. More than a dozen highly trained snipers were hiding in trees, behind rocks, and inside farm equipment parked in the nearby field. Drones were being used to maintain visual coordination.

Everything now hinged on God granting them wisdom and skill. If this ended well, Ramirez would be in custody by sunset, making a big dent in illegal drug operations across the South and Southwest. More importantly, Zach would be home with his mother, and the nightmare Danni Kemp had lived during the past several months would be over.

Although everything was weighted in their favor, it would be a tough, and costly, battle. There was no doubt Ramirez had an ambush planned. This wasn't the pickup Robert Evans had been told to expect. Drug bosses didn't sanction early retirement plans, not unless the retiree was carried away in a body bag.

The bus had been on the road for an hour when Ridge saw the sign to the right of the highway. "Our exit's up ahead." He glanced at his watch. "One o'clock. We're on schedule."

Thirty minutes later, they turned off the county blacktop onto a gravel road. The farther they traveled the fewer houses they saw. If Ramirez had wanted a remote site, he had certainly found it. And one with a landing strip. Convenient for him but not for a forty-five foot coach navigating narrow curves and never-ending hills.

"This place is in the middle of nowhere." Evans complained.

"Yup, no fancy hotels or steakhouses in sight." Ridge rolled his eyes.

Caleb smiled but decided to stay out of the conversation.

Wiley chuckled. "Before I moved from Jersey, I thought everyone in Tennessee lived in this kind of setting."

Ridge guffawed. "I may be from New York, but I knew better than that. Haven't you ever watched the television series *Nashville*?"

"Hey, boys." The bus driver called to them over his shoulder. "I don't think we're going to make it across this bridge."

Evans jumped from his seat, almost tripping over his leg irons. "You'd better not scratch this bus, Hank!"

"That's the least of our worries." The driver appeared to be unaffected by his former boss's ire. "I don't think it'll hold our weight."

Ten minutes later, while everyone stood alongside the road watching, the driver eased the massive coach between the two side rails of the tiny bridge. A phone call to the county road commissioner's office had yielded little more than "good luck, hope you make it." No one seemed to know for sure how much weight the ancient structure would withstand.

Caleb looked skyward. There wasn't a cloud above. Hopefully his prayers were going straight up. Zach's life depended on this bus making it to the other side of the bridge. They would worry about the return trip soon enough.

Seconds later, Robert Evans cringed at the sound of metal scarping metal. It was followed by a victory cry from Hank and his roadside passengers. The bridge had held the weight of the bus. Crisis averted.

About a mile up the road they saw the gated entrance to the four-hundred-acre spread. A TBI advance team had picked the lock, and with a bit of fancy maneuvering, Hank threaded the couch around a curve and through an opening not much wider than the bus.

A sullen Evans sat silently on the sofa, not lifting his chin or uttering a word. Perhaps he had realized at this point that he had more to worry about than the paint job on his coach.

Caleb pulled his cell phone from his pocket. No bars. Wiley's satellite phone would be their only means of communication out here. That and the encrypted walkie-talkie they would use to choreograph their detailed plan. They had already scored one major win. Ramirez hadn't called to change the location. Perhaps because this property had the only private landing strip within a hundred-mile radius.

As they crested a hill, they could see the tiny airstrip running parallel and to the left of the main driveway. Ridge instructed Hank to pull to a stop at the bottom of the hill, with the coach doors opening away from the landing strip.

They had twenty minutes to prepare.

Wiley keyed his walkie-talkie to broadcast into the ears of more than two-dozen men in the field. "Everybody, listen up. I won't be repeating these instructions.

"Sniper team, remember we will have a CI on the ground and two hostages in the plane. Use extreme caution. Hold your fire until all three are out of danger or unless the other side shoots first.

"Perimeter team, stay alert. As the plane is landing, on my count of three, you'll neutralize your ground targets. Don't move too soon or one of the goons may alert the pilot, and our plane will be gone."

Wiley stepped to the front of the bus to assess the on-site visual as he finalized his instructions, and a nervous looking Evans requested use of the bathroom. His guard removed his shackles first, and then accompanied him to the back hall.

Once they were alone, Ridge glanced toward Caleb. "We'll take good care of her."

"Is it that obvious?"

"You mean that you have feelings for Danielle Kemp?" His boss checked his .45 and returned it to his shoulder holster. "I've known that for a long time."

"I would never let it interfere with my work."

"I know that too, Samuels. You're a good man. We all fall prey to love at one time or another." He grinned. "Let's get this done."

With that, Ridge walked to the back to fetch the women. His final decision had been to let Danni take the risk.

At three o'clock sharp, Wiley pointed toward a speck above the rugged tree line to the north side of the landing strip. Sweat beaded on the FBI man's forehead as he waited to set everything in motion with a final countdown. "Three . . . two . . . one."

If all had gone well, Ramirez's men guarding the perimeter of the field had just been neutralized and no one had sounded an alert. Now it was up to the ATF guys to keep a watchful eye.

Within seconds of the plane rolling to a stop, Caleb saw a member of the FBI Tactical Aviation team crawl out of his hiding place alongside the runway and disappear beneath the aircraft. His job was to disable it. Once that was done, they were locked into the final confrontation.

Now for the hard part—keeping everyone alive.

Danni brushed past Caleb on her way to the front of the bus. They hadn't spoken since this morning when he'd driven her to their meeting place. He reached to take her hand and squeezed it. She looked up to find unspoken reassurance in his eyes. There was nothing left to say. If everything turned out well, there would be plenty of time to talk later.

"Are you ready?" Martin Ridge asked.

She nodded.

"In about thirty seconds, you will walk around the front of the bus with Mr. Evans. Stay together, and walk slowly toward the airplane."

Ridge turned to Rob. "Do exactly as you've been told, and we'll do our best to get you out of this alive. Keep your hands in plain sight. Stop when you reach the halfway point between the bus and the plane." He looked from Rob to Danni. "Do you both understand?"

"Yes, sir." Rob whimpered. There was no resonance to his voice. His once powerful demeanor had disappeared. His self-imposed importance had gone away, leaving a shallow man who had nothing to cling to but the people he had tried to outsmart.

"Let's do this," Wiley said.

At the bottom of the bus steps, Rob tucked his arm around Danni's waist and escorted her toward the open field. She could see the plane. It was maybe one-hundred-and-fifty yards ahead.

Once clear of the vehicle, Rob withdrew his arm, leaving her on her own. Just like he always had. But she knew the man behind her, Caleb Samuels, had her back.

CHAPTER 45

From inside the bus, Caleb and his partners watched the scene play out in front of them. Danni and Evans were almost midway between the bus and the airplane. Another step, and she would be closer to the danger than she was to him. But he had to let her go.

He'd been trained to follow protocol. To obey his superiors. This had been Ridge's decision, and he had confidence in his boss. It was better that Ridge was in charge. He wasn't as emotionally involved as Caleb was. He would see to it that they did the right thing.

The airplane door opened.

Caleb turned to his boss, who watched through field glasses. "It's Ramirez. I'd bet on it. He's surrounded by three bodyguards, all carrying high-powered rifles." He hesitated. "I don't see the hostages."

Caleb's heart took a dive. *Where was Zach?*

"Once they've cleared the plane by about thirty yards we'll make our move."

Caleb wanted to rush to Danni's side, to get this behind them, but he waited.

"Let's go," Ridge said, handing Wiley the binoculars.

Caleb, Ridge, and Jamie Wade descended the bus steps in single file, leaving Evans's guard to watch Hank and Wiley on lookout. He would be calling the shots quite literally.

As the three agents rounded the front of the Prevost en masse, Ridge raised a bullhorn to his mouth. "Halt. TBI. Put your weapons down. You're surrounded."

Caleb, Ridge, and Jamie Wade continued to walk. They were within twenty-five feet of Danni and Evans when Ramirez shouted back toward the plane.

Was he giving up or would he fight?

Someone from the plane handed Ramirez a bullhorn of his own.

"Which one of you is Samuels?"

"I am." Caleb took a step in front of his partners, closer to Danni.

Within seconds, three silhouettes darkened the door of the plane. Two adult figures and a child.

"I was expecting you, Samuels."

Caleb's chest pounded. Zach was here. And the woman beside him must be FBI Agent Cassia Kennedy.

He turned to look at Ridge, who mouthed. "Is that the kid?"

Caleb nodded, and Ridge stepped to his side. Agent Wade joined them as the goon next to Zach escorted him to where Ramirez stood.

"That boy has nothing to do with this," Ridge shouted.

Ramirez, now no more than thirty yards away, drew Zach in front of him. "I'm afraid he has everything to do with it. He's my ticket out of here. He's why I called this party."

"But why Zach?" Caleb asked.

Ramirez chuckled. "You should know the answer to that, Mr. Samuels. You had become too personally involved in this case. Unfortunately for the boy, that left me with the need to get your attention."

He clapped his hand on top of Zach's shoulder. The boy tried to pull away. But Ramirez held on.

"Don't you hurt him!" Caleb took another step forward, keeping his hands in the air. "Take me instead. I'm the one you have the grudge with." He gestured toward Zach and the woman behind them. "Let the others go."

Ramirez stood silent for a moment and then brought his hands together in mock applause. The sound echoed across the hollow. "Very well done, Mr. Samuels. I enjoyed that display of bravado."

The drug boss glanced toward Danni who was standing to Caleb's left, just beyond Jamie Wade and Robert Evans.

"I'm sure your lady was impressed. But I'm afraid I can't oblige you. I really need to get on with the reason we're here."

Caleb ran through possible scenarios. There was little time to gain the upper hand. He had two civilian lives at stake. The ATF snipers were well placed, but would they react quickly enough to take a risk?

He could feel blood rushing through the artery in his neck, pounding with every beat of his heart. An invisible clock was ticking, and it was time to make a decision.

He glanced from Wiley to Ridge to Danni, locking eyes with her for a brief second. Would she understand what he was about to do? Would Zach? *Please God.*

"Well, since you don't have anything more to say, we need to get started with our execution." Ramirez laughed. "Did I really say that? I mean with the execution of our plans."

Danni held her breath and said a silent prayer. Was Caleb about to do what she suspected? His fleeting glance took her back to Centennial Park when the three of them—Caleb, Zach, and she—had played cops and robbers on a spring day.

If she was right, she had to be ready to drop to the ground. But would Zach remember? He was a ten-year-old boy. He had to be scared out of his wits. Would he respond in time to Caleb's signal? And if not?

She prayed. *Dear Lord, help him to know.*

The odious sound of Ramirez laughter brought her out of her meditation. Caleb took one step forward with an exaggerated swagger. And then he shouted, "Fold!"

Danni dropped to the ground only seconds before gunshots rang out in rapid fire. A body fell beside her, but she didn't open her eyes. The blasts replayed over and over, ricocheting off the hills surrounding them.

Then came silence. Deathly silence. It was followed by men shouting, footsteps near her, running past.

Agent Wade reached her first, kneeling to ask if she was hurt. *Where was Caleb?*

Danni saw the body lying next to her. The one she heard hit the ground.

"It's Robert Evans," Jamie whispered. "But he's alive."

"What about . . . ?"

Caleb reached to lift her from the grass. "Are you okay?"

She nodded and grabbed him. He didn't pull away until Zach called out to her.

"Ms. Danni, you did it!" A smile spread across the boy's face. "I was so afraid you would forget!"

Danni laughed and gave him a hug.

"I'm not sure if she remembered or if she fainted," Caleb teased.

"Did you faint, Ms. Danni?"

"I'm not telling," she said, leaning forward to give Zach a kiss on the cheek. "But either way the good guys won."

"Yes, they did!" He grinned. "Oh . . . I need to check on my friend Cassia. I'll be right back."

Caleb took Danni by the hand and pulled her close. "Do I get a kiss too?"

"Happy to oblige," she said, leaning into him.

Mid-kiss, she pulled back to search his dark brown eyes. "Is this a real kiss, or are we just pretending again?"

"Which do you want it to be?" He asked.

"I'd like it to be real . . ." Her words faded into the warm afternoon air. Then she added. "And I'd like it to last forever."

He drew her to him and kissed her again.

EPILOGUE

One year later

Danni and Caleb stood in front of a weathered oak tree in Centennial Park, not far from where they had first kissed, "I can't believe you agreed to marry me." He looked into the eyes of his soon-to-be-wife.

"And I can't believe you finally asked," Danni teased.

"You two lovebirds need to keep your mind on the business at hand," Thomas Edwards, a recently retired FBI photographer, interrupted. "Stop talking, look straight into the camera, and smile. We're almost finished.

"Who found this guy?" Caleb whispered, his lips barely moving as he smiled directly into the camera.

"You did!" Danni laughed. "Remember?"

"Oh, yes. I remember now." He squeezed her hand. "I guess you can't trust me."

"That's where you're wrong, Agent Samuels." She turned to him. "I trust you with my life."

Caleb's phone buzzed. It was a text from Ridge. "Hold on, Tom." He raised his hand to the photographer. "I need to take a look at this."

A new case just came across my desk. I need you back at the office as soon as possible. P.S. Give my favorite CI a kiss on the cheek for me.

Caleb slid the phone back into his pocket and then swiveled toward his future wife. He planted a kiss on her cheek. "That was from Ridge."

She smiled. "And . . . ?"

He hesitated, then leaned forward to give her a lingering kiss on the lips. "And that was from me"

"Hold on, Sophie!" Zach and the big Newfoundland almost knocked them down. "I'm sorry, Ms. Danni. She got away from me."

Danni looked at the boy and smiled. "I'll tell you what, Zach. Why don't we put you both in our picture?"

"Sure!" Zach squeezed between Caleb and Danni.

"Sit, Sophie." Danni tugged on the Newfie's collar.

Sophie took a seat directly in front of the boy with her tongue hanging out of her mouth and an expression on her face that Caleb would have sworn looked exactly like a smile.

"Hold it . . . right there." Edwards shouted.

"Everybody say, 'Chicken!'" Caleb teased, and they all burst into laughter.

"Okay! That's a wrap!" The photographer put down his camera. "That last one was a keeper."

Acknowledgements and Special Thanks

Thanks to—

- Linda Veath and Rebecca Deel—for your help with the early draft
- Edlynn Zimmerman, Karin Warf, and Debbie Scroggins—for your encouragement
- Julie Gwinn—for your patience and guidance
- Ramona Richards—for your continued faith
- Everyone at New Hope Publishers/Iron Stream Media—for bringing this book to life
- Tom and Letha Edwards and the Big Mean Kitty web team—for your digital dexterity
- Susan Larson and the girls at FBC—for introducing me to the healing work of The Next Door, Nashville

Special thanks for your help with research:

- Tim Adair
- Kelcey Bell
- Tonya Bible
- Hendersonville Citizens Police Academy
- Ed Laneville
- Kate Tanis McKinnie
- George Offutt
- The TBI Press Office

My hope is that this story will reflect the Word, Jesus Christ, who was, is, and will be forever. I write to the rhythm of His song.

A Note to the Reader

We don't always choose our stories. They sometimes choose us. *Deadly Commitment* was a story that chose me. And, once it took hold, it wouldn't let go.

Over the past few years, we've seen the theme of deadly narcotics dominate the headlines. But during that time, the personal reality of illicit drugs destroying lives also impacted me closer to home. During the time it took me to write this book, that reality, unfortunately, stole the future of two of my extended family members.

And then there was Michael.

I met Michael several years ago when he was a manager in a small coffee shop where I wrote the first draft of this book. Michael would always greet me and other patrons with a warm smile and friendly conversation. One day when I was writing, he walked over to my table and asked what I was doing. I explained that I was working on a book, and he immediately took interest. Although I never shared details about my story, every few days he would ask how my book was coming along.

Several months passed, and then one day I walked into the coffee shop and saw a framed picture of Michael sitting on the front counter. Two dates were written beneath it. The date of his birth, and the date of his death. I was told later that he had died of an overdose.

As Michael had encouraged me in life, he continued to encourage me with his legacy. I had come face-to-face with the knowledge that good people can, and do, die from bad drugs. And, if I'd ever had any doubt, I knew then I had to finish this story.

Not long after Michael's death I became acquainted with a group of women from my church who were volunteering at The Next Door, an addiction treatment center in Nashville, and I decided to join them. It was through volunteering at The Next Door that I met countless young women who, like Rachel in my fictional story, were making their best effort to put their lives back together. Thanks to The Next Door, and facilities like them across the country, young women and men are given the opportunity for a second chance.

I hope you will check out the resources page on my website, www.kathyharrisbooks.com/resources, for ways that you can help make a difference in the lives of those who have been affected by addiction. By working together, we can help them write hope into their personal stories.

God bless you.

Continue reading for a sneak peek at the
next book in the Deadly Secrets Series
Deadly Connection

Kathy Harris

After fending off a would-be abductor, twenty-seven-year-old singer-songwriter Hannah Cassidy hides behind a car in the half-empty parking lot behind Pancake Pantry and watches in horror as her attacker grabs another woman and pushes her into a nearby car. Within seconds, the vehicle speeds away.

TBI Special Agent Jake Matheson may have planned a quiet day off and a date with Shannon—the only name her online profile revealed—for an introductory lunch, but soon after pulling into a parking space on 21st Avenue South, he hears a scream. Jake races to the back of the building and finds a frightened young woman bent forward and gasping for breath.

Jake presents his badge, and Hannah explains what she just witnessed. The pieces fall into place quickly for Jake. Shannon, who fits the same general physical description as Hannah, with long, wavy blonde hair, medium height and medium build, is most likely the victim. But what was the motive? Was this the work of an international trafficking ring or a lone wolf? Did Shannon's abductor grab her because she was in the wrong place at the wrong time? Or was she being stalked, perhaps because of her profile on the online dating app? Had the attacker confused the two women, and, if so, was Hannah Cassidy being stalked, and was she still in danger?

After the police arrive, Hannah comes to grips with what has happened. She has avoided death or injury at the expense of another woman. Guilt sets in, not only for her but for Jake, who can only assume that Shannon would be safe right now if he hadn't invited her to lunch.

Thrown together by uncanny circumstances and driven by the whys and what ifs of secrets yet to be revealed, Jake and Hannah set out to piece together the connection between them—and Shannon. Will they make that connection in time, or will it prove to be deadly?

CHAPTER 1

Present Day – August 28

Strong arms pulled Hannah Cassidy backward, her heels barely touching the pavement as her captor drug her across the half-vacant parking lot. The harder she fought the more the man tightened his grip on her throat, and each breath she drew threatened to be her last. She willed herself not to lose consciousness.

Or hope.

If she could land one well-placed kick, she could make a run for freedom. Fighting to fill her lungs with air, Hannah summoned the strength to secure her footing. Then, with a twist of her body, she landed a blow, driving her heel into the man's shin.

"O-o-ouch! You little—" He released his hold enough for Hannah to pull away.

Lunging forward, she calculated her escape. If she could make it to the main street she could solicit help from a passerby. Her ability to outrun her attacker would either seal her fate or set her free.

She chose the latter and took off running. Midway to Belcourt Avenue, she heard footsteps falling behind her. And then she heard the shrill scream of a siren.

Could it be that easy?

Turning quickly, she scanned the landscape in front of her in search of her rescuer. But the Metro Nashville police cruiser rolled past on Wedgewood Avenue, lights ablaze, oblivious to her situation. Still, it had been enough to distract the man chasing her, who stopped to watch the police car. While he was distracted, Hannah ducked behind a nearby vehicle.

Barely breathing, she peered through the window of the SUV that shielded her from her attacker. She watched as the man hesitated, glanced over his shoulder to look for her, and then took off running in the opposite direction.

Now taking her breaths in gulps, Hannah watched as her former captor grabbed another woman. The girl, who appeared to be a college student, dropped the books she had been carrying. Papers littered the sidewalk in front of her and scattered into the street.

The young woman's neck jerked backwards as her assailant lifted her feet from the ground and dragged her toward a light-colored sedan. The man opened the back left-side passenger door and tossed the girl, her body now limp, into the car. Then he slammed the door. Seconds later he jumped into the driver's seat and sped away, heading up the hill toward Belmont University and, perhaps, the interstate highway just beyond.

Hannah's gut churned as she replayed the last few minutes of her life. *The stranger's arms wrenching her throat, choking, squeezing, dragging her.* How had she managed to escape? And if she hadn't, would her fate have been the same as the young girl who had just been whisked away?

She knew the answer. And it drove her to her knees.

Jake Matheson pulled his dark gray Toyota Tacoma into an empty parking spot on Belcourt Avenue near 21st Avenue South. Glancing into his rearview mirror he ran his hand through his short-cropped hair and gathered his composure. If this went as usual, he would be on his way home in an hour with zero connection and even more doubt that he could ever find someone special in his life again. Even after a year, the pain of losing Rylee still stabbed him in the gut.

He switched his phone to mute and tucked his Tennessee Bureau of Investigation Special Agent's badge into his back pocket. His date, whom he only knew as Shannon from her online profile, deserved an uninterrupted conversation. And one without the complications of knowing about his difficult job.

When he stepped out of his truck, a blur of movement caught his attention. Someone, a young woman, had fallen in the parking lot. He slammed his door and ran to her side.

"Are you okay?"

"No—" She appeared to be shaken.

"Are you hurt? Can I help you up?"

"I'm not hurt," the woman said, raising her face to him.

Jake grasped her by the shoulders and lifted her to her feet. After leaning her against a nearby vehicle, he recognized the splotches on her neck as strangulation marks.

"What happened?"

She shook off the question. "I'm the lucky one . . . I managed to get away. But another woman"—she pointed toward Wedgewood Avenue—"the man who attacked me. He took her."

Jake scanned the parking lot. "Where? In a car?"

She nodded.

"Can you describe the car for me? And the woman?" He pulled his phone from his pocket preparing to dial 9-1-1. "What about the man?"

"They were in a light blue, or maybe a silver, sedan. An Audi, I think."

"Could you read the plates?"

"No, not the plates. But the girl was wearing a pink blouse. With ripped jeans. And . . ." She closed her eyes. "She must have been a student because she was carrying books. They fell everywhere."

Jake scanned the parking lot, finally focusing on the pile of books and scattered papers on the sidewalk and in the street. He looked back to the woman in front of him.

"What's your name?"

"Hannah . . . Hannah Cassidy."

"Hannah, my name is Jake. I'm a TBI agent. Do you remember anything about the man who attacked you?"

Her eyes clouded. "No . . . I'm sorry. I didn't see his face. He was dragging me backwards." She put her hands to her neck. "I couldn't breathe."

"I understand." Jake dialed 9-1-1.

"I remember he was tall," Hannah said. "He towered over me. And he was dressed in a light-colored polo shirt, maybe even silk. And khakis." She shook her head. "It all happened so fast."

"You're doing a good job, Hannah. Hold on while I—"

"9-1-1. How can I help you?"

"Yes. This is Jake Matheson. I'm a special agent with the TBI. A woman has reportedly been abducted. I have the witness with me. We're in the parking lot behind the Pancake Pantry, at the corner of 21st and Wedgewood. You're looking for a silver or light blue Audi sedan with two passengers. The victim is—" He gestured to his hair.

"Blond," Hannah said. "Long blond hair. About the length and color of mine."

"The victim is blond." Jake repeated. "She's wearing a pink blouse and torn blue jeans. The suspect is tall. Medium build?" He looked to Hannah again. She nodded. "He's wearing a polo shirt and khakis pants."

"We're sending a car, Agent Matheson. Will you be on the scene?"

"I'll be here. With the witness."

Jake hung up the phone. "Hannah, are you okay to stay here by yourself for a minute? I want to secure the evidence."

"Yes."

Hannah was either a woman of few words, or she was in shock. Jake guessed the latter considering the unfocused look in her eyes. He ran to his truck, pulled gloves and an evidence bag from his trunk, and then slammed the hatch door shut.

After checking on Hannah again, he sprinted across the parking lot where he found three books lying on the sidewalk. He snapped a photo to document their position and then stepped into the street to retrieve a notebook that had landed in a lane of traffic.

Jake froze when he read the name on the cover.

Shannon Bridges.

The woman he had planned to meet for lunch.

**If you enjoyed this book, will you consider
sharing the message with others?**

Let us know your thoughts at info@newhopepublishers.com.
You can also let the author know by visiting or sharing a photo
of the cover on our social media pages or leaving a review at
a retailer's site. All of it helps us get the message out!

Twitter.com/NewHopeBooks
Facebook.com/NewHopePublishers
Instagram.com/NewHopePublishers

New Hope® Publishers, Ascender Books,
Iron Stream Books, and New Hope Kidz are
imprints of Iron Stream Media,
which derives its name from Proverbs 27:17,
"As iron sharpens iron, so one person sharpens another."

This sharpening describes the process of discipleship,
one to another. With this in mind, Iron Stream Media
provides a variety of solutions for churches, ministry leaders,
and nonprofits ranging from in-depth Bible study curriculum
and Christian book publishing to custom publishing and
consultative services. Through the popular Life Bible Study
and Student Life Bible Study brands, ISM provides web-based
full-year and short-term Bible study teaching plans as well
as printed devotionals, Bibles, and discipleship curriculum.

For more information on ISM and
New Hope Publishers, please visit

IronStreamMedia.com
NewHopePublishers.com

More fiction you may enjoy . . .

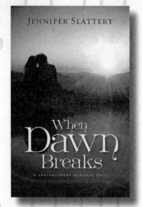

Author Jennifer Slattery